PRIVATE
DUBLIN

THE PRIVATE NOVELS

A list of more titles by James Patterson appears at the back of this book

JAMES PATTERSON
& ADAM HAMDY

PRIVATE
DUBLIN

CENTURY

CENTURY

UK | USA | Canada | Ireland | Australia
India | New Zealand | South Africa

Century is part of the Penguin Random House group of companies
whose addresses can be found at global.penguinrandomhouse.com

Penguin Random House UK,
One Embassy Gardens, 8 Viaduct Gardens, London SW11 7BW

penguin.co.uk

First published 2025
001

Copyright © James Patterson, 2025

The moral right of the author has been asserted

Set in 12.25/18.25pt ITC Berkeley Oldstyle Std
Typeset by Jouve (UK), Milton Keynes

Printed and bound in Great Britain by Clays Ltd, Elcograf S.p.A.

The authorised representative in the EEA is Penguin Random House Ireland,
Morrison Chambers, 32 Nassau Street, Dublin D02 YH68

A CIP catalogue record for this book is available from the British Library

ISBN: 978–1–529–93641–4 (hardback)
ISBN: 978–1–529–93642–1 (trade paperback)

MIX
Paper | Supporting
responsible forestry
FSC
www.fsc.org   FSC® C018179

Penguin Random House is committed to a
sustainable future for our business, our readers
and our planet. This book is made from Forest
Stewardship Council® certified paper.

For those who seek the lamp beside the golden door

CHAPTER 1

THUNDEROUS APPLAUSE FILLED the auditorium, and the filmmakers beamed as though the claps and cheers were dollar bills. I glanced at Justine, who was applauding politely. Even in a theater full of stars, she shone the brightest. Her wavy brown hair fell against the crimson cocktail dress she'd chosen for the premiere. It had a daring slit that showed off her long, tanned legs, and I could hardly take my eyes off her.

"What did you think?" she asked.

"Pretty good," I replied. "Alan will do well from it."

Alan Bloom was a former client, now friend, who was one of four producers of the movie we'd just watched. He was standing near the screen with the director, cast, studio executives and other producers. A *Star Wars* movie is always a big deal, and this, the first in a new trilogy, looked set to dominate the summer box office. The clamor of the crowd was as much a celebration of Hollywood's continued ability to captivate global audiences as it was a response to the movie.

After a standing ovation, people began filing out of Los Angeles's famous Samuel Goldwyn Theater, and Justine and I followed our neighbors into the aisle. Alan caught up to us as we joined the crowd thronging through the nearest exit. He looked wired. Like me, he was in a tuxedo, but he wore his better. Mine felt constrictive, ill suited to my line of work. Alan's fitted like a second skin. Combined with his perfectly coiffed salt-and-pepper hair, tan and dazzling smile, it gave him the appearance of a Bel Air James Bond, buzzing after the completion of a successful mission.

"Jack . . . Justine!" he called over the heads of the people around us. "What did you think?"

"You've got a great movie," I replied. "Congratulations."

"I loved it," Justine said. "I think it's going to be a hit."

Alan's smile broadened. "Thanks. It's always such a relief when a movie plays well."

The crowd swept us through the double doors into the marble lobby of the Academy, more precisely the Academy of Motion Picture Arts and Sciences. It's the headquarters of the organization that runs the Academy Awards and, in many ways, represents the seat of creative power in Hollywood.

The party was in full swing as we entered. Servers distributed drinks and canapes and the room was packed with chattering people abuzz with the energy of success. Deals were being made, careers enhanced, networks strengthened. Alan settled beside me and Justine as we sheltered beside a column.

"These things are always so hectic," he remarked, grabbing a glass of champagne from an agile server. "You want one?"

Justine shook her head. "The atmosphere is intoxicating enough."

"I'm driving," I said.

He nodded and took a gulp. "I need something to settle the nerves."

"Don't feel you have to babysit us," Justine told him. "If you need to work the room, go hustle."

Alan scoffed. "If it didn't look bad, I'd be on my way home to tuck myself up with a good book."

"A producer who reads," I said with a chuckle.

"That's a cheap shot," he replied with feigned hurt. "You guys are my cover. If anyone tries to cut in, just start talking about per diems, catering budgets, or something equally dull. Save me from schmoozing."

Justine and I grinned at Alan, but my smile fell away as soon as I registered a frighteningly familiar sound. The violent staccato of machine gunfire.

I heard screams and peered round the column to see a charge begin. People near the steel-and-glass entrance to the Academy pressed deeper into the lobby, their faces reflecting horror and panic, as a man in a ski mask stalked into the building after them. Behind him I could see a couple of fallen security guards. The paparazzi and fans who'd gathered around the red carpet had dispersed, and people were yelling frantically. I caught cries of "cops," and "ambulance."

"We need to move," I said, an instant before the masked gunman sprayed the room with bullets. "Now!"

The press of people turned into a panicked stampede, and screams joined a chorus of horrified cries as most people tried to flee back into the auditorium. Others attempted to escape through fire exits or doors to the service sections of the building. Some were gunned down as they ran.

I pushed Justine and Alan toward the auditorium, and as we moved, I locked eyes with the gunman. He hesitated for a moment before letting off a volley of bullets in my direction. I ducked into the short tunnel that led to the theater as the walls around me puckered and splintered under the impact of so many bullets.

The shooter was using some kind of machine pistol. I knew if he got into the auditorium there would be an absolute bloodbath, so I crouched against the wall by the doors to the lobby and ignored my thundering heartbeat. Behind me, people were pressing through the short tunnel into the theater.

Justine glanced back, but I gestured for her to follow the crowd to safety. As the shooter's shadow fell into the mouth of the tunnel, I rose, rounded the corner, and grabbed his weapon. A blast of gunfire erupted, spitting flame and lead from the muzzle. The bullets thudded into the wall and ceiling, raining plaster and dust onto us. I drove my shoulder into the shooter's chest, and as he collided with the wall, I caught him with a right hook that dazed him. I grabbed the gun and wrenched it free, but as I was about to turn it on him, I heard a sound that sickened me.

"Jack," Justine said, anguish and pain palpable in her trembling voice.

I glanced over my shoulder to see her in the doorway to the auditorium. Alan was trying to support her as she clutched her stomach. A spreading bloodstain was turning her dress a deeper shade of red. She fell to her knees and looked at me pleadingly.

"Jack," she said, "I'm sorry . . ."

I staggered toward her and barely registered the shooter push past me and run for the exit.

"Save the planet!" he yelled as he sprinted into the street. "Two degrees is extinction . . ."

The words jolted me to my senses and, for a split second, I thought about giving chase, but Justine needed me. I ran to her side and handed Alan the pistol.

"Hold this in case he comes back," I said as I supported Justine.

"I'll call 911." Alan took his phone from his pocket and stepped away to dial.

I registered a few other people around us using their phones, speaking hurriedly to emergency operators, friends or family. I stroked Justine's face. "Stay with me, Justine. Stay with me."

"I'm cold, Jack," she replied weakly. "I'm so cold."

"Someone, help!" I yelled, as her strength gave out and her eyes rolled back in her head.

CHAPTER 2

THE SHOOTING HAD received sensational coverage. The paparazzi, who had been there to cover the premiere, had captured and shared video footage of the masked gunman yelling his environmental creed, and the media had already dubbed him the Ecokiller. Unsure whether he was still armed, security and passersby had kept their distance, and the perp had fled into the night, slipping away in the confusion caused by his onslaught before the cops arrived.

I was in the waiting room at Cedars-Sinai Hospital off Beverly Boulevard, watching the unfolding coverage on my phone, trying to glean any useful pieces of information that might help me identify the shooter, while doctors performed emergency surgery on Justine. The brief ambulance ride from the theater had been the most stressful experience of my life. I could tell from the paramedics' grave expressions and artificially calm voices that she was in serious danger.

I hadn't been allowed into the emergency room. Hours ago a nurse had told me Justine was being taken for emergency abdominal surgery. Since then I'd tried to distract myself with my phone, my hands shaking with fear for her. My heart thudded with anger at the thought of the monster who'd done this, my body flushing hot and cold as I replayed the attack in my mind over and over again. It didn't matter which websites I visited, which news reports I watched, I couldn't shut out the memories of my own failings. I chastised myself for my stupid mistakes. If I'd done things differently, if I'd been better and faster and stronger, Justine would have been at my side now instead of fighting for her life in an operating theater.

"Jack!" a familiar voice called across the crowded room.

Eighteen people had been wounded and four killed in the attack, and most had been brought to Cedars-Sinai, so the place was packed with the victims' family and friends.

I turned to see Maureen Roth, Private's technology guru, entering the room. Known to everyone at Private as "Mo-bot," she was a computer geek extraordinaire. At fifty-something, she was a salutary lesson in the unexpected. Her tattoos and spiky hair suggested a cold, hard rebel, but she had the warmest heart and was thought of by many at Private as their second mom, someone they could go to with their problems. The only thing about her that hinted at a softer side, and spoke to her age, were the bifocals, which I always said looked like they belonged to a

Boca Raton grandmother. She managed a team of six tech specialists in the LA office and oversaw dozens of others in Private's international units. She was followed into the waiting room by Seymour "Sci" Kloppenberg, Private's world-renowned forensics expert. A slight, bookish man, he dressed like a Hells Angel biker, which was where his heart probably lay because he was always restoring old muscle bikes. These two were among my oldest friends and most trusted colleagues and it was comforting to see them.

"How is she?" Sci asked.

"She caught two in the stomach," I replied, scarcely able to believe what I was saying. "She's in surgery still."

"I'm so sorry, Jack," Mo-bot said, and gave me a reassuring hug.

"She's going to be okay," Sci remarked. "Justine's a fighter."

I nodded, but my experiences of losing people in the field told me it didn't matter how strong or determined a person was, a bullet could be the ultimate arbiter of life or death.

"What happened?" Mo-bot asked. "I've seen the news, but how did the guy get in?"

"Looks like he shot door security and then came in and started blasting," I replied.

"Media are saying he was disarmed by a guest. You?" Sci asked.

I nodded. "If I'd been quicker . . ." I trailed off.

"I bet you were as fast as anyone could have been," Sci told me. "You did good, Jack."

I nodded again, but his words rang hollow. It was hard to view my response as anything other than an abject failure when the woman I loved was currently fighting for her life in an operating theater.

"Cops spoken to you yet?" Mo-bot asked.

I shook my head. "I've been told to expect a detective, but I think they're giving me space while I deal with this." I nodded in the direction of the double doors that led to the surgical area. "I don't have much to tell them. The shooter was masked, so I didn't get a look at him. He was about six-one, well built, strong and fast."

"They're calling him the Ecokiller," Sci remarked.

"He yelled a bunch of stuff about the planet as he escaped," I replied. "I want us to find him."

Mo-bot put her hand on my shoulder. "You did well, Jack. If you hadn't been there, who knows how many more might have died. But this isn't on you. Focus on Justine. Let the cops handle this. Sci and I will help."

I looked at Mo-bot and her reassuring smile wilted under the severity of my stare. I wasn't angry with her, but my anger at the man who had put us here shone through. "I can't do that, Mo," I told her. "I need to find this guy and make sure he answers for what he's done."

CHAPTER 3

THAT NIGHT, I dreamed of flames and the screams of those I couldn't save when my Marine Corps CH-46 Sea Knight had been shot down in Afghanistan. I'd been a chopper pilot for the Corps before taking over Private from my old man, and since then had turned his ramshackle outfit into the world's largest private detective agency. I'd faced danger and death more times than I cared to remember. However, the loss of those men, the jarheads I'd served with, hurt most of all. Even though the NCIS investigation had concluded there had been no way to avoid the crash, I'd still felt responsible. It didn't matter what the investigators said, or how many people told me I'd done my best. All that mattered was the blood and honor of the field, and I carried my failure with me. It tormented me still when I was low or troubled. To this day, memories of that crash and the ghosts of those men were guaranteed to make me feel as low as humanly possible, but now my failure to protect Justine had become a new nadir, a low from which I could only recover if she did. In my dream, I fled the scorching heat of the fire, abandoning the bodies burning in the wreckage, but when I turned, I saw Justine kneeling on the rocky ground, clutching the gunshot wounds in her belly, blood spreading across the front of her red dress.

"Mr. Morgan," a voice cut in, and I felt a hand on my shoulder.

I woke with a start to see Dr. Gurdasani, a woman in her mid-thirties, smiling at me gently.

"Mr. Morgan," she repeated, "Ms. Smith is out of surgery and just surfacing from the anesthetic. It's early, but we think she's going to pull through."

"Can I see her?" I asked.

"In a little while," Dr. Gurdasani replied. "Once we've got her comfortable."

A "little while" proved to be ninety of the slowest minutes I've ever experienced. I'd sent Mo-bot and Sci home shortly after 3 a.m. so I messaged them while I was waiting to let them know Justine was out of surgery and recovering. They both wished her well and asked me to send them updates. With nothing more to do and my desire to see her filling me with impatience, I tried distracting myself by pacing the now quiet waiting room and checking my phone for updates on the shooting. There wasn't much more to go on, and the sensational stories about the Ecokiller focused mostly on newly released details about the gunman's victims. The four dead were two security guards who'd been on the door, a server who'd been working shifts to help put herself through UCLA, and a junior studio executive who was being hailed as a hero for shielding his colleagues as they escaped through a fire exit. Social media photos accompanied the news pieces, and I felt nothing but sympathy for their loved ones. I tried not to imagine the suffering of such loss, but it was difficult to push past the dark imaginings that had tormented me in that hospital, a place where the line between life and death was at its thinnest.

Finally, when my patience was ragged and frayed, Dr. Gurdasani beckoned me from beyond the ward doors.

"You can see her now," she said, and I didn't bother trying to play it cool but snapped to the medic's side like a faithful dog.

We walked to the recovery ward in silence, passing rooms containing surgery patients wired to monitors and connected to drips. Despite this display of frailty, I wasn't prepared for what greeted me when Dr. Gurdasani led me into Justine's room. Her dark hair was lank and had been tied back from the face that had been so bright and alive only a few hours ago, now pale and clammy. She lay in a bed, a light blanket supported on a frame draped over her bandaged abdomen. I saw she was connected to two drips and guessed one was fluid and the other antibiotics or some sort of medication. A monitor tracked her heart function and a catheter led to a bag hooked to the side of her bed. Her eyes opened as we entered. They were bloodshot and sunken into shadow, and her pupils looked faded. A CPAP oxygen mask covered her nose and mouth, and there was a gentle rush of air with each breath.

"Justine," I said.

Her eyes filled with tears as she registered me moving toward her.

"You can't stay long," Dr. Gurdasani said. She'd hung back by the door. "Justine needs her rest."

I stood by the bed and gently clasped her hand. It was cold and there was hardly any strength in her fingers.

"I'm going to stay right here until I can take you home," I told her.

She closed her eyes and a couple of tears spilled from them and rolled down her sunken cheeks. She shook her head, the gesture so slight as to be almost imperceptible.

I lingered. In the quiet broken only by the humming of the machines surrounding her, I realized Justine was trying to talk. I leaned close to her and she strained to be heard through the oxygen mask she wore.

"Find him." Her voice was a hoarse whisper. "Find the man who did this to me."

CHAPTER 4

DR. GURDASANI USHERED me out of Justine's room after a few minutes. I'd wasted our time together by protesting about her request, telling her I needed to stay by her side and be with her throughout her recovery. Justine had smiled faintly, which I'd found encouraging because it took strength to express gentle derision. She'd told me she didn't want me lurking around, that being cooped up in hospital with her would drive me crazy. She was angry at the man who'd put her in that bed and wanted justice if not revenge.

I knew when I was beaten and followed the doctor out with a last "I love you" spoken over my shoulder to Justine. She looked so vulnerable lying there, relying on machines to keep her alive, and I felt the heat of anger flush through me. She was right: the man who'd done this must answer for his crimes. I needed to find him—not just for her, but for the people he'd killed and the others he'd wounded.

I sent messages to Mo-bot and Sci, letting them know what Justine had said, and asking them to come to the hospital to keep vigil with her in my absence. They were more than colleagues to us both, they were good friends, if not our surrogate family.

Twenty-five minutes later, I met Mo-bot in the corridor outside of Justine's room.

"How is she?" Mo-bot asked.

"The doctor says she's going to recover, but she looks so weak," I replied.

"She's not weak though," Mo-bot said sternly. "We know that. You want to wrap her up in cotton wool and protect her, but she's not a doll. She's a strong woman and she's resilient. If she's asked you to find this guy, it's because she doesn't want you moping around feeling sorry for her. She wants you to do what you do best."

I nodded slowly. "Moping around?" I asked with a faint smile.

"Moping," Mo-bot replied with a nod. "Or pining. Take your pick. Either way, you won't be helping her. You'll just be sitting out here, desperate to be useful, and I can stay with her while *being* useful." She patted the laptop bag slung over her shoulder. "Go do what she asked. Find this guy. I've arranged for Sci to come visit this afternoon. We'll make sure there's always someone here in case she needs anything."

I hesitated, and Mo-bot looked at me severely. Being the

company mom wasn't all hugs and reassurance. Sometimes she used that persona to be stern and intimidating.

"Okay," I responded. "Call me if there's any news or you need anything."

"Of course," she said. "Now get."

I gave a last lingering look at the door to Justine's room before I said, "I'll call you later."

Mo-bot nodded, took a seat in an armchair, and watched me leave.

I made my way through the hospital and stepped out into bright June sunshine, feeling a little disorientated and bewildered. A couple of passersby eyed me quizzically and I realized I must look a sight, still dressed in a tuxedo, my black bowtie hanging loose around my unbuttoned collar.

It took me a moment to compose my thoughts, but I quickly figured out where I needed to go. A short cab ride later, I was back on Wilshire Boulevard near the Academy. A police cordon had been established around the building, and the street was peppered with news crews recording pieces or milling around, waiting for updates. It was a little after 10:30 a.m., and tourists and local gawkers were gathered near the perimeter line, taking photos of the crime scene and avoiding the cops instructing spectators to move on.

I could see crime-scene investigators in white coveralls working the lobby, meticulously photographing and cataloging evidence from the scene of the shootings.

I took out my cell and called Mo-bot.

"That was quick," she said when she answered.

"I need to know who runs security at the Academy," I replied.

"Not wasting any time," she remarked. I heard her tapping her keyboard. "Jenny Powell. Ex-FBI."

"Thanks," I said, before hanging up.

I walked over to the cordon and approached a young officer with a friendly demeanor, who sized me up and took in my tux.

"A little late for the screening," she said.

"I was here last night," I replied, and her playful smile fell.

"I'm sorry, sir."

"I have an appointment with Jenny Powell," I lied. "Jack Morgan. I run Private, the detective agency."

"Just a moment, sir," she said, stepping away to confer with someone on her radio. A minute later, she returned. "You can go through, Mr. Morgan." She indicated a gap in the cordon. "Use the staff entrance on the side of the building."

"Thanks."

I passed between two bollards that broke the police tape line.

The area around the Academy felt like a battlefield the day after a gunfight: subdued, quiet, touched by horror. Los Angeles bustled in the background, but here in this small corner of the city, people were coping with the aftermath of a traumatic event.

Inside was no different, and when I went through the staff entrance, I found a woman with short blonde hair waiting for me in the lobby. She wore a long black evening gown but no makeup. Her exhaustion was plain to see. Shadowed, red-rimmed eyes stood out against her pale face.

"Mr. Morgan," she said. "I'm Jenny Powell. I see you've also been up all night."

"I've been at the hospital. My girlfriend was injured in the attack," I replied.

"I'm so sorry," she said. "I recognized your name from the guest list, and I know Private by reputation. How can I help?"

"Well, I'm here to offer you my help actually," I replied. "I have a personal interest in finding the man who did this."

She hesitated before saying, "I can understand that. I can't do anything that might interfere with the police investigation." I was about to protest, when she added, "But I'd be happy to introduce you to the detective in charge, and if he okays it, then we'll see what we can do. Follow me."

CHAPTER 5

I FOLLOWED JENNY Powell through the luxurious contemporary building to a security room located on the second floor. The large, windowless space was dominated by a bank of monitors on one wall. Half a dozen desks were occupied by men and women in suits who were reviewing CCTV footage while a middle-aged man with pinched features and a haunted expression leaned against a coffee station watching them. His dark brown uniform and epaulets told me he was a senior security officer for the Academy.

A guy in a dark blue suit perched on the edge of the desk nearest the wall of monitors, studying video footage of the entrance to the building taken just before the shooter entered.

"Detective Mattera," Jenny said as we approached. "This is Jack Morgan."

"Mr. Morgan," he said, stepping away from the desk to shake

my hand. He had curly black hair and bright, watchful eyes. "My name is Salvatore . . . Sal. You're on my list of people to talk to. I understand one of your colleagues was injured in the attack."

I was impressed he was on top of the details. "Girlfriend and colleague," I replied. "And yes, two gunshot wounds. She's recovering at Cedars-Sinai. They think she's going to be okay."

"Glad to hear it," Sal said.

"I wanted to offer my support to the Academy and to the LAPD if appropriate, and to direct Private's resources into helping find the guy who did this."

Sal's eyes narrowed. "For revenge?"

"Justice," I said.

He nodded toward his colleagues busy reviewing the CCTV footage. "You don't think we've got this?"

Jenny shifted uncomfortably.

"I know you've got this," I responded. "My offer isn't a reflection of any lack of faith in the LAPD. I also know what it's like at the heart of an investigation like this and how useful it can be to have more minds and bodies to throw at a problem."

Sal pursed his lips as he considered my words.

"And I know what my team can add even to the most experienced group of investigators."

Sal nodded. "Okay. If Ms. Powell is happy, I won't look a gift horse in the mouth. Particularly not this one. I know your organization, Mr. Morgan, and I'm not too proud to say you're right. It could give us an advantage. I want to find this guy before he skips town. If he hasn't already left."

"The Academy won't have any problem with you assisting, Mr. Morgan," Jenny said. "And we want to thank you for your intervention last night."

"Yeah," Sal agreed. "I've seen the footage, and it confirms what the witnesses said about you stopping the guy. If you hadn't stepped in . . ."

"We're grateful," Jenny said when the detective's voice trailed off.

I nodded, though I wasn't interested in the recognition. I'd done what I hoped anyone with my training would have done, given the opportunity. "What have you got?"

Sal nodded toward a laptop beside him. "We've been reviewing footage, pulling anything useful." He selected a clip on the computer. "This is from the intersection of Santa Monica Boulevard and Century Park East and it shows the shooter stepping off a bus twenty minutes before the attack."

I looked at the image on-screen, which showed the man rolling down his ski mask as he left the bus on the busy street.

"He's pulling his mask down," I remarked.

"Or adjusting it," Sal responded. "Either way, there's a chance he was photographed without it on the bus. I was about to head to the depot. You want to come along for the ride?"

I nodded. "Sure."

CHAPTER 6

DETECTIVE SALVATORE MATTERA looked like he was on his way to star in a cologne commercial. He looked stylish and rugged in a fresh-off-the-rack suit. I sat beside him in his black Lincoln Aviator, aware of how rumpled and grubby my tux felt and how disheveled I must look next to him. I rubbed my chin and felt rough stubble.

"I need a shower," I remarked, and he looked at me and smiled.

"I was on a stakeout once and our suspects got antsy. Me and my partner couldn't leave our tiny attic in the neighboring building for three days otherwise we'd have broken cover. I was pretty ripe by the time our relief could take over."

I grinned, warming to the guy. "How many years on the job?"

"Twelve. Six as detective," he replied, keeping his eyes fixed on the road.

We were heading toward the headquarters of the Big Blue Bus corporation on 7th Street in Santa Monica and were stuck in slow-moving lunchtime traffic. We slowed to a crawl as we passed each exit.

"How did you get into the PI business?" Sal asked.

"My dad started Private. I took it over from him a while back and set up offices internationally," I replied. "But LA will always be our home."

"There's nowhere like it." He gestured at the eight-lane high-way and the endless lines of cars in both directions. "Though this probably isn't the best place to illustrate that sentiment."

I started to agree but he turned to look at me, an earnest expression on his face. "I don't know whether it's the ley lines or whether the ancient gods spilled some kind of potion here, but this place is special." He hesitated. "Why else would every other bum on the planet want to live here? Come on, people!" He gestured to the nose-to-tail traffic.

We both laughed, and I was grateful for his easy company.

As we turned off the freeway, I received a message from Mo-bot saying she'd managed to speak to Justine who had said to tell me she was feeling a lot better. The message boosted my spirits and I felt revived as we pulled into the parking lot beside the Big Blue Bus building. The street outside featured a line of vehicles, familiar to anyone who has lived in or visited LA. The security guard on the gate pointed us in the direction of a space, and once Sal had parked, we headed into the two-story glass-and-steel building. On the other side of the lot, I saw buses lined up for cleaning and servicing, a fuel depot and a drivers' lounge.

Inside, a friendly receptionist took us to the depot manager's office, where a forty-something man in a white shirt and black pants was waiting for us.

"Detective Mattera?" he asked.

Sal nodded.

"I'm Ray Jenkins," he said, offering his hand. "Depot manager."

Sal shook it. "Mr. Jenkins, this is Jack Morgan. He runs Private, a detective agency that's assisting us with our investigation."

Ray and I shook hands, and I could tell he was sizing me up, trying to figure out exactly how a scruffy man in a tux was involved with this investigation.

"One of my colleagues was injured in the shooting," I revealed, and that seemed to put his mind at ease.

"I'm sorry to hear that," Ray replied. "One of your colleagues, Detective Landis, called and told me all about what you're looking for. I pulled the footage from the Route 5 bus you caught on camera last night. It's all set up."

He gestured at his PC and we gathered around his desk to get a view of the monitor. The window behind us overlooked the yard, and the walls of the office were lined with photos of buses and groups of employees. I got the sense he was a man who took pride in his work, and the footage he'd cued up reinforced this view.

"Here," he said, leaning forward to use his mouse.

He clicked a video file, and the interior of one of the buses traveling through LA at night appeared on screen.

I immediately saw the shooter making his way from the back of the bus to the center doors.

"He got off at Santa Monica and Century Park," Ray said, before scrubbing back through the video.

"He has his mask on," I remarked to Sal, who frowned and nodded. I could tell he shared my disappointment.

"See stranger things than ski masks when you ride the bus," Ray said absently as on-screen passengers embarked and disembarked in reverse while he reprised the bus's journey.

The shooter stayed in the last row of seats for the whole trip. He didn't talk to anyone and no one went near him, maybe because of the mask.

"He gets on the bus in Santa Monica near the ocean," Ray said, before switching to another file, "and before that, he rides the Route 9."

He scrubbed back through footage of another bus, and daylight filled the windows. The landscape in the background was wild and mountainous. I watched the shooter rise from his seat and walk backward before disappearing from the footage. Ray rewound a little further and then allowed it to play again.

On-screen, the shooter boarded the bus, paid the driver and took his seat.

"That's the stop on Sunset at the edge of Temescal Canyon," he said. "Route serves the Palisades, but we don't get many passengers joining it there. I spoke to the driver, Curtis Tucker, and he says the guy was masked when he flagged down the bus. You want to talk to him? It's his day off, but I can ask him to come in."

"I don't think that will be necessary," Sal replied. "One of my colleagues can go to Mr. Tucker's home and take his statement. See if he caught anything that might be useful. Can you send that footage to my office?"

"Sure," Ray said. "I'll get right on it."

"Use this email address." Sal handed him a card.

"What now?" I asked the thoughtful-looking cop.

"How do you feel about another drive?" he replied.

CHAPTER 7

WE FOLLOWED THE Route 9 bus line via Rustic Canyon, heading through one of LA's most desirable neighborhoods. Along tree-lined Chautauqua Boulevard, we caught glimpses of mansions set behind high walls and imposing gates. They nestled in gardens shaded by trees large enough to have been around when movies played without sound.

Sal and I talked about the job, his years on the force, the harder edge the world had developed in recent years that made it a more dangerous place for anyone in law enforcement. He told me that when he'd first started as a beat cop out on patrol, he would talk to drunks and addicts and they would be reasonable and generally comply with his instructions. Now, the twin scourges of opiate addiction and anti-police sentiment meant that if a cop approached anyone, they would almost invariably be subjected to hostility and violence. Sal said he was glad he only rarely had contact with the street nowadays, but he felt sorry for newly minted beat cops trying to navigate such a volatile landscape.

We talked about the screening and my experiences in the attack. Sal was driving and couldn't take notes, so he recorded my account on his phone for transcription later. There wasn't much to tell. The Ecokiller, as the media had dubbed him, was looking to make a political statement, and had chosen the highest-profile movie release of the year as the target of his violence. He was strong, reasonably well trained, and smart enough not to have shown his face during transit. He wore nondescript clothes that covered any distinguishing features or markings.

As we drove beyond the lush gardens that were nourished by water drawn by pump, pipe and faucet from rivers hundreds of miles away, the mountains returned to their natural state: rugged, dry, covered in rough scrub. We rose into the hills, following Sunset Boulevard, which bent and curled like a snake.

We finally reached the bus stop on the corner of Sunset and Temescal Canyon, and Sal took a right and pulled onto a grass median that split the two lanes of the canyon road. The trailhead was directly in front of us and the bus stop to our rear, with the Pacific Ocean beyond. Up ahead were trailers and a makeshift camp of tents. The press called this place Sanctuary City, an encampment of the homeless that had sprung up in the foothills of Temescal Canyon, drawing more desperate people each and every day while the city fought legal battles in the courts to dismantle the camp and move the inhabitants on.

"Hard Luck City," Sal said, nodding toward the first tents, just visible through the trees.

It was the name cops and city workers gave to the place and was more accurate in my opinion. This wasn't a sanctuary, at least not one the people living there could depend on for any length of time.

"You think our guy might have come from there?" I asked.

"It's possible," Sal replied.

We got out, and I immediately felt the early-afternoon sun baking my black tux. The grass was tinder-dry and the ground hard beneath my feet. I took off my jacket and left it in Sal's Lincoln. He wandered around, hands on hips, surveying the location.

"Busy," he said, observing the steady flow of traffic on Sunset.

"But people don't stop here," I replied. "They drive up the hill to park in the Canyon lot." I gestured beyond the makeshift encampment.

I took out my phone and called Mo-bot.

"What can I do for you, Jack?" she said when she answered.

"I'm going to send you a location," I replied. "Can you check vehicle GPS signals half an hour before . . ." I lifted my head toward Sal. "When did he get on the number 9?"

"Six-fifteen, according to the footage," he replied.

"So, let's make it from five-thirty," I told her. "Any vehicle that stopped at this location and was parked here or in the Canyon lot until after the shooting."

"Okay," Mo-bot said. "I can ask our friend in Maryland. Should be a breeze for him."

Mo-bot was referring to a Department of Defense analyst called Weaver, who had worked with us during the Monaco investigation when we'd thwarted an attempt on the life of Eli Carver, the Secretary of Defense.

"Thanks," I replied.

"I'll call as soon as I have anything," Mo-bot said, before hanging up.

"Impressive," Sal remarked. "Can you really do that?"

"With a little help," I told him.

"Would take me at least a week. If I could get a warrant," he sighed.

"It won't compromise your ability to build a case, will it?" I asked, suddenly concerned I might have jeopardized the chances of Justine's assailant facing justice.

"If it comes to something, no one needs to know how we got there," Sal replied.

I nodded, liking the experienced cop more with each passing hour.

"We should check the camp," he said. "Canvas folk. In case our guy did come through there."

"Sounds good," I said, and we started walking toward the encampment nestled in the trees.

CHAPTER 8

THERE WERE A handful of trailers, but most of the people occupying the encampment lived in tents. Portable gas stoves filled the air with the scents of coffee and hot food. A local homeless charity had set up a mobile kitchen, where volunteers were handing out bowls of noodles. A couple of uniformed cops loitered by their bicycles near the perimeter of the impromptu settlement, watching the comings and goings of the people who'd settled into their own rhythm in this place.

The first news reports on Sanctuary City had started about a month ago, but the encampment had already been going strong. No one knew quite when the first people came or why they'd chosen this place, but it had wrong-footed the authorities who didn't know how to handle the mass clearance of people from a natural space that was surrounded by some of the most expensive homes in California. The optics, as many commentators had remarked, wouldn't be good. So, the city had settled for litigation that would ensure everything was done by the book, and in the interim word had spread. California was a desirable destination for people without homes because of its good weather and the justified belief the West Coast was still somewhere dreams could come true.

Sal and I split up and took different routes through the camp. I stopped to talk to anyone who looked approachable and was struck by how many of the people here had stories of bad luck; three or four big calls that hadn't gone their way, many involving medical emergencies, and they'd speedily found themselves on the wrong side of the tracks. There were some drug users and people with clear mental health issues, but I moved swiftly on from them if they weren't responsive or coherent. For the most part, people were friendly and tried to be helpful, and I found myself wondering about Sal's assessment of the changes he'd seen as a cop. Maybe, as the saying goes, when you're trained to be a hammer, after enough time, you start seeing nails everywhere.

There were unexpected little signs of domesticity in the camp. A Welcome mat outside of one of the rusty trailers. A collection of plants in small pots lined up by a tent. A dog with a jaunty bandana tied around its neck. People often talk about what makes us human in terms of our intellect, emotions or spirit, but perhaps humanity is to be found in these small expressions of our souls. The sign tacked to the side of a tent that reads "Strangers are friends you haven't met," or the warm smile of one of the volunteers doling out food to someone in need.

I crouched beside a lady in a wheelchair who was busy sewing a patch onto a jacket.

"I wonder if I could ask you some questions," I said.

She eyed me carefully. She looked to be in her mid-fifties, but homelessness could age a person, so it was hard to be sure. She had curly gray hair that fell to her shoulders and wore a faded Madonna T-shirt. Her face was tanned and lined, but her eyes still sparkled with vitality.

"Cop?" she asked.

"No," I replied. "I'm trying to help a friend who got hurt last night."

She nodded. "Friend who lives here?"

I shook my head. "No. But the person who hurt my friend might have passed this way."

"What did he look like?" she asked.

"About six feet tall. Black jacket, black pants, my build or thereabouts," I replied.

"Face?"

"He was wearing a mask," I said.

She frowned as she thought about this and relaxed her expression before she spoke. "We have good people here. Peaceful. You have to be decent to live in a community like this with no locks on the door." She gestured at the nearest tent, which I could only assume was hers. "No one has much, but we like what we have and want to hold on to it, and when we're crowded in like this, there needs to be trust. No one here hurt your friend. Least not anyone I know of."

"Thank you," I said, rising to my feet.

"You're welcome," she replied. "A lot of people from outside misunderstand what this place is."

I looked at her expectantly.

"It's home," she said. "A place where we can feel safe. Where we can look after ourselves and those close to us."

"Thank you again," I said, and she nodded.

I turned and spotted Sal some distance off in the camp. He was finishing up with a thin, gray-haired man in his early sixties. My phone rang before I reached them, and I saw Mo-bot's name on-screen.

"Go ahead," I said after I'd greeted her.

"Weaver says one hundred and eighty-three vehicles passed the bus stop between five-thirty and six-fifteen," Mo-bot replied. "Just over sixty of them went up to the parking lot, but all of them left before the Academy shooting."

My heart sank.

"So, they can't belong to the shooter, but there was one vehicle that stopped on the corner of the intersection, right by the bus stop, and it paused for less than a minute at five-forty-six p.m. A Honda Prius registered to an Uber driver called Ahmed Subry. It came from the south, stopped, and then went back the way it came."

"Dropping someone off?" I suggested.

"Looks that way," Mo-bot replied. "I'll send you Subry's details."

"Thanks," I said. "And please pass on my appreciation to our friend in Maryland."

"Already done," Mo-bot told me, before hanging up.

"Anything?" Sal asked as he headed my way.

My phone vibrated with an incoming message from Mo-bot. "Looks like he might have taken an Uber up here." I checked my phone. "Driver is called Ahmed Subry. He lives in Ladera Heights."

"Let's go," Sal said, and we headed back through the settlement toward his car.

CHAPTER 9

AHMED SUBRY LIVED in a small house on Hill Street, a blue-collar neighborhood on the outskirts of Ladera Heights, touching the edges of Inglewood. We caught the start of the evening rush hour as we went south on the 405, and I watched light from the setting sun touch the cars ahead, making them glow brightly like colorful lanterns strung in an endless line. The sky turned copper and by the time we reached Subry's house, the first stars had pierced the deepening purple of the night.

I followed Sal along a path that bisected a small, well-kept yard. A Honda Prius was parked on a short driveway to our left. The front door stood behind a metal security grille and Sal rapped the frame so it clattered loudly.

"Go away," a man yelled from inside.

"Los Angeles Police Department, Mr. Subry," Sal said. "Open up."

I waited a couple of steps back. A woman spoke sharp words in Arabic, and moments later the door opened and Ahmed Subry, thirty-something, peered through the gap hesitantly. He wore a traditional galabaya, a long tunic commonly worn in the Middle East instead of comfortable lounge wear or pajamas. Behind him a woman held a girl of about eight close to her.

"Identification," Subry said.

Sal produced his shield. "My name is Detective Mattera. This is Jack Morgan. He is a private investigator who is helping us with our inquiries."

"Inquiries into?" Subry asked, his concern palpable.

"You hear about the shooting at the Motion Picture Academy last night?" Sal asked, and Subry looked blank.

"The *Star Wars* movie," I suggested, and saw realization dawn.

"Yes, of course. Those poor people," he said somberly. "What does that have to do with me?"

"We believe you might have given the suspect a ride yesterday. Taken him to a bus stop near Temescal Canyon," I responded.

Subry's eyes widened. "The Irishman?"

"Irish?" Sal asked.

Subry nodded. "Yes, I think so. Irish. I know the accent because it sounds like people are singing when they talk."

"Where did you pick him up?" I asked.

Subry thought for a moment. "The Hyland Inn, in Van Nuys."

"I know it," Sal said. "You run a dashcam?"

Subry shook his head. "I had one, but someone stole it. Crime in this city . . ." He suddenly remembered who he was talking to and trailed off.

"It's okay, Mr. Subry," Sal assured him. "I believe crime in this city sucks too."

"You think this Irishman was a guest at the Hyland?" I asked.

"I think so," Subry said. "He came out of room 205."

"Let's go," Sal said, heading for his car. "Thank you, Mr. Subry. I'm going to arrange for an artist to visit and work on a composite of the man you saw."

"I start work in an hour," Subry protested.

"We appreciate your cooperation," Sal said. "Don't go anywhere, please, sir. Not until one of my colleagues has given you the okay."

Subry looked crestfallen as he watched us head for the Lincoln.

Sal was already on his phone. "Do you mind driving?" he asked as he unlocked the car. "I need to make some calls."

"Sure," I replied.

I got behind the wheel, pressed the start button and the engine came to life.

Salvatore got in beside me, giving instructions to one of his team as I put the car in drive and started for Van Nuys.

CHAPTER 10

SAL TURNED ON the siren, and the lights in the front and rear windows had a miraculous effect on the traffic on the 405. Cars parted, allowing me to cut across the eight-lane highway to the carpool lane, where I could make fast progress north. The engine roared and the suspension rocked and bounced as we raced by lines of almost stationary traffic.

Sal spent the journey on his phone either texting or calling, coordinating with his team and the SWAT response unit that was dispatched to the scene. A police car had been deployed to the Hyland Inn, and a uniformed officer had confirmed with the manager that room 205 was still occupied by a man who fit the shooter's height and build. The officer had obtained a copy of the Irish passport the man had presented on check-in. Sal flashed his phone screen at me, and I saw a pug-faced man with a broken nose and dark, curly hair.

"Passport in the name of Colm Finlay," Sal said. He spoke into his phone. "Thanks for the ID, Officer Stotter. Find somewhere quiet to watch the place without alerting the suspect."

I understood Sal's game plan. The uniform had been sent to verify the lead, seemingly visiting the motel as part of a routine patrol. The cop would pull back to a place of concealment to make sure the suspect didn't leave until we and the rapid response SWAT team arrived. It was sound policework, and I was impressed by Sal's quick thinking and adaptability.

It took another twenty minutes of fast, traffic-weaving, bump, brake and accelerate driving to reach the motel, and we were there before the SWAT unit. Sal cut the lights a block from the place, and I made a point of slowing his Lincoln as we drew close.

My heart was thundering with the adrenalin rush of the drive, but I forced myself to remain calm. I couldn't give our presence away. The Lincoln had to look like just another vehicle as we took a right off Sepulveda Boulevard, past the blue-and-gray colonial-style motel, and pulled into the parking lot round back. The two-story accommodation block was arranged in a horseshoe around a small garden that was fringed by tall palm trees. I took a spot in the far corner of the lot, parking so the tail of the car was pointed toward the motel rooms. Sal and I could see the door to room 205 by looking in the side mirrors, but the tall head rests would make any casual observer think the Lincoln was empty.

"Where are you?" Sal said into his phone, which was now on speaker.

"Outside of Starbucks on the other side of Sepulveda,"

Officer Stotter replied, and I saw his vehicle parked about a hundred yards away in the parking lot across the street.

Sal used his radio to contact the SWAT team. "What's your ETA, Winston?"

"We're five minutes out," a man said. "Sit tight, Sal."

"I guess we do what the man said," he told me, but my attention was drawn to a blue Toyota Camry rolling to a halt near the motel accommodation block.

The driver, a heavy-set, bald man in his fifties, got out and went to room 205. He knocked on the door and said something, before returning to his vehicle.

"I think we've got a problem," I remarked.

Sal glanced in his wing mirror as the door to room 205 opened and our suspect filled the frame, a holdall slung over his shoulder and a small suitcase by his side.

"He's leaving," I said. "What should we do?"

The man glanced around furtively before walking to the car.

"We let him roll, we risk losing him," Sal said. "I say we take him here, once he's in the car. You good with that?"

I nodded.

"Winston," Sal said into the radio, "we've got a situation. Suspect is leaving. We're going to have to make a move."

"Dammit, Sal," Winston replied, but the detective didn't wait to hear any more and muted the radio so he could focus on his phone.

"Officer Stotter, the suspect is on the move. Blue Toyota Camry. We're going to have to take him. Get over here and back us up," Sal said.

"Yes, sir," Stotter replied.

We watched the suspect climb into the back of the Toyota, and the moment he shut the door, Sal nodded. I hit the start button, flipped the gearshift into reverse and gunned the engine. The tires screeched as the car surged back and I hit the brakes, so we stopped directly ahead of the Toyota. Sal jumped out, drew his pistol and pointed it at the suspect.

"Get out of the car now!" he yelled. "You're under arrest."

The terrified driver raised his hands, but a split second later, a bullet burst through his forehead, punching a hole through the windshield and spattering it with blood. The Ecokiller had shot the man through the back of his skull and followed up with a volley of shots aimed at Sal, who dodged behind the rear of the Lincoln.

I ducked down, leaning against the passenger seat as the side windows shattered and showered me with glass. The noise of gunfire was deafening, and I could smell gun smoke in the air. My exit was blocked by the immobile Toyota, so I opened the passenger door, hauled myself across the seat and tumbled out of the car onto the asphalt beside Sal. He was crouched by the rear wheel.

"Shit," he said, clasping his gun.

I heard Stotter's siren blaring as he raced across Sepulveda Boulevard toward us, but the sound of his approach must have spurred the shooter because he made a move, opening the rear door of the Toyota and racing from the vehicle back toward his motel room. He barged the door open with his shoulder, fired a couple of wild shots in our direction, and disappeared into the darkness beyond.

CHAPTER 11

SAL RAN ACROSS the small courtyard garden to the exterior wall of room 205, and I joined him on the other side of the doorway. Other guests were peering through their windows or standing in doorways, and traffic had stopped on Sepulveda to let Officer Stotter pass. Another couple of shots zipped from the motel room, aimed in our direction, and the crack of the gunfire thundered in my ears. Muzzle flash illuminated the room briefly as the shooter fired again, and I saw his shape outlined toward the back.

Officer Stotter skidded into the parking lot and killed his lights and sirens as he screeched to a halt. Sal waved him toward the rear of the accommodation block, and I watched the uniformed cop steer his vehicle to the back of the building.

I gave Sal an over-emphasized shrug, indicating my need for instruction.

"We wait for the back to be covered and then I'll move in," he whispered.

My heart was thumping in my ears, and I was very conscious I was unarmed. I'd taken the decision years ago only to carry a weapon when strictly necessary. Concealed carry on a regular basis was a recipe for gun theft or accidents, so I hadn't armed myself last night before the premiere. I was regretting my decision now though, and more so when we heard a brace of shots from the back of the building. A man cried out and then came a third shot. I had no doubt Officer Stotter had run into trouble.

Sal ran into the motel room and rolled clear of the door. I followed him and saw the very basic room was empty. I checked under the unmade bed and found nothing.

Sal went into the bathroom.

"Jack," he said, and I ran into the cramped room and saw an open window. "Get the car."

Outside, we heard an engine rev, and I prayed the shooter hadn't killed the uniformed cop.

"I'm going after him," Sal told me, and hoisted himself through the window. "He's got Stotter's patrol car."

I sprinted out of room 205 and ran across the lot to Sal's Lincoln. There were more sirens in the distance, and a crowd was gathering around the motel.

I heard further gunshots and screeching tires as I jumped behind the wheel. I started the car, threw the gearshift into drive, and steered it toward the end of the accommodation block.

I took the corner at speed and entered an alleyway that

wrapped around the rear of the motel. I could see a patrol car racing into the distance beyond the other end of the alley. Sal was halfway along it, crouched beside Officer Stotter, performing CPR. I pulled to a shuddering halt beside the men, and the car threw out a plume of dust behind me.

Sal stood and staggered back from Officer Stotter, and as he moved, I saw three gunshot wounds in the cop's neck. The police officer was dead.

"Come on," I said, watching the black-and-white patrol car disappear around the corner, bouncing as it jumped the curb and joined Sepulveda Boulevard. "Come on, Sal. We can't do anything for him. But we can catch that scumbag."

My words snapped Sal to his senses. He ran to the car, climbed into the passenger seat and said, "Go!"

My foot was already on the accelerator. As the Lincoln gathered speed Sal got on the radio.

"Dispatch, this is Detective Mattera. Officer Stotter is down, in the alleyway behind the Hyland Inn. I did what I could, but . . ."

He trailed off, and for a moment I thought he might break down, but he composed himself. "We are in pursuit of a suspect heading north on Sepulveda in Officer Stotter's patrol car."

"Copy that," the dispatcher replied. "All units be on the lookout for patrol vehicle seven-zero-four-nine-five. Suspect is believed to have been involved in an officer shooting and is to be considered armed and dangerous."

The radio filled with responses from nearby patrols. Cops all over the world share the same sentiment—harm one of their own at your peril.

By the time we hit Sepulveda, it sounded as though an army was being mobilized to catch this guy.

Sal turned on the lights and siren and I wove through the traffic, pursuing the patrol car, which also had its reds and blues going.

"You get that, Winston?" Sal said into his radio.

"We got it," he replied. "We'll go for an intercept."

"Suspect turned off Sepulveda onto Kittridge Street," Sal said, and I zipped past stationary traffic to reach the intersection.

I swung a hard left onto a quiet road lined with retail units and warehouses. I slowed down as I saw the patrol car abandoned in the middle of one lane. The driver's door hung open, but the engine was still running.

"Trap?" I suggested.

"Could be," Sal replied. "We move carefully."

I nodded. Pursuits were frustrating because a violent suspect could often flee with much less caution than those on his tail.

I rolled up behind the patrol car and Sal got out, gun at the ready.

CHAPTER 12

SAL CROUCHED LOW and approached Officer Stotter's vehicle. The engine purred ominously as he closed in, arms outstretched, pistol raised. I stayed back, unarmed, conscious of the fact the gunman might be lying across the front seats. Salvatore got an angle on the interior.

"Clear," he said, before leaning through the driver's door and popping the trunk.

He moved round the back of the vehicle and lifted the lid to reveal a semi-auto shotgun in the trunk-space locking mount. He unlocked the quick release and handed me the gun along with a box of shells.

"For use in self-defense only," he told me.

The Benelli M4 tactical shotgun came with a pistol grip and was a reliable weapon that carried six shells. I checked the gun was fully loaded and emptied the box of twenty-five further shells into my pockets, splitting them between the side pockets of my tux.

The surrounding buildings were all occupied apart from one warehouse directly left of the patrol car, which looked empty and derelict. A demolition notice was pinned to the gates, and a strip of the mesh fencing had been torn open at some point in the past and curled back through regular use by intruders. The warehouse beyond was covered in graffiti and peppered with broken windows. A late-twentieth-century build, it was a large, functional place that stood three stories high. A lot of places to hide in there.

"Should we wait?" I asked, feeling more confident with a gun in my hands.

The sirens weren't far off.

"He might slip out the back," Sal replied, before speaking into his phone. "Winston, we're outside of a warehouse on Kittridge Street. Suspect has fled into the building on foot. Tell dispatch to notify responding units. We are going into the building after him."

"Copy that," Winston replied. "We're no more than three minutes out. We'll have your back."

Sal pocketed his phone and started toward the hole in the fence.

"Quickly and quietly, sweep the place," he said. "Check the exits. Make sure he hasn't escaped."

I nodded and followed him through the fence. We double-timed it across the disused parking lot and were about sixty feet from the main entrance when the yard erupted with the crackle of gunfire.

Sal went down almost instantly, caught by the shooter, who was using a sub machine gun to shell us from a second-floor window. I replied with my shotgun, knowing it had little chance of doing serious harm at that range, but it was noisy, and few people could stand tall in the face of a semi-automatic at any distance.

My gamble worked. The shooter backed away from the window. I kept firing as I rushed toward Sal, who was on his back, moaning.

I grabbed his pistol, which had fallen a few feet from him, and fired a brace of shots at the window. The FN 509 carried seventeen rounds in its magazine, so I used it to tell the shooter I had a more accurate short-range weapon.

"You okay?" I asked Sal.

I could see he wasn't. His right arm had been shredded, and an unknown number of bullets had pierced his abdomen. Blood was spreading rapidly across his shirt front. I saw the shooter back in the window and fired the pistol again, unleashing another pair of bullets to send the man cowering away.

I dropped the shotgun, grabbed Sal by his good arm and dragged him with my left hand, while laying covering fire with my right. My shots weren't accurate, but they shattered what remained of the window and did exactly what I'd intended, scaring the shooter off.

I pulled Sal back through the fence and dragged him behind the patrol car. I found a fresh clip in his holster and reloaded the pistol. Staying alert to danger, I put the detective in the recovery position and used his belt to tie a tourniquet around his mangled arm. I spoke to him constantly, encouraging him to hold on while we waited for help, which, judging by the incoming scream of sirens, was only seconds away.

CHAPTER 13

I STEMMED THE bleeding from Sal's arm and talked to the badly wounded, delirious man, keeping him conscious until the first police units arrived. SWAT were on the scene, and the team medic sprinted over to me. The unit commander, who I assumed was Winston, was a few yards behind.

"Jeez, Sal," he remarked.

The medic got to work immediately, and I stood and faced the SWAT commander.

"Jack Morgan," I said. "I was working with Detective Mattera."

"John Winston, SWAT team leader," he replied. "Shooter?"

"Second-floor window," I said, pointing at the location. "Just above the entrance."

"This man needs to be moved to a hospital immediately," the medic said.

"Ambulance is two minutes out," Winston said. "We're going in."

He assembled his unit near their van and issued instructions. I crouched to help the medic apply pressure to Sal's wounds as more police vehicles approached, sirens blaring. I couldn't hear everything he said to the team, but it was clear they were going to sweep the building.

The ambulance arrived moments later and pulled to a halt a few feet away from the patrol car. Two paramedics jumped out of the vehicle and ran over to us, carrying gear bags.

"What have we got?" the lead responder asked.

"Multiple gunshot wounds to his arm and abdomen," I replied. "Bleeding pretty bad."

"Tourniquet is holding," the SWAT medic advised.

The lead paramedic sank onto her knees beside Sal and opened her bag.

"Name?" she asked.

"Detective Salvatore Mattera," I replied. "He likes to be called Sal."

She nodded. "We've got this now, sir. Thank you for every-thing you've done." She turned to Sal. "Detective Mattera . . . Sal . . . my name is Rosa. I'm going to check you over."

Sal groaned, which was a good sign. He still had some con-nection to what was going on around him.

I got to my feet and stepped back while Winston and his team moved into the building, expertly covering each other until they were inside.

I looked down at Sal's pistol, which was still in my hand, and saw my knuckles were white from clutching the grip. I hoped I'd got lucky and winged the shooter with one of my shots.

I walked across the street and sank onto the curb as more cop cars arrived. Soon patrol cars and unmarked vehicles filled the road around the warehouse, drawing people to the doorways, windows and lots of the surrounding businesses. Uniformed cops were instructed to form a perimeter by a watch commander, and somber-faced men and women in suits clustered around Sal.

After a few minutes, my phone rang and I saw Mo-bot's name on-screen.

"Go ahead," I said.

"You okay?" she asked, sounding relieved. "The tabloids are reporting the Ecokiller has shot a cop. LAPD chatter picked up on scanners and from anonymous department sources."

I shook my head at the thought grim news like this could break even before the cop's family had been told.

"I'm fine," I assured her. "Detective Mattera got shot too. He's in a bad way."

"I'm sorry, Jack," Mo-bot said.

The crime scene was getting even busier. A mobile command unit was pulling up at the end of the street, and the first citizen journalists were on the scene with their phones.

"It's turning into a circus here," I said, and then I noticed one of the cops who'd just arrived break away from a group of detectives and head in my direction. She walked with confidence and wore an expensive gray pantsuit. "I've got to go," I told Mo-bot. "I'll keep you posted."

"I'm Captain Linda Brooks," the suited woman said as I hung up. "SWAT medic says you saved Sal's life."

"I wish I could have done more," I replied. "Jack Morgan." I offered her my hand.

"Private," she said as she shook it. "Sal told me you were helping him. I'm his commanding officer. What the hell happened here?"

I sighed, and glanced over at Sal, who was being lifted onto a gurney. "We pursued the suspect known as the Ecokiller. We were concerned he would escape from the building, and as we moved in to prevent that, he opened fire."

"Shit," said Brooks. "Sal should have known better. He shouldn't have tried playing the hero."

One of the paramedics approached us. "We're moving him now, Captain."

Across the street, the SWAT medic and one ambulance service responder lifted the gurney to full height and pushed Sal toward the vehicle. The paramedic held a drip above the injured man's head.

"Gotta go," said the lead paramedic, jogging to the ambulance.

Linda and I followed, and she touched Sal's shoulder as he was lifted into the vehicle.

"You stay with us, Sal," she said. He looked at us with glassy, unseeing eyes before the paramedics got busy around him.

Moments later, the doors were slammed shut, the engine rumbled to life, and the siren sounded as the vehicle began its dash to the hospital.

"You'd better take this," I said, offering Captain Brooks the pistol I was still holding. "It's Sal's. I used it to lay down suppressing fire so I could pull him clear."

She took the gun from me without comment and slipped it into her waistband.

As the ambulance joined Sepulveda Boulevard and raced away, Winston emerged from the building and jogged across the disused parking lot to the gates which had been forced open.

"Building is clear," he said as he approached us. "The suspect is in the wind."

CHAPTER 14

IT WAS LATE by the time I got to the hospital. I was still in my tux from the previous night, and it was now grimy with the residue of a traumatic day. I desperately needed a shower, but I'd arranged to meet Mo-bot and Sci and wanted to check on Justine.

I'd been interviewed by Captain Brooks and a Detective Philips, who was seething at what the shooter had done to Sal. I gathered he was a popular figure in the department. I gave them the same account I'd given Brooks when she'd spoken to me at the scene, but with much more detail. While I was being deposed at the precinct, Brooks got word Sal's condition had stabilized enough for surgery. The news had buoyed the cops' spirits, and I could understand why. I know about the camaraderie people develop when serving together or while working dangerous jobs. Today it was Sal who had fallen victim to a

shooter. Another day and it could have been a different colleague whose life was brutally disrupted, carted away in an
ambulance to fight off the cruel grasp of death. Plus, Sal seemed
to be a genuinely good guy. I'd warmed to him during our brief
time together.

Finally, when Linda was satisfied she had everything she
needed, I was told I could go. I immediately caught a cab to
Cedars-Sinai. Mo-bot was due to hand over to Sci, but said she'd
wait for me so we could discuss what had happened.

"She's awake," Mo-bot told me, as I neared Justine's room.
"She wants to see you."

Mo-bot and Sci were seated either side of the low table directly opposite the door. Mo-bot was on her laptop, and Sci was
reading a book on classic motorcycles called *The Art of Speed*.

"Boss," he said with a nod. "You look like you've been in the
wars. A stylish war, but a war nonetheless."

I tipped an imaginary hat at him. "It hasn't been the best day.
Give me a few minutes."

He and Mo-bot nodded, and I opened the door to Justine's
room carefully in case she was resting.

She was lying with her head at an angle, so she could see past
the frame that kept the blanket off her belly. I was pleased to see
she was no longer on supplemental oxygen. The mask had gone.

"Hey," she said quietly.

"Hey," I replied. "How are you?"

"Okay. They say it's going to take a while."

I knew from experience that the mental aspects of recovery
could be as challenging as the physical.

"There's no rush. Take all the time you need," I said.

"Mo told me about the cop who died," Justine responded. "Poor guy. Are you okay?"

I nodded. "I was lucky."

"LAPD will be all over this," Justine remarked.

"Yeah. And the guy just went for another cop too." I took her right hand and squeezed it gently.

"I changed my mind," she said. "I don't want you ending up like me. Or the cops. This guy is far too dangerous."

I nodded. "I get that."

I hated the idea of giving up on a chase, but my place was at Justine's side, and the cops would hunt this man to the ends of the earth. There wouldn't be a rock he could hide under in this whole city or the world beyond.

"My ally in the department got taken out, so I'm probably not welcome in any case. I'll go home, have a shower, grab a change of clothes and see if the hospital can set me up with a cot in here."

"I already asked," Justine revealed. "It's against policy. Visitors need to leave by nine. Security personnel are permitted to be present by special arrangement, which is why Sci and Mo-bot were allowed to loiter outside for so long."

"Then I'll join your team of loiterers," I told her. "And when I'm not here, I'll stay at the Four Seasons down the street." The upscale hotel was only a few hundred yards from the hospital.

Justine smiled and squeezed my hand in reply, making a point of showing her returning strength. Her grip still felt weak, but I was encouraged by the effort she'd made and pretended it hurt.

"Ow."

"Wuss," she replied, and I leaned down to kiss her.

"Get some sleep," I said. "I'll be here when you wake up."

She nodded and watched me leave.

I joined Mo-bot and Sci in the corridor.

"News reports say it was carnage," Mo-bot revealed, turning her computer to show me the sensational coverage of the Eco-killer's latest violent rampage. "You okay?"

I nodded. "Another cop just got shot up pretty bad, but I was lucky."

"I doubt that," Sci remarked. "Experience tells me luck doesn't come into it with you."

"What now?" Mo-bot asked.

"Cops run with it," I replied. "We stand down."

They exchanged glances of surprise

"Justine doesn't want me in harm's way."

"But she told you to—" Mo-bot began before I cut her off.

"She was coming out of anesthetic then. She was scared and angry. Confused even. And that was before two cops were mown down. I get where she's coming from now. This guy is danger-ous, and half the cops in the city are hunting him. I'd only get in the way."

"Makes sense," Mo-bot remarked.

"I'm going home to shower and grab some stuff and then I'll take over here. We can split the days and make sure she's got someone with her all the time until she's discharged."

CHAPTER 15

I SLEPT UNEASILY. I was back in the wreckage of my Sea Knight, the searing flames scorching my skin as my comrades cried out all around me. It took a moment for me to make the disorientating transition from dream to reality, realizing the sound of their screams was in fact my phone ringing.

I rubbed my face and sat straighter in the chair outside of Justine's room. A nurse walked by, pushing a dispensing trolley that had morning meds laid out in neat rows. I pulled my phone from my pocket and saw Mo-bot's name flash on-screen. The tiny clockface read 7:03 a.m.

"Yeah?" I answered.

"No good morning?" she replied.

"It's too early."

"Someone's in a bad mood," she observed.

I felt groggy but had managed a few hours of broken sleep. I rose and walked to the door of Justine's room. Glancing in through the observation window, I saw she was fast asleep, her face flushed and relaxed, suggesting it was a deep, peaceful rest.

"Morning," I conceded. "Is everything okay?"

"We need to meet," Mo-bot said. "Are you at the hospital?"

"What's going on?" I asked, stepping away from the door so as not to wake Justine.

"It's the shooter. LAPD put out an APB, but it was too late to stop him leaving the country. He managed to escape the warehouse and there're now photographs of him boarding a flight to Dublin, Ireland, at LAX, and . . . well, you need to see them. Justine too."

"What?" I asked. "Why? Why would she need to see anything?"

"Are you at the hospital? You need to meet us," Mo-bot pressed.

"Us?"

"Sci is coming too," she said.

"Yeah, I'm at the hospital," I replied.

"See you in twenty," she said, before hanging up.

I wondered what could be so urgent and why she wanted me and Justine to see the photos from LAX. I didn't dwell on it for too long though. I knew the time would pass more quickly if I was busy, so I grabbed the overnight bag I'd brought from home and went to the bathroom, where I brushed my teeth, had a wash and changed my clothes, opting for a lightweight black pullover and jeans. I left the men's room looking casual but respectable, certainly not like someone who'd snatched a few hours' sleep in a hospital corridor. I went downstairs and found a coffee shop where I ordered a double espresso, which I took back to our observation point outside of Justine's room.

Mo-bot and Sci were waiting by the time I returned, both of them frowning and agitated.

"What is it?" I asked, recognizing the signs of trouble.

Mo-bot opened her satchel, took out her laptop and set it on the low table between the chairs.

"The APB reached the airport too late for Homeland Security to put him on the no-fly list, and he was traveling on a different passport," Mo-bot said. An image of the Ecokiller filled her screen. He was standing at a check-in desk, smiling as he spoke to a flight attendant.

Anger rose in me at the sight of the man who had caused so much harm.

"He must have been on his way to the airport when you and Detective Mattera found him at the motel," Sci remarked.

"Looks like he went straight there after the shootout at the warehouse," Mo-bot said. "Smart. Taking advantage of the fact APBs and port alerts take time."

"This isn't our fight anymore," I said, glancing at the door to Justine's room. I desperately wanted to go after this man and bring him to justice, but my place was here. "We're done."

"You might not feel the same way when you see this," Mo-bot told me. "I got it from the file the Department of Homeland Security shared with LAPD," she said as she switched to another photo.

This one showed the gunman with his shoes and shirt off,

being searched by a Homeland Security officer in an airport cubicle.

"Someone must have got a bad vibe from him, because he was flagged for a fingertip search," Mo-bot said.

"Or maybe they picked up gunpowder residue on a swab," Sci remarked.

"Either way," Mo-bot went on, "he got asked to strip."

She moved to another photo which showed the Ecokiller from the rear, his shoulders and back bare. The exposed skin was covered in tattoos, and I saw why Mo-bot had wanted to meet immediately. Among skulls and other insignia was a tattoo of three fleur-de-lys inside a Jerusalem Cross. The symbol was inked on his left shoulder blade, and I recognized it as the insignia of Propaganda Tre, the secret society we thought we had destroyed in Rome, and whose subsequent attempted assassination of US Secretary of Defense Eli Carver we had thwarted in Monaco. The malevolent group extended its reach into the realms of politics, finance and organized crime, and was set on using chaos as the means of acquiring ever more power and wealth.

I realized in a moment of heart-pounding, adrenalin-fuelled clarity that Justine and I had not been the chance victims of a random shooting.

We'd been the intended targets all along.

CHAPTER 16

I UNDERSTOOD WHY Mo-bot had insisted on meeting me at the hospital, and she and I exchanged a somber look. When I'd been in Italy to open our new office in the Eternal City, we had become embroiled in Propaganda Tre's conspiracy to take over the Vatican and other positions of power in Rome. Justine and I had subsequently been targeted in Monaco as part of an attempt at revenge by the group, and here I was once more looking at the distinctive tattoo that signaled the gunman's membership of the secret criminal group. In Monaco, one leading member of Propaganda Tre had escaped, Raymond Chalmont, the owner of the casino which the group had been using to launder money from its criminal activities. I had tried to find him as had the Monégasque, French and US authorities, but the trail had gone cold in Tangier. Chalmont had strong motives for revenge having lost everything of value that he had—his home, family, friends, status and business—staking it all on an attempt to assassinate Eli Carver, the US Secretary of Defense.

For a while after the events in Monaco I'd been worried but, over time, I'd lowered my guard. It was clear now that I'd made a catastrophic mistake.

"This was targeted," Sci said.

I nodded. "Is our man still in the air?"

Mo-bot shook her head. "Flight landed in Dublin over an hour ago. LAPD notified the Irish police, the Garda Síochána, but the alert came too late."

"Damn," I said, and started pacing in frustration, trying to figure out the best course of action. "I've got to go there," I said at last.

"I don't think—" Sci began, but Mo-bot cut him off.

"He has to." She turned to me. "You want us to tell Justine?"

I glanced at the door to her room and shook my head. "I can't leave without her knowing."

Mo-bot looked pointedly at the door.

I walked over to it reluctantly. I knew this wouldn't be easy but couldn't see that I had any other choice. I knocked gently and, after a moment, heard a faint, "Come in."

I stepped inside, steeling myself.

"Hey," Justine said, sitting up a little straighter in bed. She knew me too well and must have clocked something in my expression. "What's wrong?"

I propped myself against the edge of the bed and stroked the back of her left hand.

"How are you?" I asked.

She still looked too pale, but there was more color in her face than yesterday, and her eyes didn't seem as dull.

"It's too early to say for sure," she replied. "But I think I feel better. A little at least. What's the matter?"

"The man who shot you," I began, before hesitating. "There's no easy way to say this. He left the country after being strip-searched at the airport. He had a Propaganda Tre tattoo."

I'd seen her bracing for bad news, but she couldn't have prepared herself for the shock of this revelation.

"No," she said. "That would mean . . ."

"I think he came here to kill us," I finished her train of thought. "We were the intended targets."

We sat in near-silence for a moment, the stillness broken only by the sounds of the machines around her.

"He went to Ireland," I said. "I have to go after him."

"No," Justine responded. "You can't, Jack. It's too dangerous."

"I have to," I said. "It will take weeks for LAPD to work through the red tape with the Irish police, by which time his trail will have gone cold. I don't have any of those constraints. I can get on the next flight and find him."

She tried to speak but I held up my hand to stop her.

"Mo-bot and Sci will stay with you in case they try again." With these words, I saw the severity of our situation hit home for her. "We won't be truly safe until I've found this man and whoever sent him."

"Jack . . ." she began, but couldn't continue. Tears filled her eyes.

"I'll get support from our London office," I said. "It's the only way. The one chance we've got of putting Rome and Monaco behind us and staying safe, once and for all."

She was silent for a long while and I saw her struggling to think of alternatives, but in the end acceptance washed over her. She looked at me and nodded.

"You're right," she whispered. "You have to go."

She took my hand and squeezed it, and I felt genuine strength in her grip this time.

"I love you," I said.

"I love you too," she replied. "Come back to me, Jack. You hear me? Come back in one piece."

CHAPTER 17

I LEFT THE hospital and went to the office to grab the go bag I kept there for urgent deployments just like this one. At the wheel of my Mercedes SLS, a very expensive thank-you gift from a grateful client, I turned into the parking garage beneath our building. I stopped at the bottom of the ramp to give the sensor time to recognize my license plate, and the shutter rose to allow me inside.

After sliding the Mercedes into my parking space, I took the elevator up to Private's offices on the fifth floor, and emerged into the lobby where Michelle and Dewayne, our two receptionists, were already at their shared desk. Both were on the phone fielding calls, but they smiled and waved when they saw me. I didn't linger but hurried into my corner office, which overlooked Wilshire Boulevard and offered a view of the City of Angels coming to life for the start of another working day.

As I sat at my desk, booking my flight, I received a call from Emily Knighton, the manager of Private London. I'd tried her on my way from the hospital and had left a message for her to call me as soon as possible.

"Emily," I said.

"Jack," she responded. "How are you? And how's Justine?"

Word of the shooting had spread throughout the Private network.

"I'm fine," I replied. "Justine is in hospital, but it looks like she's going to be okay."

"That's such a relief. What can I do for you?"

Emily had been a Royalty and Specialist Protection Officer in Protection Command until she'd taken over our London office two years ago. Tough and dedicated, she was someone I knew I could rely on.

"I'm flying to Dublin tonight. I arrive tomorrow afternoon. Do we have anyone with local knowledge of the city?" I asked.

"Yes," she replied. "A handful. I'll see who's available. Send me your flight details and I'll make sure you're met at the airport."

"Thanks," I said.

"Does this have something to do with the shooting?" she asked.

"It looks like Justine and I might have been targeted for the attack at the Academy."

My response prompted a sharp intake of breath from Emily.

"It was meant to look random, but it wasn't. He tried to throw us off the scent with that eco statement. But it was revenge, for Rome and Monaco."

Our European offices had all been involved in the Monaco operation and the entire organization had access to the Rome case file so I knew Emily would pick up on what I was saying.

"I'm sorry to hear that," she replied. "Send me everything you've got and I'll make sure it goes to the operative assigned to you. We'll also see what we can dig up from here."

"I appreciate it," I replied. "Speak soon."

"Safe travels," she said, before hanging up.

I completed my reservation for the next flight from LAX to Dublin, grabbed my go bag, and headed for the airport.

As I crawled toward the airport in slow-moving morning traffic, watching the sunlight gleaming off the rainbow of cars ahead of me, I thought about our current situation. Fate had set Justine and me on a collision course with Propaganda Tre in Rome and, rather than leave us in peace, they'd sought revenge. First, they'd kidnapped Justine in Monaco and had attempted to blackmail me into assassinating Eli Carver. Now they'd tried again, and as I thought about her lying wounded in hospital, my anger grew stronger. I knew we'd never truly be safe until I found the man responsible for the shooting and used him to implicate those who'd sent him to kill us. I wondered whether Raymond Chalmont could be behind this, even though he didn't strike me as the type. He was careful and cunning; his first instinct would be for his own survival, which meant stay-ing hidden. Revenge attracted unwanted attention and was a costly business, particularly when it was unsuccessful.

I reached the airport a little before noon and spent the rest of the day in the first-class lounge, counting down the hours, coordinating with Mo-bot to send Emily everything we had on the investigation so far. There wasn't much to go on besides the photos of the shooter taken from surveillance cameras outside of the Academy. Mo-bot had been able to get a copy of the passport the shooter had presented at LAX, made out in the name of Colm Finlay. It was fake, but at least it gave us a full, head-on image of the man. And we were able to give Emily details of the flight he'd boarded, which pinpointed his arrival time in Dublin.

With the case file on its way to London, I exchanged WhatsApp messages with Justine for a short time. I was keen not to tire her, but wanted to keep her connected to what I was doing.

Finally, after hours of waiting, my flight was called for boarding and I got to my feet and headed for the gate and the Airbus A330 that would take me to Ireland.

CHAPTER 18

YEARS OF COMBAT experience as a Marine and then as head of Private had taught me to sleep whenever the opportunity presented itself. I drifted off as the aircraft reached cruising altitude and woke for the breakfast service, about ninety minutes out from Dublin. I had a black coffee and watched the Emerald Isle come into view as we began our descent. I hadn't had any dreams, at least none I could remember, but the sight of the distinctive green landscape on the very edge of a different continent prompted me to think of my last trip to Europe. My mind filled with images of me and Justine on what should have been a romantic vacation in Monaco, a trip that had ended in turmoil and danger.

I hadn't intended to fall in love with a colleague, but I wasn't sure a civilian would have been able to cope with the stresses, hazards and unpredictable nature of my work. Justine was one of the world's leading criminal profilers and had years of experience of operating in this arena. She understood the landscape of law enforcement as well as she did the criminal mind, and recognized that sometimes we had to make personal sacrifices to do the right thing. Being away from her now in order to come to Ireland was one such sacrifice for me. My heart wanted to be with her, never leaving her side as she continued her recovery, but my experience as a detective and a veteran told me I had to neutralize this threat.

We continued our descent as we flew over the west coast of Ireland and moved from roiling seas crashing against rocky shores to a rich, fertile green landscape. I could see cows grazing in fields beneath puffball clouds, a tractor motoring up a gentle hill toward a field-stone barn, cars winding along single-lane roads that crisscrossed the landscape between high hedges, large expanses of wild bog and thick forests. In the distance, a town lay nestled between hills at the mouth of a wide estuary. This looked like a beautiful, peaceful country; it was hard for me to imagine such a bountiful, gentle environment as the source of the horror that had invaded my life. Then I recalled Ireland's troubled past, both recent and ancient, and reminded myself that darkness can thrive wherever people's hearts are turned by ambition, greed or anger.

Situated on the East Coast of Ireland at the mouth of the River Liffey, Dublin is home to a little over half a million souls and its mix of architecture reflects a history that stretches back more than a thousand years. Peppered among the post-war homes and contemporary retail parks and office blocks were castles and ruins so old they seemed to have merged with the landscape, making the myth and magic that are commonly associated with Ireland feel real. The flight touched down at 2:30 p.m. on a warm and sunny day.

I cleared Customs and Immigration in under an hour, and as I went into the Arrivals hall, I saw a woman holding up a sign with the word "Private" on it. She was early thirties, athletic, had long black hair tied in a ponytail, and wore a dark green pantsuit. Her keen gaze suggested a sharp mind and there was a flash of recognition in it when I approached.

"Mr. Morgan, my name is Andrea Harris. Emily Knighton sent me from the London office."

She spoke with a London accent but there were Irish undertones to her voice. She stepped forward and shook my hand.

"Nice to meet you, Ms. Harris," I responded. "Call me Jack."

"Everyone calls me Andi," she said with a bright smile. "Welcome to Dublin, Jack."

CHAPTER 19

"I USED A gray name to hire it," Andi told me as I placed my bag in the trunk of a black Ford Kuga.

Gray names were identities belonging to real people we paid to allow us to book hotel rooms, car rentals, Airbnb homes and other practical hires in their name when we didn't want to leave a paper trail. Private had to operate within the law, but sometimes our activities required straining legal limits, and gray names were one way we did this.

"I used a different name to rent a place in the city center," she said as we got into the car.

She started the Ford, revved the engine a little too long, and drove out of the white multi-story parking structure at speed. She was an aggressive driver, bordering on reckless, but I said nothing as we darted along the airport service roads, weaving through the traffic, passing rental cars, and red and white Bus Éireann coaches.

While Andi got us clear of the airport, I used my phone to message Justine, Mo-bot and Sci, to let them know I'd arrived safely.

"Have you been to Dublin before?" Andi asked, as we joined the motorway.

"No," I replied, taking in the greenery that surrounded the busy six-lane highway.

"Your loss," she said, flashing a cheeky smile. "I was born in London, but my dad was from the old country, and I spent a lot of time here as a child. When Emily asked for a volunteer, I jumped at the chance. And not just because I'd get face time with the big boss."

It was my turn to smile. Her enthusiastic and irreverent energy shone through, and I found it endearing.

"Or should I call you the ultimate boss?" she asked playfully. "Anyway, I know this place like a home from home and have a lot of friends here. We're staying in Fitzwilliam Square, in the heart of the action."

I'd done some research on Dublin at the airport and the city had a reputation as one of the most welcoming capitals in the world. Situated on the Irish Sea, covering less than 120 square kilometers, with a port to the east and lush countryside in every other direction, it was the economic powerhouse of Ireland and home to more than ten percent of the country's population.

"Emily gave me the case file you sent," Andi continued. "So, you're looking for this Finlay fella, or whatever his real name is. Any leads? Where do you want to start?"

"We've got his flight details and arrival time," I replied. "We should start at the airport. Get access to security footage and track his movements. He'll have left the airport in a private vehicle, cab or public transport, any of which could give us a trail to follow."

Andi crinkled her nose, signaling she wasn't keen on my suggestion. "I don't want to disagree with the big boss, but I've got a better idea."

CHAPTER 20

ANDI HAD RENTED us a beautiful four-story redbrick town-house in Fitzwilliam Square, an upscale, historic Georgian area in the heart of Dublin. Set in the center of a long terrace, the house faced south, overlooking mature trees that lined the edge of a well-manicured garden. We were within a stone's throw of several embassies and there was a visible police presence in the area, as well as national and private security patrols around the grand buildings that flew the flags of other nations. I spotted Hungary, South Africa and Canada as Andi navigated the streets to our assigned parking spot outside of our temporary home.

I grabbed my bag from the trunk and Andi led me inside an elegantly decorated house, complete with period features. Intricate plaster reliefs surrounded the light fittings, a picture rail ran around the tops of the walls, and there were elaborate marble surrounds to the two fireplaces I could see from the hallway. Floorboards were old and worn and covered with over-sized rugs, and the furnishings were all antique. Andi took me upstairs to a similarly refined bedroom on the second floor. A king-size bed stood against the wall to my left, directly opposite two large sash windows overlooking the garden in the center of the square. There was an en suite bathroom off the other side of the room. I placed my bag on a couch that was set between the windows.

"Nice view," I remarked, looking down at the green space. Beyond the stately surrounding trees was a long wide stretch of lawn that formed the green heart of the neighborhood, with a further avenue of trees on the other side of it. The terrace of brick-built town houses on the far side of the square looked much the same as the one that stretched away to either side of us.

"My room's even better," Andi responded. "I'm directly above you. I didn't imagine a progressive boss would object to his sub-ordinate having the best room."

I smiled. "No objections at all."

"Good," she replied. "Do you want to shower before we get going?"

I nodded. "I'll be quick."

She left the room and shut the door behind her. I took in my new accommodation as I undressed. A large Persian rug covered most of the floorboards. The wool was worn in places, suggesting a long history rather than neglect. Black-and-white photos of Dublin's gracious center dotted the walls, and the walnut dresser had a polished brass ship's compass as a centerpiece. Someone had gone to great lengths to give this place the welcoming feel of a high-end boutique hotel. The ethos continued in the bathroom, which was well stocked with quality toiletries and luxurious towels.

I wrapped one around me as I stepped from the shower, feeling much better for having shed the residue of a transatlantic flight. I put on a white shirt and dark gray two-piece suit.

"Looking sharp," Andi remarked, as I came downstairs.

She was leaning against the wall by the front door.

"Where are we going?" I asked.

"To see an old friend," she replied enigmatically, but her mysterious expression broke immediately into a smile. "An old cop friend. I can't lie. Never been able to keep a straight face. Even as a joke or to wind up my big boss."

"Must make you terrible at poker," I remarked.

"I wouldn't go near cards. Or magic tricks," she said seriously.

She exhaled dramatically as though releasing a pent-up burden. I wasn't sure whether it was part of her patter or if she was genuinely troubled by dishonesty.

"We're going to see Conor Roche. He's a police intelligence officer with the Garda. He and I worked together on a joint operation when I was with the Metropolitan Police in London."

Andi drove us west through the city. We took the route along Parnell Road, passing charming old terraces, post-war houses and shopping centers. Even though there was the diverse architecture found in any European capital, Dublin seemed to have been constructed on a human scale, its atmosphere warm and homely. This city of half a million souls could make even strangers feel like they belonged. After a while we joined the South

Circular Road, which took us north through the commercial district, over a stone bridge that spanned the River Liffey. Finally, after driving through a large park, we reached Garda Headquarters, made up of several huge brownstone blocks that looked like old army barracks. The complex was set on a large, high-security campus.

We parked in the visitors' lot, which was beside the main gate, and after Andi had pulled into a space and killed the engine, she sent a text message. She received a reply a moment later.

"He's on his way."

I watched a couple of joggers running round the perimeter of the park opposite, and saw a car go through the security protocols at the main gate of the Garda Headquarters, which involved an undercarriage search using a camera and a sweep with a sniffer dog.

"There he is," Andi said a few minutes later, when a man in an aviator jacket, navy blue pullover and jeans sauntered out of the main building.

I watched him stop at a silver BMW in the staff lot and rummage inside for a stick of gum, which he chewed lazily as he approached.

Andi and I stepped out of the car. Conor Roche couldn't have been more than thirty, but up close he looked rugged, his face as craggy as the west coast cliffs I'd flown over on my way here. He was lean, his cheeks almost pinched-looking, and his head was topped by a crop of curly brown hair.

"Conor, this is Jack Morgan," Andi said.

He stepped forward and offered me his hand. "Mr. Morgan, it's an honor to meet you. The Moscow operation was incredible."

He had a thick Dublin accent.

"Nice to meet you too, Detective Roche. And, please, call me Jack."

"Conor," he replied, before turning to Andi. "What can I do for you?"

"Jack and our chief profiler were attacked in Los Angeles a couple of days ago," she said.

Conor nodded. "The Academy shooting. LAPD sent an alert saying the shooter skipped to Dublin."

"Yeah," I responded.

Andi showed Conor a photo of the suspect on her phone. "Recognize him?"

"Dublin is a small place compared to London, but we don't all know each other," Conor protested.

"You're police intelligence. Can't be too many assassins with the stones to gun down innocents in a foreign country," Andi remarked.

Conor frowned. "True. But I still don't know him."

"What about the tattoo?" I asked, and Andi swiped to a magnified image of the distinctive fleur-de-lys inside a Jerusalem Cross. "This is the insignia of a criminal group I encountered in Italy called Propaganda Tre."

Conor shook his head. "Never seen it before, but I'll run a search and ask around."

"We'd appreciate it," Andi said.

"Thanks," I added. "Anything you can find out would be a great help."

"I'll see what I can do," he said as he backed away.

We watched him head through the gates toward the central wide two-story building. Andi said, "Sorry. I hoped he'd be able to give us something immediately. He always has his ear to the ground."

"I'm not surprised he doesn't know anything. Propaganda Tre is another level of devious," I replied.

She nodded. "Airport?" she suggested.

"Airport," I confirmed.

CHAPTER 21

ANDI TOOK CHESTERFIELD Avenue, a road that cut through Phoenix Park, a broad expanse of parkland planted with ancient oaks and other mature trees. I exchanged messages with Emily Knighton in London, asking her to try and get us an appointment with someone from Dublin Airport security. We moved into a residential suburb before turning onto a large highway that cut through open countryside to the north-east of the city. Emily messaged as we left the highway and joined the airport service road to say that Amanda Doyle, the head of security, had agreed to meet us.

"Emily got us in to see the director of security," I told Andi as I typed a short message of thanks.

"That doesn't surprise me," she replied. "Emily is quite persuasive, and the Private name opens a lot of doors."

I knew we had a good reputation with law enforcement and

our clients, but it had never occurred to me that our brand awareness and value was more widespread than that.

"It shouldn't be a shock," Andi continued. "You've built an incredible organization and staffed it with some of the best ex-cops and soldiers in the world. Not that I'm boasting, of course."

"Sounds a little boastful," I replied.

She smiled. "Maybe a little. Word of your exploits filters out, Jack. And the rest of us aren't doing too badly, even if our successes don't always make the headlines. You should be proud of what you've accomplished."

I didn't pay much mind to superstition, but I did believe pride went before a fall and wasn't interested in reflecting on what I'd achieved. It was more than a job. Helping people to right wrongs was my calling, and as long as there were cases to solve, I wouldn't ever stop. I didn't say anything to Andi though because I didn't want her to think I was ungrateful for her kind words.

When we arrived at the airport, she parked in the multi-story short-stay car park and asked an attendant to direct us to the executive offices, located near Terminal 2.

We made our way to the contemporary building at the heart of the airport campus and checked in at reception. After a short wait in the bright, airy lobby, Amanda Doyle's assistant, a man who introduced himself as Simon, took us up to the executive suite. He noted my American accent and made polite conversation about a trip he'd made to LA a few years back, and how Hollywood had left a huge impression on him. I wasn't in the mood for small talk, but Andi was very adroit and stepped in to keep Simon engaged.

The executive offices were located on the fourth floor and the high windows offered unrivalled views of the main runway and aircraft stands.

Amanda Doyle was waiting for us in her large, modern corner office. Late forties, she had short brown hair and a serious demeanor, which wasn't surprising given the nature of her job. She wore a black ankle-length skirt and a red blouse.

"Mr. Morgan, Ms. Harris, your colleague in London said you have an urgent request. Please take a seat."

She directed us to three armchairs that were arranged opposite a couch.

"Tea? Coffee?" she asked.

"I'm okay," I replied.

"Me too," Andi added.

Amanda nodded at Simon, who shut the door behind him as he left the room.

"Thanks for giving us your time," I said, easing myself into one of the chairs.

Andi sat beside me, and Amanda took the couch.

"It's the least I can do," she replied. "I know Private by reputation . . ." Andi shot me a "told you so" look ". . . so I wasn't going to pass up the chance to meet *the* Jack Morgan."

I smiled and glanced at the floor bashfully. I didn't cope well with praise or notoriety.

"Well, thank you," I said. "We believe the man behind the Academy shooting, the supposed Ecokiller, boarded an Aer Lingus flight from LAX to Dublin the day before yesterday."

Amanda nodded. "We got the alert from the Garda, but it

came too late to stop him at the border. It wouldn't have mattered in any case."

I frowned. "How do you mean?"

"We reviewed the gate footage," Amanda replied. "He never left the plane. And we checked the cameras at passport control. No one matching the suspect's description came through, and no one used the Colm Finlay passport."

"Did he board another flight at LAX?" Andi asked.

Amanda shook her head. "We don't think so. Pre-takeoff passenger count was two hundred and sixteen, but when we counted at the arrival gate, two hundred and fifteen got off, meaning the suspect managed to leave that aircraft without being detected somewhere between Los Angeles International and Dublin Airport."

CHAPTER 22

AMANDA TOOK US to a security control room where we went to a small audio-visual suite that lay off the main office and reviewed the camera footage for ourselves. We spent another hour studying every single angle and found no sign of the shooter from any of the cameras trained on the aircraft from the moment it reached the stand. If he'd disembarked at Dublin Airport, he'd done so like a magician performing a vanishing act.

Disappointed, we sat in silence while Andi drove us back to the city. I wondered whether the man known to us as Colm Finlay had somehow faked his boarding of the flight to Dublin and had in fact taken another plane. If so, he could be anywhere in the world by now. But how did that explain the discrepancy in the headcount at LAX, after the aircraft door had been closed, with that at passport control in Dublin?

"How could he get off the plane without anyone or any

cameras seeing him?" Andi asked. Her frown suggested she shared my frustration with the mystery.

"Either he was never on the plane and the headcount at LAX was wrong," I suggested. "Or he jumped out somewhere over the Atlantic."

Andi smiled at my unhelpful suggestions. "Or someone smuggled him off the aircraft," she replied. "And we just haven't figured out how."

"An insider at the airport?" I said.

"Why not?" she responded. "This group has people every-where, right?"

I nodded slowly. It was certainly possible.

Andi's phone rang and Conor Roche's name flashed on the central console screen. She answered the call on the car's Blue-tooth audio.

"Go ahead, Conor," she said. "Jack is with me."

"I couldn't find anything on your tattoo, but I checked the Interpol alerts and this Propaganda Tre is linked to a street gang called the Dark Fates," he said.

Andi glanced at me and I nodded. The Dark Fates had been Propaganda Tre's paramilitary arm in Rome and Monaco, the muscle to the other group's brain.

"Well, the Dark Fates started showing up on our radar here about a year ago. Street thugs, but more organized than the usual gangsters. Drugs, extortion, that sort of thing. There was an altercation in a pub called the Night Watch three weeks ago. Officers picked up a ketamine dealer who is tied to the Fates. Goes by the name of Joe McGee."

"You got any known associates or an address?" I asked.

"I couldn't possibly give you his address," Conor replied. "That would breach all sorts of confidentiality laws. But I could brief you in person if you meet me at number three Bessborough Avenue, East Wall."

Andi smiled. "Bit of an odd place to meet."

"It is, it is, I'll grant you," Conor said, "but that's just me. Odd. I'll see you there sometime soon."

He hung up and I made no attempt to hide my bafflement as I looked at Andi.

"East Wall is one of the rougher parts of the city. The road he named is a residential street. My guess is he just gave us McGee's address without putting himself at risk if the call was recorded."

"Smart," I said, grateful for the renewed hope that came with Conor's lead.

CHAPTER 23

THE WALLS OF the pub were steeped in the misery of ages. Once white, they were now brown with the stains left by decades of cigarette smoke, quite possibly exhaled by the very men who looked down at us from a mosaic of framed black-and-white photos. These mementos of Dublin's industrial history were displayed in the White Horse, a pub on Bessborough Avenue, about thirty meters away from the short terrace that Conor Roche had identified for us in his call.

"I bet you've never been in a place like this before," Andi said, grabbing a handful of peanuts from a pack she'd split open and placed on the table between us.

She'd also popped a packet of Taytos, which she'd told me were the best brand of potato chips in the world. Neither held any interest for me. My eyes were fixed on number three, not far from the eastern end of the terrace.

"Not exactly like it," I replied, glancing round the old, run-down pub. "But there are places like this the world over."

It was true. This place was a shelter from the storm of life for the locals who struggled against the bitter wind of poverty and the rain of misfortune. Hardship was writ large in the streets of East Wall, from the old cars, derelict warehouses, graffiti-covered brickwork, and homes in need of more than a touch of tender loving care. It showed on the face of the publican too, an alabaster-pale man in his fifties, whose skin was blemished with the red route map of burst blood vessels that were the hallmark of a heavy drinker. We were the only customers in his tiny establishment, and he was nursing a pint of ale that never seemed to run dry.

"Poor places?" Andi asked.

I nodded. "And hard. I've been in many of them."

"Your legend says you're a man of privilege," Andi responded.

I scoffed. "Legends are just stories designed to make the teller feel important. They aren't the truth. I've led a life no easier or harder than most."

She pursed her lips. "War, death, pain? I wouldn't say yours was no harder than most people's."

I was uncomfortable with the direction this conversation was taking but was saved from having to reply by the sound of my phone. Justine was calling.

"Keep watch," I said to Andi, gesturing to the house as I got to my feet and stepped through an archway into a seating area at the back of the pub.

"Justine," I said as I answered. "How are you?"

"Tired," she replied. "But okay. Where are you?"

"In a pub," I said. "We're following a lead."

"We?"

"Andi Harris. She's a detective from the London office with good local knowledge."

"What's the lead?" Justine asked.

"A member of the Dark Fates who was arrested here a few weeks ago. We're watching his place."

"The Dark Fates . . . they're in Dublin?"

"Yes," I replied. "They've been getting into street crime locally."

"I thought we were done with all this after Monaco," Justine sighed.

"We were done with them," I said. "They weren't done with us."

She was silent for a moment.

"I don't want to go through this again," she said at last.

"You won't," I assured her. "It ends here."

"I love you, Jack," she replied.

"Love you too."

"I'll check in later," she said. "I better go now. The doctor is here."

"Keep me posted on what they say," I responded. "And make sure you rest."

"I will," she said before hanging up.

I turned to see Andi standing in the archway.

"Come on," she said, and I followed her back to our table to see an unmarked white Mercedes van parked outside of number three.

The green front door opened and a man appeared in the doorway. He had straw-blond hair and a face that looked to have been set in a fierce scowl since birth. His skin was pasty, padded out by debauchery.

"It's him," Andi said, showing me the mugshot taken after Joe McGee's arrest. Conor had emailed it to her.

Joe closed the front door behind him and hurried through his tiny front yard to the waiting van. As he opened the passenger door and jumped inside, I started for the exit.

"Come on," I said to Andi. "We need to follow him."

CHAPTER 24

WE JOGGED AWAY from the pub along Bessborough Avenue and reached our Ford SUV as the van took a right at the end of the street. Andi jumped behind the wheel and I climbed in beside her. She gunned the engine and slid the car in drive, before pulling out and speeding to follow the van.

"Right," I said, and she swung the wheel and took the turn at speed, pressing me against my armrest.

We straightened up on a main road that was lined with run-down stores and homes. A funeral parlor, a place that advertised beds, but which had its graffiti-covered security shutters locked up tight, a wig and toupée emporium, along with other odd businesses that survived at the margins of society.

We saw the Mercedes van as a brief flash of white, racing beneath a steel railway bridge in the distance. Andi stepped on the gas and closed the gap. Within seconds, we were no more than thirty meters behind, trailing the vehicle over every bump and pothole in the road. I used my phone to take photos of the van and its license plate.

We came to a major intersection by Annesley Bridge and took a right along the river. A park fronted the other bank, and to our right were small terrace houses painted shades of gray, blue and cream. We kept going south-east until we reached the port area and then followed the van through the Dublin Port Tunnel toll booths and into the mouth of a two-lane subterranean highway that would take us beneath the northern suburbs of the city.

Andi drove expertly, using buses and trucks to keep our pursuit concealed. She allowed other vehicles between us and the van as we sped through the busy tunnel. When we finally emerged, we joined the M1, heading north. We passed the airport and were soon in open countryside, speeding along a highway flanked by tall trees whose branches were thick with leaves.

We drove like this for more than half an hour, passing Lusk, a town to the north of Dublin. The further we went, the lighter the traffic became, making subterfuge difficult, so Andi simply kept her distance, allowing the van to slip to the very edge of our safe field, the point at which we could be reasonably certain we wouldn't lose it.

After another twenty minutes, we saw it leave the motorway. The sun was kissing the tops of the trees, bathing everything in a rose-gold light, and as we came off the highway and followed the van over a bridge, I caught a glimpse of the Irish landscape rolling on toward Dublin. For a moment I almost forgot all the dark reasons that had brought me to this place, too busy admiring one of the most beautiful expanses of lush countryside I'd ever seen.

"People never really leave Ireland," Andi remarked. "You carry this country with you forever."

I nodded and was brought back to reality by the sight of the van weaving around a roundabout and taking a turning onto a narrow country lane.

We followed for another hour, trailing it into remote countryside as darkness swept in. Andi kept her distance and used the car's GPS map to see potential turn-offs ahead. Most of the lanes wound for miles without intersections, which allowed her to let the van run on ahead. We could be satisfied with distant glimpses of its roof over the tops of hedges. It was a masterclass in undetected pursuit.

Shadows and silhouettes replaced solid color, and the landscape took on a monochrome beauty in the moonlight.

Finally, more than two hours after we'd left the pub, the van slowed as it passed the gates to a large property. Andi killed the lights and slowed the Ford, so we were crawling as we passed the same entrance. The black-and-gold sign displayed by the gates featured a prancing horse above the words "Kearney Stud."

In front of us, the van's brake lights flared cherry red as it pulled into a turnout. Andi stopped some distance behind and we watched as four men, including Joe McGee, jumped out of the vehicle, pulled ski masks over their heads, and scaled the high wall that surrounded the stud farm.

"What do we do?" Andi asked.

"We keep going," I said, unclasping my seatbelt. "We follow them."

I stepped out of the car and headed for the high stone wall and whatever lay beyond.

CHAPTER 25

THE GROUND UNDERFOOT was springy with moss. As I reached the wall, I heard Andi come up behind me.

"Are you sure this is a good idea?" she whispered.

I nodded but she pursed her lips, suggesting she didn't agree. She didn't voice any objection though, so I clasped my hands together and held them out like a sling, offering her a boost over the wall.

She frowned and smiled dismissively before taking a short run-up, grabbing the capstones and hauling herself over.

I copied her move but scuffed my shoes and snagged my suit as I dragged myself up and over with far less elegance. I pivoted and dropped into the shadow of a large bush. I crept toward Andi, crouched by the trunk of an ancient oak tree.

She beckoned me to hurry and signaled for me to stay low.

When I joined her, I saw why. We were in a small hollow and

flashlights were visible beyond a rise, moving through woodland, illuminating the otherwise ghostly trunks and branches. Now and then, I caught sight of the silhouettes of the masked men.

I nodded at Andi and we set off after them, taking great care to keep low and ensure we maintained our cover by moving from tree to tree, and using the surrounding foliage to obscure us.

As we drew nearer, I heard indistinct whispers, footsteps, clothes brushing against branches and leaves, and heavy breathing. They weren't being anywhere near as careful as us, which was good because the noise they made gave us more cover.

The flashlights went off and I stopped, raising my right fist to Andi to signal a halt. We froze and I glanced over at her as the usual sounds of the night filled my ears. The breeze through the trees, rustling leaves, the hoot of an owl, the high squeak of a rodent somewhere in the distance. Satisfied we weren't the reason for the flashlights going dark, I crept on and Andi followed. Soon we came to the edge of the wood. Beyond the trees was a paddock where three horses grazed lazily in the silver moonlight. To our right was a large stable block, and directly ahead a substantial Georgian farmhouse, which was surrounded by more stables and outbuildings.

I crouched under a low-branching tree and surveyed the stud farm.

"Horse thieves," Andi whispered. "They would normally take the grazers unless they're after a particular horse."

Her theory was sound, and I nodded.

"We should check the stables," she suggested.

I nodded again. We rose and started toward the stable block, but after a few paces we were frozen in place by the sound of a terrible scream piercing the night.

CHAPTER 26

THE SHRIEK HAD come from the farmhouse. Andi and I immediately ran toward the building. The grand old home stood three stories high, its long sash windows offering glimpses into a comfortable family room and a formal dining room as we moved from the lawn to the terrace and skirted around the house. I saw shadows moving through the dining-room door, and light spilling from the doorway opposite.

I nodded at Andi and we kept moving around the house. We skirted the north-east corner, hugging the wall, and saw golden light through a picture window. A ceramic teapot and a basil plant on the sill told me this was a kitchen. Beside the window, the back door stood ajar, light slicing through the gap between it and the frame.

I sensed movement on the other side and slowed even more,

so my steps were almost painfully deliberate. I glanced round and saw Andi doing likewise, advancing silently across the terrace slabs until she was to the right of the doorway and I was on the left.

There was a grid of glazed panes set into the door, and I peered through one to see a masked man stalking through the kitchen. He glanced around the room before peering through the interior doorway and then looking straight toward the back door.

I knew the kitchen lights would make me difficult to spot, and that night would turn the windows into mirrors, but still I ducked back, unwilling to take any unnecessary risks. I looked at Andi, pointed into the kitchen and held up one finger. I could see only one man, but I knew the others were somewhere in the house. Their muffled voices were audible, though their words were indistinct.

I held up my hand and pointed at my chest before indicating the doorway. Andi nodded, clearly understanding my intention to enter the building.

I peered inside again and saw the masked man had turned away from the back door and was looking into the interior of the house. I took a deep breath and eased the door a little wider. I almost cursed when the hinges creaked. My heart, which had already been pulsing adrenalin to my extremities, went into overdrive as the masked man turned to face me, his wide eyes making his shock palpable.

I took advantage of his surprise to rush him. He cried out as

I body-slammed him against a large, American-style double fridge. He tried to reach into his jacket, and I guessed he was going for a gun, so I punched him in the gut, and as he buckled, forced his head down into my knee.

The blow knocked him out. I caught him and eased his fall to minimize noise.

"Let him go," a man's voice said, and I turned to see one of the other masked invaders standing in the inner doorway. He aimed a pistol at me.

I raised my hands and stepped forward, edging closer to my captor.

"Who are you?" he asked.

I was saved from having to answer by the sound of the back door slamming against the wall. The masked gunman instinctively pointed the pistol at the open doorway, and I exploited his mistake and launched myself at him as he tried to swing the weapon in my direction. But I was already inside his reach and blocked his gun hand before driving my right fist into his cheek. He staggered back, clutching his face, and caught me with a lucky blow to my head. The weight of the gun connecting with my temple made stars fill my vision. I couldn't see clearly, but I felt the gunman punch me in the stomach and then hit my head with the gun again.

This time I went down, but I tried to focus. I needed to find my reserves of strength, but my head was swimming and my limbs were weak and unresponsive. I was in grave danger and had a vague sense of a shadow sweeping toward me. I was pretty sure it was the gun.

A loud crack startled me, and the sickening sound was followed by a grunt. The shadow in front of me fell away to one side. As my senses returned, I realized the masked gunman had collapsed at my feet and that it was Andi standing behind his prone body, holding a heavy black frying pan.

CHAPTER 27

"THANKS," I WHISPERED.

She nodded, placed the pan carefully on the kitchen counter, and stepped nearer.

"You okay?" she asked quietly.

I touched my temple gingerly, and the spinning world came into sharper focus as the feeling I might black out receded.

"I'll be fine," I told her. "Let's go."

I heard voices coming from somewhere in the house, muffled and unclear words being spoken by two men, their deep voices with the distinctive Dublin accent, tone hostile.

"Take the gun," I whispered.

Andi leaned down and grabbed the pistol from the man she'd knocked out. Meanwhile I searched the jacket of the guy I'd incapacitated. He'd been reaching for a telescopic metal baton, the kind riot police use for crowd control.

I took it and flicked it to full extension. It locked with a satisfying click. I lifted the masks off both the unconscious men and saw faces I didn't recognize. Joe McGee was still somewhere inside the house.

I moved through the kitchen doorway into a large entrance hall. To my left was the formal dining room I'd seen from outside, and to my right a double-door front entrance. Ahead lay a sitting room, furnished with sagging but comfortable-looking old sofas and chairs and fine mahogany heirloom pieces.

Andi drew alongside me and pointed upstairs. I nodded. The men's voices were clearer now, and I could also hear a child sobbing and a woman muttering soothing words.

I moved to the stairs and started up them. When I glanced over my shoulder, I saw Andi behind me, gun raised in the ready stance. Her face was stern, her eyes hard, her whole demeanor at odds with the easy banter of earlier. I could see why Emily had hired her. I felt confident I had someone capable as my back-up.

We paused on the wraparound landing to listen to what was clearly a confrontation.

"Don't you dare hurt them," I heard a man say.

"Then give us what we want," a second man replied.

The voices were coming from a doorway across the landing.

"Do it," the second man said.

I heard a thud and then a child screamed.

"Mummy!" a boy cried. "Leave her alone."

"Stop!" the first man yelled. "Leave them be or I'll kill you all."

There was another blow, and then more screaming and pleading from a woman and children.

I looked at Andi, who nodded. We crept across the landing to the open doorway. I peered inside and saw a large bedroom. One of the masked men was standing by a seating area, holding a gun on an indignant middle-aged man in jeans and T-shirt.

The last home invader was by the bed, where a woman and two children, a boy who couldn't have been more than ten and a girl who looked about twelve, had been bound with cord at ankles and wrists and were lying face-down on the mattress. Their masked tormentor was holding a telescopic baton and used it to strike the woman hard on the back.

I gave Andi a furious glance and she signaled to the man by the couch and pointed at herself. I nodded. Together we rushed into the room, startling the home invaders, who had been confidently in command.

"Joe!" the man by the couch said as he turned his gun on Andi.

So the guy beating the woman was our target, the member of the Dark Fates Conor Roche had identified.

My fury rose as he turned to face me. I ducked as he swung at me with his baton. I glanced back to see Andi dodge the gunman's aim. His bullet went harmlessly by her, but the sound was deafening and my ears rang in the aftermath of the gunshot.

I struck Joe McGee on the shins with my baton, two sharp blows with the weighted bulb, one on each leg. He jumped back and yelped.

Andi aimed her pistol at the gunman, but before she could

shoot, the male captive jumped up and grabbed his assailant, making it impossible for her to find a safe target.

Joe recovered and came at me, but I parried his flailing blow with my baton and drove my shoulder into his chest, pushing him away from the bed and slamming him against the wall beside a grand fireplace. There was the clatter and smash of ceramic as his hand floundered around the mantel, searching for purchase, knocking figurines of horses onto the slate hearth.

Behind me, I heard another ear-splitting gunshot and looked round to see the masked assailant knock down the homeowner, dazing him. He spun quickly and caught Andi on the side of her head with the butt of his gun, sending her flying.

Her pistol tumbled from her hand and spun across the rug toward the bed. I dived for it and shots rang out as I wrapped my fingers around it. There was more gunfire while I scrabbled for cover behind the bed.

I heard a rush of movement and risked breaking cover to see both masked invaders fleeing through the doorway.

I ran after them but was forced to a halt by more gunfire. Bullets splintered the door frame where I had been standing a split second before.

Downstairs, there was further movement and someone shouted orders.

"Jack," Andi said, and I turned to see her struggling to stand.

I ran over and helped her up.

"You okay?" I asked.

"I will be," she said. "Go."

I hesitated, but she nodded and pushed me toward the door.

I ran through it, across the landing and down the stairs. The first floor was deserted, the men we'd knocked out were both gone, and now the front door was hanging open.

I should have been grateful to be alive. Instead I was frustrated to have lost a potential lead to the man who'd shot Justine.

CHAPTER 28

I RETURNED TO the bedroom and found Andi untying the woman. The man was working on the boy's bonds. Both children were crying.

I went to the girl and started loosening the cord that bound her ankles.

"It's okay," I said soothingly. "They've gone."

"Dad," the boy said, as his father freed him. He threw his arms around the man's neck and sobbed into his shoulder.

"I'm sorry," the man told his son. "I'm so sorry."

"They could have killed us, Noah," the woman said tearfully.

"Are you okay?" he asked anxiously.

She nodded. "Sore. But I'll live." She turned to her children. "Mummy is alright, kids."

Andi untied her wrists and she hurried over to the man and their son. A moment later, when I'd freed her, the girl joined them.

"I'm sorry," the man said, embracing them all. "I should never have . . ." His voice trailed off when he registered Andi and me. "Thank you so much," he told us. "Thanks, both of you."

"If you hadn't come," the woman added, "I don't even want to think about what might have happened."

She drew her children closer.

"Mr. and Mrs. Kearney?" Andi asked.

It was reasonable to guess the stud farm was named after the family.

The man nodded. "Noah and Mary. This is our girl, Molly, and our boy, Ben. Are you okay, Ben?" He returned his attention to the boy.

"It hurts," Ben cried, rubbing his back.

"We need to take him to the hospital," Mary told her husband.

He nodded. "It's not safe here. Take the children to the car and I'll get some things."

Mary looked at us uncertainly, as though we might interfere with the family's plans.

I stood to one side. "I'm not here to force you to do anything," I assured her. "You can leave anytime."

She ushered the children to their feet and steered them from the room. I heard them sobbing all the way down the stairs.

Noah went to a walk-in wardrobe and got busy throwing belongings into a large holdall.

"Why isn't it safe for you here?" I asked. "What did those men want, Mr. Kearney?"

He paused and moved to the doorway.

"You a cop?" he asked. "You're a Yank, that's for sure."

"I'm not a cop," I replied. "But I am an American."

"Fed?" he suggested, sizing me up.

I shook my head. "I'm a private investigator. My name is Jack Morgan, and this is my associate, Andrea Harris."

He frowned. "I might be many things, but I'm no grass," he said, before he resumed packing.

"Those men hurt your family," Andi responded with more than a hint of exasperation. "If we hadn't been here . . ."

Noah glanced anxiously at the doorway. "Which is exactly why I'm no grass. What do you think they'll do to me next if they find out I've been talking to the likes of you?"

"We would never betray your confidence," Andi assured him.

Noah sneered. "And exactly what have I done to deserve such undying loyalty? Who are you again? You don't know these people. What they're capable of."

I stepped forward and produced my phone. "I know exactly what they're capable of. They've already tried to kill me more than once. My girlfriend was shot by this man." I held up a photo of the man we knew as Colm Finlay. "I think he's connected to the gang who were here tonight."

Noah frowned at the picture and, in the quiet that followed, I heard Mary yell from outside.

"Come on, Noah!"

"I know those were dangerous men, Mr. Kearney," I said. "Please tell us what they wanted with a horse breeder."

"It's because they're dangerous that I can't tell you," he replied, sounding exasperated and clearly itching to be gone.

"They tortured your wife and terrorized your kids," I countered. "Why?"

Still he hesitated to speak.

"And your best solution is to run away, is it? Believe me, that never solves a problem like this," I told him. "I want to stop them doing the same thing to innocent people. Help me."

He wavered, and I could see he was wrestling with his conscience.

"Please, Mr. Kearney, if you can tell us anything at all," I said.

"I'm no grass, but you'll find what you're after at the Ballycorus at Leopardstown tomorrow," he said in a low voice.

With that he slung the holdall over his shoulder and headed for the door. He stopped on the threshold and glanced back.

"Check the winners' enclosure after the second race. You'll find your answers there," he said. He hesitated then added, "And thank you again for what you did tonight. I mean that."

He gave us a respectful nod and left to join his family.

CHAPTER 29

NOAH KEARNEY SHOWED us out of his home and we watched him lock up. He told us nothing more, but Mary thanked us again before he joined her and the children in a Mercedes GLS and drove them into the night.

"Why do you think he wants us to go to the races?" Andi mused.

"Doping?" I responded. "Gambling? Something sufficiently criminal to get a family home invaded and children tortured."

Andi scoffed, "In these parts, that could be a pretty long list."

We started through the woods toward the perimeter wall and our car.

Over an hour later, after taking the winding route back to the city and stopping for an Indian takeout from a restaurant Andi recommended, we were sitting at the kitchen table in our rental house in Fitzwilliam Square, spooning food from plastic containers into our bowls.

The deep scent of spices filled the air, and I caught hints of fennel, cumin, fenugreek, garlic and coriander. Andi's recommendation was justified. The food was delicious. From the achar gosht, a hot lamb and lime pickle dish, to the chicken tikka masala, everything was perfectly cooked.

"Good, huh?" Andi said.

"Really good," I replied. "Great choice."

She took a swig from a bottle of beer. The owner had insisted we have four to accompany our meal, and I found the lager refreshing, even if the act of opening my mouth to eat or drink still sparked flashes of pain where the guy had clocked me with his gun.

"You think we should report the incident?" I asked, lowering my bottle to the table and rubbing my jaw gingerly.

"If they wanted it reported, they would have called it in," Andi responded. "Whatever Noah Kearney is up to, it's shady, but I'll tell Conor tomorrow and he can decide whether the Garda needs to make it official."

"Good call," I said.

"I've been known to choose good restaurants and make excellent work choices," she replied. "With men it's a whole different kettle of fish."

I didn't respond. The kitchen suddenly seemed very still and small.

"I'm attracted to dangerous relationships," she went on. "Ones that aren't always good for me." She took another sip of beer. "You know what I mean?"

I was sufficiently experienced to recognize unsafe territory.

"Life can be challenging like that," I replied. "I think I'm done." I got to my feet and took my bowl to the sink. "Leave the dishes. I'll do them in the morning."

She watched me closely, her expression almost sullen. Had one beer been too much for her?

"I've got some calls to make," I said. "Personal stuff. You'll have to excuse me for being bad company, but I'm done for the day. Goodnight, Andi."

I left the kitchen without waiting for a response and hurried upstairs, wondering whether I'd misinterpreted her words by reading them as an invitation. When I reached my room, I shut and locked the door. Just in case.

I phoned Justine immediately but didn't really settle into the conversation until I heard Andi climb the stairs a few minutes later. I couldn't tell if I'd imagined it or whether she really did pause outside of my room, but as Justine was bringing me up to speed with the latest from her doctor, I heard Andi climbing the last flight of stairs up to her room. The floorboards creaked and shifted above me, and her door closed audibly.

"Are you with me, Jack?" Justine's voice brought my mind back into focus.

"Yes. Sorry. I was just replaying the day," I replied.

"Busy?" she asked.

"Yeah."

"Dangerous?"

I hesitated. I hated lying to her, but there was no point in having her worry. I didn't want anything impeding her recovery.

"Not particularly," I said. It wasn't dishonest. The day had been representative of my life in recent years. "It was interesting. We've developed a lead that we'll follow up tomorrow." I kept it vague. "How are you?" I asked. "How do you feel?"

She paused. "I already told you, Jack."

"You told me what your doctor said."

She sighed. "You're right. I'm feeling okay, all things considered. I get tired easily and out of breath, but they say that's normal."

"You need to take it so easy, Jus," I responded. "Rest and recuperation. No stress and no pushing yourself."

"Yes, boss," she scoffed.

We talked a little longer, but I could hear fatigue come into her voice. After we'd exchanged words of love, I told her I was tired and needed to sleep. We said goodnight, then I opened my secure mailbox and sent a message to Mo-bot asking her to check into Noah Kearney and see if she could find any connection to the Dark Fates or Propaganda Tre.

She replied quickly to tell me she was on it.

Satisfied Justine was okay, secure in the knowledge Mo-bot would find anything there was to be found, and exhausted by the day's testing events, I took a couple of Advil to numb the worst of the pain and got ready for bed.

CHAPTER 30

I WOKE TO messages from Justine, telling me how much she loved and missed me, and Mo-bot, saying she hadn't yet been able to identify a link between Kearney and the Dark Fates or Propaganda Tre, but that she was still digging. On the face of it, Mo-bot told me, Noah and Mary Kearney's business seemed legitimate and quite successful. They bred and trained some top-tier racehorses, and there were no allegations of irregular dealing against them. Not the sort of people one would typically associate with a dangerous criminal enterprise.

I replied to both messages, put my phone down, and went to my bathroom to shower and prepare for the day ahead. I emerged from the piping-hot water feeling refreshed and eager to discover why Noah Kearney had sent us to the races.

I put on a dark gray suit and black shirt, a smart outfit I felt wouldn't be out of place at the races. Once dressed, I went downstairs to find Andi at the kitchen table, sitting where I'd left her last night. She was wearing a long green dress and seemed a little sheepish as she cradled a mug of coffee between her hands.

"Can I get you one?" she asked. "It's not freshly brewed, but still pretty good."

She stood up awkwardly and moved to the counter, where she'd placed a cafetiere of coffee and a clean mug.

"I'm fine," I replied. "What time is the first race?"

"One-twenty," she replied. "So we have plenty of time."

She paused, and I sensed she had more to say.

"I think we should get there early. Check the lay of the land," I suggested, trying to keep us focused on the investigation.

"Listen," she said, "I just wanted to apologize in case anything I said last night made you feel uncomfortable. I think I was feeling the effects of exhilaration and beer, and I don't want you to get the wrong impression."

"You've got nothing to worry about," I replied. "You did an outstanding job yesterday, and I owe you my life."

She smiled, clearly relieved.

"It can be difficult to see the line sometimes, particularly in situations like this, when we're living the job, but you were off the clock last night. A human being, rather than a detective."

"A flawed human being," she added quickly.

"A decent human being," I countered. "You didn't say anything wrong, so there's nothing to worry about."

"Good," she said before draining her coffee. "In that case, let's take a mosey out to Leopardstown and see what we can find."

An hour later, after heading south-east through Dublin, we

turned off and joined a line of traffic heading toward the race-track. Even though it lay directly beside the motorway, it took us thirty minutes to join another line of cars being directed toward race-day parking.

Dating back to the nineteenth century, Leopardstown Race-course is built around a large grandstand and has capacity for up to 10,000 fans. Judging by the crowds thronging toward the complex, today would be a test of the upper limit. With more than 200 acres of course and training facilities, Leopardstown is a respected course that hosts some significant Irish racing fixtures.

We were waved into a space at the very edge of the parking lot by a marshal in a high-visibility vest.

"Thanks," I said to Andi as she cut the engine.

"No problem," she replied.

"I wonder what they do when it rains," I commented as we traipsed through the long grass between rows of cars.

It was a fine day and the ground was firm, but in fouler weather, I could imagine a quagmire that might trap people and their vehicles.

"Bring wellies," Andi said with a sideways grin. "And prepare to get muddy."

We collected day passes Andi had bought online, and I slipped a lanyard over my head, so the pass rested against my chest like a medal. We joined a gaggle of excited racegoers to have our passes checked and were waved through security.

The grandstand was alive with anticipation. Most people were here for a fun day out, and even though it was almost two hours until the first race, some had already started drinking. There were a few professional gamblers who gathered in small, serious groups and checked their phones obsessively, looking at prices, running reports and rumors about horses' form.

Our passes got us general admission and we found a spot in the main stand, not far from the winners' enclosure, which lay to the east of the grandstand and was surrounded by hospitality and office blocks.

I'd never before taken much interest in horse racing, but I could sense the anticipation and excitement building. Andi and I walked the complex in the run-up to the first race, checking out the hospitality venues, which were all packed. We couldn't see why Noah Kearney had sent us here. Finally, feeling some-what frustrated, we returned to the main grandstand just in time for the first race.

I couldn't help but be swept up in the buzz and thrill as the horses were settled for the start and calm descended over the course for a moment before the starter sent them off, which sparked roars and cheers throughout the huge crowd. There were screens dotted around the grandstand and a large one positioned almost opposite the crowded venue, and Andi and I watched the magnificent, highly trained thoroughbreds speed around the course, spurred on by some of the best jockeys in the world. The sport of kings had the spectators up on their feet, hands in the air, cheering, jeering and venting their excite-ment or disappointment, and Andi and I joined them, standing for a better view of the horses thundering around the last bend, jostling for the lead. One, called Hunter's Lodge, was pulling away from the pack, and quickly established his dominance. The excitable commentator broadcasting over the public address system was yelling the horse's name, and judging by the crowd's reaction it must have been popular with the punters because a thunderous roar went up as its lead lengthened. The jockey pushed the animal to give its all. The cheering reached a crescendo as Hunter's Lodge crossed the finishing line comfortably in first place. This took place directly opposite the grandstand and the crowd there was the thickest and most vocal. As the horses slowed to a trot, the crowd dispersed and with the clamor dying down, I heard the delighted chatter of people all around us who'd backed the winner.

"We should check out the winners' enclosure," I shouted to Andi above the furor.

"Kearney said the second race," she replied.

"I know, but it won't hurt to be there watching the comings and goings in advance."

Andi nodded, and we joined the flow of people leaving the stand to collect their winnings or buy commiseration drinks. We worked our way through the grandstand, following the signs for the winners' enclosure.

We stepped outside and tracked a group of men in tailored suits who showed their passes to a steward at a gate. Beyond it was a paddock, parade ring and a small seating area.

"Passes," the steward asked us as he waved the group of men through.

"Is this part of the general ticket?" I asked, accentuating my American drawl.

"I'm afraid not, sir," the steward replied. "This is the winners' enclosure, for owners, their guests and select passholders. You're welcome to use the main grandstand and any of the facilities in that part of the course."

"Jack." Andi nudged me sharply, and I immediately saw why.

Across the enclosure I saw a man step out of a building. He was followed by an entourage of bodyguards, who were scanning their surroundings. They carried themselves with the posture and bearing of military men and all of them knew how to move around their principal to maximize the effectiveness of their close protection. One of the bodyguards recognized me the moment we locked eyes across the enclosure. I understood then why Noah Kearney had sent us to this place.

This was the shooter from Los Angeles, the man who'd put Justine, Salvatore Mattera and eighteen others in hospital and five innocent victims in the ground. Here was the man I'd pursued across the Atlantic to Ireland.

CHAPTER 31

HE BOLTED, TURNING back the way he'd come and darting through the doorway, almost knocking over two ladies in elegant dresses. I didn't hesitate but pushed past the steward, who yelled at me to stop. Ignoring him, I jumped the waist-high gate and picked up speed as I ducked under the paddock's metal rail and sprinted across the enclosure. The steward yelled at me again, and when I looked right, I saw the horses from the first race being led down from the finish, with a celebratory procession of people surrounding them. They were still some distance away and didn't impede my progress as I sprinted across the grass and ducked under the railing on the other side.

The other three suited men who'd been with the shooter still surrounded their principal and stood ready, but I wasn't interested in their man, or not at least at that moment, so I didn't engage with them as I ran toward the building.

I barged past a couple coming out, ignored yells from the man, and shot along a corridor lined with hospitality suites toward a junction at the end. The startled glances of a group of women told me my target had gone right, and sure enough, when I turned a corner, I saw the shooter up ahead sprinting toward an exit about thirty feet away. He glanced back and the sight of me must have spurred him on, because he picked up his pace. I was equally motivated by the prospect of catching him, and my lungs heaved as my legs fired like pistons and propelled me toward him.

"Stop!" I commanded. "Stop that man!"

A long interior window offered a view of a lavish bar, and I caught bemused looks from the people inside, most of whom were busy enjoying the sponsor's champagne. A few called out words of encouragement to me and sounded quite drunk already.

The shooter burst through the exit and slammed it shut behind him. I barreled out moments later and felt strong hands on my shoulders. I was pushed forward and lost my balance, hitting the ground hard. I rolled onto my back and saw he'd waited beside the door to surprise me with a sneak attack.

I knew he'd be on me instantly and leaped to my feet to face him. He came at me as I was rising, with a roundhouse kick aimed at my head. I blocked it and stood into him, so my shoulder caught the underside of his knee, sending him toppling backward.

I threw a punch and landed a blow on his cheek. He staggered back, dazed, before turning tail and running away across a paved garden area toward a stable block.

I could see grooms exercising some fine racehorses, and stewards and owners gathered in small groups to observe the spectacle. To the north was a paved yard full of horse boxes and cars.

The shooter sprinted across to the stables, and I realized that our chase was attracting more and more attention. People all around looked our way, surprised and puzzled by the frenetic action taking place in the yard. I heard people burst through the doorway behind us, and when I glanced over my shoulder, I saw the steward from the gate leading a couple of security officers. They were all shouting at me to stop. The steward called out to his colleagues ahead of me.

"Stop him!" he yelled, pointing at me, and more stewards and course personnel moved in my direction.

Ahead of me, the shooter barged through a door leading into the stable block and I followed. I stopped instantly when I realized I had the man cornered in a tack room. We were surrounded by saddles, bridles and other riding gear. I eyed him coldly as I shut the door behind me, and very deliberately slid the bolt closed.

The shooter took off his jacket as I stepped away from the door. There was hammering from the other side of it and a clamor of voices, which I ignored.

I removed my suit jacket and squared up to the man who'd shot Justine, eager to fight.

CHAPTER 32

HE CROSSED THE paved floor and threw a jab, which I dodged. Another right and then a left hook, which all found nothing but air. He was fast and a skilled fighter. I got the impression he was feeling me out, trying to get the measure of me as we moved around the tack room.

The noise from outside grew louder, and I heard people hitting the door with something so heavy that it shook in its frame.

The shooter stepped forward and caught me with a front kick to my shin, which hurt a lot. I tried to shake it off, but he didn't give me a moment and came at me with a flurry of punches. As I covered up to protect my face, he went for my body. He was powerful and quick. Punches were expertly delivered to my ribs and kidneys, but he had no idea I wanted him close and had lured him in.

When I had my chance, I grabbed his shoulders and pulled him into a head butt, my forehead connecting viciously with the bridge of his nose and making it crack. He tried to stagger back and I helped him on his way, dropping my shoulder and charging him into the wide wooden support that held up a mezzanine balcony encircling the tack room. He grunted as his back hit the beam and the air was forced from his lungs. With my head down, I punched his soft, yielding gut, driving my fists against him with all my strength. The support meant his body had no give and he took the full force of my blows. I felt him wobble as his legs lost their strength, but his arms caught me with a lucky one–two punch in the ear and cheek and I had to disengage and step back to let the pain subside.

He took the opportunity to run up the stairs onto the balcony and I chased him, trying to grab his ankles. I caught him when he was on the penultimate step. He stumbled and fell onto his hands and knees. He thudded into the thick boards, and, eager to press my advantage, I ran to seize him, but he kicked out and his foot found my face, heel connecting with my chin. I tumbled back down the stairs.

Battered and bruised, my ego wounded, I got to my feet and shook off the impact. I looked up to see him sprinting along the balcony toward an alcove.

I thundered upstairs and followed, but when I rounded the turn that had obscured my view, he was nowhere to be seen.

A small window to one side was hanging open. I peered through and saw him running across the roof of the neighboring single-story structure.

I climbed through the window and ran after him, matching him stride for stride.

When he reached the end of the building, he jumped without hesitating and I saw him sprint across the packed parking yard beneath. I followed, making the same leap and falling onto a narrow grass verge. I rolled, got to my feet, and as I ran after him, saw the shooter jump into a BMW 5-Series, gun the engine and speed toward the gate.

"Stop him!" I yelled, running up the drive in futile pursuit. "Stop him!"

My words must have been lost to the distance because the guard on the gate raised it and allowed the powerful car through.

I heard a vehicle race up behind me and thought about commandeering it, but when I turned, I saw it was a course security van. It screeched to a halt. Four guards spilled from inside and tackled me to the ground.

My cheek pressed against dirt, I was restrained forcibly with the four guards yelling at me to stay down. Through their legs, I saw a group of stewards and more guards running toward me, and behind them was Andi, her eyes full of dismay.

CHAPTER 33

LEOPARDSTOWN'S HOLDING ROOM was an eight by twelve feet cell in the main administration building. It was bare apart from a metal bench, bolted to the floor. The walls were gloss-painted and a single strip light was recessed into the ceiling behind a sturdy metal grille.

The security guards had frog-marched me from the owners' parking lot to the rear entrance of the administration building and manhandled me through the first door along. I guessed this cell was used to cool off any particularly troublesome drunks, or, as in my case, secure a person safely until the Garda arrived. There were police on site and nearby, providing crowd control and directing traffic, so I doubted I would have to wait very long.

Sure enough, I soon heard footsteps outside, and the heavy lock clicked open at the turn of a key. The door swung wide. I rose from the bench, expecting to be taken away, but instead I was surprised to see the man who had been at the heart of the shooter's close protection detail. He entered the room like he owned the place. There was no sign of any of his bodyguards.

"Good morning, Mr. Morgan," he said, offering me his hand. "My name is Lawrence Finch."

I didn't shake it. He shrugged and presented me with my phone and wallet, which had been confiscated by the security guards.

"I believe these are yours."

"Thank you," I replied, pocketing them. "Do you work here?"

He smiled. "No. My horses race here. I sit on the board as a non-executive director. I'd like to know why you were chasing Sam."

"Sam?" I asked.

"Sam Farrell," he said. "He's part of my security detail. Or at least he was until he bolted like a hare chased by a hound."

This man had the easy confidence that came with money and power. His two-piece double-breasted blue herringbone suit had been tailormade and hung perfectly from his muscular shoulders. The gray flecks in his dark brown hair and the wrinkles around the corners of his eyes suggested he was in his mid-forties.

"How long has he worked for you?" I asked.

"Three months," Lawrence replied. "He was with the Garda in their serious crime unit before that. Impeccable references."

So Farrell was a cop, I mused inwardly. That would explain how methodical the shooter had been and how he might have been able to disembark the plane without detection. He probably had contacts at the airport. His profile also fit Propaganda Tre's usual modus operandi, which was to recruit people in positions of power and authority. I wondered if I was looking at a fellow member now or whether Lawrence Finch was a mark, the target of Sam Farrell's plans. Either way, I knew I couldn't trust him.

"What line of business are you in, Mr. Finch?" I asked.

"Construction," he replied. "Horse racing is just a passion of mine. An expensive one."

"I can imagine," I said.

"I've spoken to the course management and they have agreed not to involve the police," Finch said, "but I really must insist that you answer my question, Mr. Morgan. What did you want with Sam? And why did he run?"

He'd given me no clue as to his guilt or innocence but I saw no risk in telling him the truth, particularly since it would ease my release.

"The man you know as Sam Farrell was the perpetrator of a mass shooting at the screening of a movie in Los Angeles three days ago," I replied.

"The Ecokiller?" he asked in disbelief. "I saw something about it on the news."

"There was no Ecokiller, or rather it was a sensational cover story designed to throw the media and police off his trail and mask the truth," I said. "My colleague and I were the intended targets of the shooting."

Finch's mouth opened and closed a few times, and his eyes

widened in disbelief, but whatever he was thinking remained unspoken. If he was part of the conspiracy, he was an incredibly talented actor.

"So, I tracked him here and almost caught him," I went on. "And now you will understand why I was chasing him. I want to find out why he tried to kill us and who sent him."

Lawrence Finch collected himself. "I can understand, Mr. Morgan, and I want you to know that I'm very sorry you weren't able to catch him."

He hesitated.

"I'm not sure how to respond to something like this, other than to say I will help you and the police in any way I possibly can."

CHAPTER 34

"JACK," ANDI SAID, the relief in her voice palpable.

She pushed past Finch and then hesitated. I thought she was debating whether to give me a hug. In the end, she handed me my suit jacket, which she must have recovered from the tack room.

"Andi Harris, this is Lawrence Finch," I said, brushing off the worst of the dust. "The shooter is a man called Sam Farrell. He's former Garda and works for Mr. Finch."

"Used to," Finch said as he offered Andi his hand. "I think this is grounds for termination. Of employment, of course," he added.

"Garda?" Andi responded quizzically as she took Finch's hand. "A cop turned killer?"

"I've encountered them before," I said.

"Mr. Finch, I know you from the papers," Andi remarked.

"The stories aren't always true. Believe only half of them," he responded.

"Which half?" she asked.

"Whichever half makes me look the best," he replied with a grin, which quickly faded. "I'm shocked by Mr. Morgan's revelation and was just saying I want to help however I can."

"You could hire Private to find your man," Andi said without skipping a beat.

I paused midway through slipping my arm into the sleeve of my jacket.

"This is a personal—" I began, but he cut me off.

"Of course," he said. "If it would help to have more resources at your disposal . . ."

"It would," Andi replied.

I couldn't argue without making her look foolish, and she had a point. Running this as a billable investigation would enable me to direct Private's resources without any guilt whatsoever.

"Then it's settled," said Finch. "Come by my place tomorrow. You can do a client induction or whatever it is you do, and I can arrange for you to see Sam's quarters."

"He lived with you?" I asked.

"On the estate," Finch replied. "All our staff have quarters on the property."

Andi's eyes widened as she caught my gaze. I could tell she was impressed by such wealth.

"Until tomorrow," Finch said. "I'll make sure there's no nonsense with the Garda after this incident."

"Thank you," I replied. "I'll have to report everything I know to them and to LAPD. This man is wanted there. I hope it won't cause you any embarrassment when I let them know where he worked."

"Why would it? The Garda hired him before I did. He was a police officer for fifteen years. This is their embarrassment not mine," Finch replied. "See you tomorrow."

He gave Andi and me a polite nod and left.

"That was bold," I said when I was certain he was out of earshot.

"Ah, he can afford it," she replied. "I think he's Ireland's fourth-richest man. Or maybe the third. And I bet his companies have ongoing requirements for specialist investigators."

"Always be closing." I smiled. "It gets us inside his circle at the very least."

"You think he's involved?" Andi seemed surprised.

"The shooter works for him," I replied.

"And the Garda before that. Like he said," Andi countered. "Even the best of us can make mistakes."

"True," I conceded. "And that's why I want to check out Finch thoroughly. See if this was a mistake or collusion."

"Paranoia is never wrong when you've been at the hot end of a gun," she said.

"Exactly. Justine is in hospital because we weren't paranoid enough," I replied. "Let's get out of here, before they change their minds about handing me over to the cops."

She smiled, nodded, and I followed her out.

CHAPTER 35

THE CLEAR SKY of a crisp evening was dotted with stars and there was a slight chill in the air, so Andi laid a fire in the living-room fireplace of the house in Fitzwilliam Square. We sat there working at a large table beside the pizza boxes that had contained our dinner.

I was reviewing the publicly available information on Lawrence Finch. He was powerful, well connected, and his multi-billion-euro property empire gave him deep pockets. Horse racing seemed to be more than a hobby to him. It provided him with an entry into high society, which bolstered the power and influence he'd obtained through his businesses. There were photo-library images of him photographed with European and Middle Eastern royalty, and movers and shakers from all walks of life and from all over the world. He was precisely the sort of person Propaganda Tre would recruit. I zipped

everything I'd found on him into a digital folder and called Mo-
bot. It was early afternoon in Los Angeles.

"Jack," she said when she answered the video call. She was in
the tech room at Private's Los Angeles headquarters, and I could
see a couple of her staff behind her. "How are you?"

"Still alive," I replied. "I'm here with Andi Harris from the
London office."

Andi, who had been reviewing filings from Lawrence Finch's
companies, rose and walked around the table to crane into
shot.

"Hi," she said. "I've taken some of your online seminars on
tech trends, but we've never met."

"Nice to meet you," Mo-bot responded. "What can I do
for you?"

"We found the shooter," I said. "He's a former cop called Sam
Farrell. Worked a special unit in the Garda here in Ireland."

Mo-bot sat up a little straighter and made a note of the
man's name.

"Sam Farrell," she remarked. "Former cop. Wow."

"Now works security for a guy called Lawrence Finch. He's
an Irish property developer and racehorse enthusiast," I said.
"He's offering to help, but he fits the profile for Propaganda Tre,
so I'd like you to dig into him. See if you can find any links to
Monaco or Rome and how far we can trust him, because my
working assumption is not at all."

"Will do," Mo-bot replied. "Have you spoken to Justine
recently?"

"Not since last night," I replied.

"You should give her a call," Mo-bot said. "I think you might be pleasantly surprised."

I was puzzled by these cryptic words but didn't need any excuse to phone Justine.

"Will do," I assured her.

"I'll keep you posted on Farrell and Finch," Mo-bot said, before she disconnected.

I called Justine immediately, and Andi returned to the other side of the table and resumed her research. I stepped out of the room into the hallway as the phone rang. I pulled the door shut to give myself some additional privacy when Justine answered.

She was smiling, which instantly buoyed my spirits.

"Hey, Jack," she said. Her tone was lighter than it had been since the shooting.

"Mo told me you've got a surprise or something," I replied.

"Watch," she said, and I saw her place the phone down on a surface nearby.

She steadied herself and then walked to the bright window. She wore a hospital gown and her legs looked pale and weak, but she was walking. She reached the sill and leaned against it for a moment before starting the return journey. Her forehead was pricked with beads of sweat, and she was breathing heavily, but there was a look of grim determination on her face. I felt myself inwardly urging her on, praying for her success as though her journey across that hospital room was the 100-meters Olympic final. She made it finally, breathing a sigh of relief when she rested her hands on the bed.

"What do you think?" she asked, reaching for her phone.

"Amazing," I replied.

"Well, I think you've done enough." A nurse came into view and blocked Justine's path: "You need to get back in bed and I need to reconnect your lines, so you'll have to hang up."

"Sounds like you're being well looked after," I said, and the nurse gave the camera a withering look.

"I know it isn't much, but it feels like a million miles to me," Justine said.

"I'm so happy for you, Jus, and proud too. But listen to the nurse. Don't push yourself too hard. You need to focus on your recovery," I said.

"I won't," she replied. "I promise. Got to go."

She hung up and I pocketed my phone. I was relieved to see her walking, but my happiness was blighted by a sense of anger. She should never have been in that hospital bed in the first place. I was furious at the man who'd wounded her so badly, and angry at the people who had sent him. I needed to track him down. Again.

CHAPTER 36

THE FOLLOWING MORNING, I rose early and joined Andi in the kitchen, where she was making coffee. I wasn't a big breakfast eater and it seemed she wasn't either, so a cup of the strongest java was sufficient to kickstart our days.

She'd opted for jeans and an oversized pullover, and I was probably overdressed by comparison, in a charcoal gray suit and white shirt.

"Anything from Maureen?" she asked, sipping her coffee while she leaned against the counter.

I was seated at the kitchen table, my mug of coffee cooling in front of me.

"Nothing yet," I replied.

"So, we could be about to consort with the enemy?" Andi remarked playfully.

"Perhaps," I replied. "He fits the bill."

"That he does," she agreed.

"So, we'll be careful about what we tell him. See what we can learn about Sam Farrell without giving anything away," I said, and Andi nodded.

Once we'd finished our drinks, we got into the Ford and headed out of Dublin. The city was still slumbering at 8:30 a.m. on a Sunday morning. As we went west along Long Mile Road, a broad, four-lane avenue, and past a school set in large grounds, I saw the turrets of a castle rising above the trees. Through the gates of the medieval structure stumbled a group of men who were obviously part of a bachelor party. The groom-to-be wore a bridal veil and they all sported bachelor tour T-shirts and carried pint glasses as they made their way onto the street.

Andi drove us through West Dublin, out past the industrial estates and retail parks, and soon we were beyond the city, traveling through the countryside on the motorway, which took us further inland. The sun was a brilliant gold against an azure sky, and unusually there wasn't a cloud to be seen. This promised to be a hot day.

Lawrence Finch lived on the Ballagh Estate in a magnificent stately home called Ballagh House, a Palladian country seat built for a member of the Irish House of Commons in 1726. Internet research had revealed an impressive mansion with wings to either side, linked to the main building by long galleries. The estate around his home comprised over 1,000 acres and included Ballagh, a village of 150 souls. The property dated from the time of the Viceroy, or Lord Lieutenant of Ireland, when Ireland was under direct rule by the English. Like many of the big estates in

England, Ballagh House's influence extended beyond the boundaries of its property into the lives and society of the wider community. The grand house was not just a manifestation of wealth, but also of power.

We left the motorway some thirty miles from Dublin and took winding country lanes to the village, where we passed a young priest finishing a beautifully drawn chalkboard image advertising Mass and inviting people into his ancient stone church.

At some point the road leading from the village had been turned into an avenue of cedar trees, which now reached across from both sides to create a high honor guard of interwoven branches for every passing motorist. I thought of how these trees must have looked as saplings and how they now towered above us. It was a beautiful realization of a long-term vision and alerted me to the fact that we were approaching a very special place indeed.

Ballagh House could not be seen from the road, and its gate-house was larger than most mansions. A security team of three men in dark suits did an excellent job of sweeping the car and even checked the underside of the vehicle with a drone on caterpillar tracks.

When they were done, the leader of the trio phoned the house, and for a moment I was worried Finch might have forgotten our arrangement, but I needn't have been concerned. We were waved through, and Andi waited for the high wrought-iron gates to open before following the broad red tarmac drive through ancient woodland.

The house itself lay at the end of a three-mile approach and I glimpsed it first through the boughs of some ancient oaks. Its full grandeur only became apparent when the trees thinned and gave way to impeccably manicured lawns, stretching away to either side of the drive until they met white metal park railings with flower-filled meadows on the far side. Beyond the meadows were streams, a lake, and on the surrounding hillsides, paddocks filled with horses grazing.

The tarmac gave way to deep gravel as we neared the house, and the Ford crunched its way around a grand fountain in the middle of the turning circle. The photos I'd seen of Ballagh didn't do the place justice, and the five-story home still fulfilled its original purpose of signaling its owner's wealth and power. Andi slowed to a halt near a stone staircase leading up to the studded double doors of the grand entrance.

Lawrence Finch was waiting for us at the bottom of the steps and greeted us warmly as we stepped out of the car. After he'd said hello and welcomed us to his home, he turned to a taciturn man standing beside him. The guy had the unmistakable posture of a veteran and the hardened eyes of someone who'd witnessed death up close.

"This is Jackson Kyle," Lawrence said. "He runs my security detail. The two of us will show you around Sam's quarters and answer any questions you might have."

"Thank you," I replied.

"Would you like tea or coffee? A bite to eat, perhaps?"

Andi and I shook our heads.

"Well," said Finch, "in that case, let's get started."

CHAPTER 37

HE LED US along a path that bisected the ornamental gardens to the west of the house. We were surrounded by perfectly trimmed hedges and summer flowers in beds bursting with color.

"Quite the place," Andi observed.

"Isn't it?" Lawrence replied. "I never expected to own anything like this when I was growing up in Carran out on the west coast, but I'm not going to complain about life blessing me so."

The two of them were walking ahead of me and Jackson, who wore a frown that seemed so natural to him that he could have been born with it.

"You don't seem happy to have us here," I remarked.

"I'm not," Jackson confessed. "It means I didn't do my job properly. I'm supposed to be able to spot threats and this eejit was a serious threat to Mr. Finch."

"Don't be too hard on yourself, Jackson," his boss told him.

"I can't be hard enough," his security head countered. "Once the Garda and LAPD get their acts together, this place will be crawling with cops, which will be unavoidable, so I'm going to remain unhappy about the presence of Mr. Morgan and what it says about my performance."

Experience had taught me how insidious a betrayal of trust could be and I knew the toll it exacted. I'd trusted Father Vito, the priest in Rome who'd helped me resolve some questions about my faith, only to discover he'd been lying about his identity and was at the heart of the crime I was investigating. If someone could betray you without you being aware, what other threats were you blind to? It was corrosive to one's self-confidence and that was a serious problem in this line of work.

"We all make mistakes," I responded.

He nodded, but the frown never left his face.

Finch took us across a walled garden to the old stable block, four rows of loose boxes set around a cobblestone courtyard. Lawrence led us through the archway into the courtyard and gestured at the two-story blocks that surrounded us.

"These used to be the stables for the house. Horses, grand carriages . . . that sort of thing. They're a bit basic for stables now, so we converted them into staff accommodation. This was Sam's."

Finch seemed impervious to the scale of priorities that remark indicated. He nodded at Jackson, who stepped toward a green door marked with a brass number 5. He produced a key and opened the door, before leading us inside.

I'd been expecting a tiny studio apartment, but instead we entered a vaulted living room. The conversion made use of the double height of the building. The hay loft had been turned into a sleeping area and there was a bathroom and kitchen located at the back of the property beneath the loft floor.

The place was furnished like a hotel, clean and new, with a hint of style but not much soul. Sam Farrell's personal effects were dotted around the place: bills, books, an iPad, running kit on the back of a chair, muddy trail shoes on the hardwood floor nearby.

"What can you tell us about him?" I asked.

"Joined three months ago. Exemplary record with the Garda. Serious crime unit. Well liked here. Quiet. Enjoyed a run and the occasional beer with the lads. Not much else to say," Jackson replied. "He was a typical ex-cop. Certainly raised no red flags or gave any hint that we'd hired a killer."

"I don't think anyone could have spotted this," Finch remarked. "What possessed him?"

"Do you mind if we look around?" Andi asked.

"Will it interfere with the police investigation?" Finch asked.

"We'll be careful," I assured him.

"Then please go ahead," he responded. "That's why you're here. To find out why he did this and where he is."

"Thanks," Andi said.

"We'll leave you," he went on. "Come up to the main house when you're finished or if you need anything."

"Thank you, Mr. Finch," I responded, and he nodded an acknowledgment and left with Jackson trailing him.

Andi and I spent three hours in Sam Farrell's small home, conducting a meticulous fingertip search, looking for anything that might give us a clue to his connections or motivations. We found nothing. I managed to unlock the iPad and found old movies and music. There wasn't any search history and no messages or emails. He was clearly careful about his digital footprint. The absence of evidence wasn't helpful and at the end of our search, out of ideas or physical space to investigate, Andi placed her hands on her hips and looked at me.

"I think this is a dead end," she said.

"I agree," I replied, making no attempt to hide my disappointment. "Whatever secrets this guy has, he doesn't keep them here."

CHAPTER 38

AS WE WALKED back to the main house, our search a bust, I puzzled over how we could develop new leads. It was very unlikely Sam Farrell would return. We'd searched the place thoroughly and hadn't found anything sufficiently important to draw him back, and a man of his experience and skills would know it was only a matter of time before the Garda established a watch on the house. As a Dublin local with fifteen years on the police force, he was unlikely to be short of friends or places to hide out. The question was how we could identify those friends and places.

The front doors stood open when we climbed the stone entrance steps to Ballagh House, so we went into the marble hallway and saw Jackson and his employer sitting in a grand drawing room to our right.

"Anything?" Finch asked as we approached.

I shook my head. "If there was, we couldn't find it."

"I'm sorry to hear that," he replied. "I was hoping for easy answers and a quick end to this."

"Can you provide us with details of any family or known associates?" Andi asked.

"There wasn't anyone I can think of, but I'll see what I can dig up," Jackson replied. "His Garda referees might be able to point us to friends and family. I'll make the approaches immediately."

"Thanks," I said.

"I'll send you my executive assistant's contact details, so you can let him deal with whatever client engagement material we need to complete," Finch told us.

"We'll get on that today," Andi replied.

We said our goodbyes and returned to the Ford. Andi frowned as we drove away from the grand estate.

"How does someone who's committed murder on another continent leave no trace of any wrongdoing?" she mused.

"Maybe that place is a front and Farrell lives his real life elsewhere," I suggested. "Somewhere that connects him to Propaganda Tre."

Andi nodded but didn't say anything else as she focused on the winding country roads that took us toward the city.

Ten minutes into our journey, my phone rang, and I saw it was Mo-bot calling.

"Mo," I said when I answered. "Go ahead."

"I'm still working on the details, but the broad picture Lawrence Finch gave you is accurate. Sam Farrell is a decorated former cop from the Garda's serious crime unit. He was a good one too."

"But?" I said.

"How did you know there was going to be a but?"

"Because we've worked together long enough for me to know your cat-who-has-got-the-cream tone."

Mo-bot laughed. "You're not wrong, Jack Morgan. Bank records show Sam Farrell made regular trips to Monaco over the last few years. They stopped last year, soon after we broke the Propaganda Tre network over there."

"I know you don't believe in coincidences . . ." I replied.

"I don't, but if I did, this would be a galactic-sized coincidence," she said. "He made at least five withdrawals from the ATM at the Chalmont Casino."

She was referring to the ATM that was once used by Propaganda Tre to help launder illegal funds for its members.

"Now *that* is a huge coincidence," I agreed.

"I'll see what else I can find," Mo-bot said.

"Thanks," I replied. "Speak soon."

I hung up and turned to Andi.

"You catch that?" I asked.

She nodded. "Our man is tied to Monaco."

"Yes. To a casino we uncovered as a major money-laundering front. So there's no doubt Farrell's part of the bigger picture."

"What do you want to do next?" she asked.

"I don't think he'll come back, but we don't have any other leads at the moment and it would be worth seeing what else we can learn about Lawrence Finch. We should stake out his place," I suggested.

"I was thinking the same," Andi revealed. "We might get lucky. Farrell might not come back, but at the very least we'll see if we can trust Private's most recent client."

CHAPTER 39

ANDI HAD COME prepared. She didn't have a full surveillance kit but had brought a basic set of gear with her from London. Two fly-silent drones, each equipped with high-resolution optical, night-vision and infra-red cameras. After driving back to the house in Fitzwilliam Square to collect the gear and change into dark comfortable clothes—I opted for black jeans, a matching T-shirt and a lightweight jacket—we returned to the edge of Lawrence Finch's estate where Andi dropped me off. We agreed I'd take the first shift and she'd relieve me just before dawn the following day.

"You got everything you need?" she asked as I hauled the gear bag out of the trunk and slung it over my shoulders.

"I'm good," I replied.

She nodded. "Okay. Mind how you go then," she said. "I'll see you at five."

She got in the car, and I watched the Ford vanish around a distant bend in the road. I shifted the gear bag to get it to settle better on my back and started toward the high wall that marked the outer perimeter of the grounds of Ballagh House.

Concealed behind a tree, I slung the bag off my back and found an electromagnetic field radiation detector, which I used to check my immediate area for any electrical signals. There were none, so I grabbed the bag and climbed the wall, dropping to the other side. I used the EMF detector to check my surroundings for signals, and its small digital display showed something on the other side of a bush at the start of a forest that stretched as far as I could see in the darkness. I took a flight case from the gear bag and opened it to reveal a fly-silent drone and remote control.

Activating the tiny battery-powered aircraft, I flew it toward the edge of the forest and used it to identify the electrical signal picked up by the EMF detector. It was a security camera attached to a metal post, and it was sweeping the ground between the wall and the forest, giving a 270-degree view of the perimeter of the estate.

I moved left, hugging the line of the wall, using the drone and EMF detector to identify the area with the largest interval between cameras. The estate was well secured, but there was a gap where the going became very uneven as the ground fell away into a ravine, forested on the far side. I packed away my gear, slung the bag over my shoulders and started my descent, following a track created by deer. With rocks either side of me and trees looming high above, I made slow progress, picking my way over the treacherous ground in darkness, but finally reached the bottom of the ravine and began to climb the tree-covered slope on the other side.

I fought my way through the overhanging branches, stopping every so often to use the EMF detector to sweep my surroundings for more cameras or other sensors, but found none. I was able to use the tree cover to come within visual range of Ballagh House.

I tracked the edge of the forest then ran across open pasture to reach the converted stable block. I climbed onto the roof of a new extension at the rear of Sam Farrell's home, which I knew from my earlier visit housed his kitchen, and forced open the picture window at the rear of the gallery bedroom. I figured there was nowhere better to be. If Sam returned, I'd be waiting for him, and the property afforded me a view of the homes of other staff, so I could build a picture of the comings and goings of the people working for Lawrence Finch.

I left the gear bag by the forced window in case I needed to make a swift escape and took the night-vision and optical cameras with me as I went downstairs into the main living area.

I settled into a chair by the window, which gave me a good view of the central courtyard. I sent messages to Justine, checking in on her, and another to Andi, telling her I would meet her where she'd dropped me off and show her the safe route to the stakeout location. She replied with a thumbs-up.

As the night wore on, I took photos of three men returning to the neighboring house. I recognized two of them from Finch's security detail at the racetrack, and the third had the same military bearing as the others. Posture and stance often gave away ex-service personnel, and if he wasn't a veteran, he moved in a way that suggested martial arts training.

I transferred the photos to my phone and sent them to Mobot, asking her to see if she could identify the men. I received a reply almost immediately telling me she was on it.

The block settled into a period of stillness and silence, so I took the opportunity to have another look around Sam Farrell's house, to see if there was anything we'd missed, but found nothing.

Shortly after 1 a.m. I heard movement at the back of the property, a scraping sound that might have been a wild animal nosing around the stables. I rose, crossed the living room into the kitchen and peered through the window above the sink. I couldn't see anything, but turned round with a start when I heard the front door open abruptly. As I ran toward the stairs, three masked men invaded the house. I tried to fight but was overwhelmed by the surge of bodies pressing forward. They forced me to the floor and one of them struck me on the head with a baton, which sent me crashing into blackness.

CHAPTER 40

THERE WERE NO dreams or nightmares, just dark oblivion, and I can't pinpoint exactly when I returned from that void to the real world. I gradually grew more aware of sound, the hum of machinery, indistinct words spoken quietly some distance away, the smell of sweat, the taste of blood, the feel of a fabric hood against my head, obscuring my vision.

I was sitting on a chair. My hands were securely cuffed; I could feel metal chafing my skin when I tried to move my wrists.

"He's awake," a man said, alerted by my futile attempts to move.

I heard footsteps and sensed someone approach.

"Let him see," another voice said. This one had a strong French accent.

My hood was removed and I squinted at the sudden glare of light. Strip bulbs blazed white in the ceiling, and as my eyes adjusted, I made out shapes: crates, pillars, walls, a large sliding metal door. I was in some kind of warehouse. The man who'd removed my hood was tanned, bearded, and wore jeans and heavy work boots. A Led Zeppelin T-shirt completed the seventies rock band roadie look. I didn't recognize him, but his companion was familiar to me.

In stark contrast to the roadie wielding the gun, the man approaching me was immaculately dressed in a cream linen suit. He had chiseled good looks, thick blond hair meticulously styled, and an air of superiority, even in this grubby place while on the run from the law. I recognized him as Raymond Chalmont, owner of the Chalmont Casino, who had fled Monaco after we'd thwarted Propaganda Tre's plans there. Chalmont had been a leading member of the group that had wanted to disrupt a European peace initiative by attempting to assassinate US Defense Secretary Eli Carver, a man I count as my personal friend. Chalmont had been the group's money launderer. When the conspiracy had been smashed, he'd left his business and family, fleeing multigenerational wealth and privilege for life on the run.

"You took everything from me," he said, punctuating his words with several blows to my face.

I glared at him. "You took it all from yourself when you got involved in a conspiracy to commit murder."

"You boy scout!" Chalmont responded angrily. "I spent months planning what I would do to you. Your death was to be public. A disgrace, a humiliation. I wanted to rob you of everything. Just like you did to me. Most of all, I wanted you dead."

JAMES PATTERSON

He moved back a step. "I still do." He clicked his fingers at his companion. "Gun."

The roadie handed him the pistol, and Chalmont raised it to my temple. He stared down at me. I wasn't sure whether he was expecting me to break down and beg for my life or become enraged in those last moments, but there was no way I was going to give him the satisfaction of revealing any emotion.

"You'd better not miss," I told him, and he frowned at me as his finger tightened around the trigger.

CHAPTER 41

"WHEN I'M DONE here, I'm going to make sure Justine Smith and your friends Maureen Roth and Seymour Kloppenberg are taken care of," Chalmont gloated while I fought to disguise mounting anger. "They will suffer for what they did in Monaco and their roles in my ruin."

This guy was born to privilege. The Chalmont family had more money than most people could ever hope to spend in a lifetime, and Raymond's father had founded the eponymous casino, which he'd passed down to his son. This man had been given every advantage, but rather than being grateful, his sense of entitlement was so powerful that he had taken up with a devious political group bent on undermining society. Propaganda Tre was a strange mix of people. There were reactionaries bent on undermining liberalism; political and economic opportunists who saw the chance for their own enrichment or acquisition of power; and ambitious criminals who thrived on the chaos the group stirred up. I think Raymond Chalmont had started as a greedy opportunist, but had become something else because of our perceived "wronging" of him. And yet he'd willingly participated in a plot to murder Eli Carver, a man committed to upholding peace and stability in the world wherever possible. There was no way I would allow myself to die at the hands of this bitter, self-deluding fool.

"Your ruin will be complete if you pull the trigger," I said.

He hesitated. "How so?"

"Every second of this conversation is being recorded," I replied. "Mr. Raymond Chalmont, member of Propaganda Tre, is currently holding a pistol to my head. He is the man responsible for my murder."

Raymond looked at the roadie. "Did you search him? I told you to search him."

"I searched him," the roadie replied. "He's clean."

"Are you sure?" I asked. "You don't know all our tricks."

"Search him again," Raymond commanded.

"It doesn't matter," I remarked. "The recording is being broadcast off-site. If anything happens to me, they will know who to come for."

Chalmont seethed. "Search him again!" he yelled, and the roadie shook his head and moved behind me.

Chalmont inched closer and pressed the muzzle of his pistol against my forehead. Behind me, the roadie unlocked the handcuffs, relieving my wrists from their bite.

"On your feet," he said.

I didn't want to make it easy for them and saw there could be an advantage to me in remaining uncooperative. I stayed completely still and earned myself a crack on the shoulder from Raymond's gun. Although painful, it was exactly the response I'd been hoping for.

"Get up," the roadie told me, as the raw sting in my shoulder died away.

I didn't budge.

When Chalmont raised his gun to hit me again, I jumped up, dodged to one side and grabbed his pistol arm. He fired instinctively and the shot hit the roadie in the gut. He went down screaming. Chalmont quickly recovered from the shock and tried to punch me with his free hand, but I sidestepped and he inflicted only a glancing blow on my back.

I stamped on his foot and he cried out and flinched, enabling me to knock the pistol from his grasp.

It clattered across the floor, and I was about to retrieve it when the sliding door opened and four men who could have been the roadie's cousins came running in. They charged at me, brandishing pistols, and I pulled their boss into a chokehold, using him to shield my body.

"Shoot him," Chalmont yelled. "Shoot!"

The men weren't as reckless as he was and hesitated, aiming their weapons at me, but not daring to pull the triggers in case they hit their boss.

Chalmont tried to elbow me, but I backed clear and punched him in the ear, which made him yelp. I dragged him back a few steps, edging toward the fallen gun.

"Let him go," one of the men yelled.

The roadie groaned in pain as he lay on the floor, clutching the wound in his stomach, and the other men looked from him to Chalmont uncertainly.

Taking advantage of the confusion, I pushed him toward his men, grabbed the gun and fired wildly in their direction as I ran for cover behind a rack of crates.

"Get him!" I heard, and the wood around me burst into a storm of splinters as gunfire erupted.

I kept running and saw an emergency exit at the back of the warehouse. I glanced over my shoulder to see Chalmont trying to wrestle a pistol from one of the gang. When he finally got it, he shot at me, the gun spitting bullets furiously, but he was too hasty and angry to find his mark, and his insistence on shooting from the front of the pack blocked the aim of the other men.

I burst through the fire exit into an alleyway and sprinted away from the warehouse. I didn't stop running until I reached a busy street full of popular retail stores five blocks away. The sidewalks were packed with shoppers. I slowed to a jog and shoved the pistol into my jacket pocket. Scanning my surroundings, I settled into a walk and joined the crowds of people milling around colorfully decorated window displays, which caught the eye in the summer sunshine. Freedom had never felt so good.

CHAPTER 42

THEY'D TAKEN MY phone, so I hurried to a bank of payphones inside Stephen's Green Shopping Centre, a large expanse of glass and ornate white-painted ironwork in the heart of Dublin, to place a collect call to the London office.

"Emily Knighton, please," I said to the switchboard operator. "It's Jack Morgan."

Moments later, Emily came on the line. "Jack, is everything okay?"

"I was attacked and abducted late last night," I replied. "They took my wallet and phone. Will you get hold of Maureen Roth in LA? She'll know how to secure my phone and will instruct someone to inform my banks."

"Are you alright? Is Andi with you?" Emily asked.

"No. I haven't seen her since last night. And I'm fine. Just annoyed I failed to identify a threat. A man we previously encountered was behind the shooting in LA. He has targeted Justine, Mo-bot, Sci and me."

"Who is he?"

"Raymond Chalmont," I said. "Tell Maureen I'm sending her a proper briefing as soon as I can."

"Will do. Anything else?"

"Can you connect me with Andi? I need to check she's safe."

"Sure," Emily replied. "Just a sec."

The line went silent for a moment before there was a ringing tone.

"Hello," Andi said.

"Andi, I've got Jack on the line," Emily told her.

I scanned the faces of the people passing by the bank of payphones, looking for danger, but saw only the disinterest of those who were preoccupied with their own lives. And in the age of cellphones, none of the other payphones were being used, so I couldn't see any immediate threat.

"Andi, I was attacked and abducted from Ballagh," I told her.

"Oh my God, Jack. Thank God you called. I went to the rendezvous as agreed, and you weren't there, so I didn't know what to do. What happened?"

"I'm not sure," I replied. "There must have been a camera I missed, or else they were keeping watch for Farrell themselves. They smashed their way into his place and overpowered me."

"Are you okay?" she asked.

"Yes. Where are you?"

"About a mile from Ballagh House. I wasn't sure what to do, so I thought I'd stay close to the estate to see if you made contact."

"Meet me back at our place as soon as you can."

"I'm heading there now," she replied, and I heard her start the car.

"I'll be with you as soon as I'm certain I don't have a tail," I said. "Thanks, Emily."

"No problem, Jack. I'll get those messages to Maureen."

"Appreciate it," I responded before hanging up.

I stepped away from the phones, alert and on edge, scanning the faces of the shoppers passing by, preparing to begin my circuitous route from the mall back to the house in Fitzwilliam Square.

CHAPTER 43

I LEFT STEPHEN'S Green Shopping Centre, but rather than going the direct route to the square, I headed north along Dawson Street, following the tram route past upscale bars and cafes until I reached Nassau Street and the grand grounds and campus of Trinity College. I went south along Kildare Street, past the historic terraces flanking the stone-built National Gallery. The whole area was a favorite with tourists and the crowds gave me plenty of opportunity to double back on myself, pause to look at the reflections in store windows and generally make sure there were no lingering cameras pointed my way or people following me. I hopped on a bus and took it a couple of stops before walking back. I went into a commercial art gallery at the end of Kildare Street and pretended to admire the contemporary paintings, while checking the sky outside for drones. When I was satisfied I was clear from pursuers, I resumed my journey heading south and then east to Fitzwilliam Square.

I'd taken so long that Andi was already there by the time I arrived, and she looked genuinely relieved to see me.

"God, Jack, are you sure you're okay?" she asked, giving me the once-over.

I knew I must look disheveled. My jeans and jacket had picked up marks and tears in the scuffles, and my face and hair were in a mess.

"I just need a shower and a change of clothes," I replied.

Before I went upstairs, I used my laptop to send Mo-bot a message on Private's secure server. I gave her the address of the warehouse I'd escaped from and asked her to find out who owned it and whether they had any links to Propaganda Tre.

Exhausted and feeling the heaviness of adrenalin leaving my system, I climbed the stairs to my room, showered, shaved and put on a fresh shirt and a fitted navy blue suit.

I returned to the kitchen and found Andi talking to Mo-bot on my laptop.

"Maureen called," Andi said. "I thought I'd better answer in the circumstances. I hope that's okay?"

"Of course," I replied, pulling up a chair and taking a seat beside her to join the video call.

"How are you feeling?" Mo-bot asked.

"Okay," I said. "Pride is a little wounded, but my body is fine."

"Does Justine know what happened?" Mo-bot asked. I saw she was in the tech room at our LA office. "Sci is with her at the hospital, but I'll be on my way over at sun-up."

"I haven't told her," I replied. "I don't want to worry her. She should be focused on getting better."

Mo-bot nodded. "I understand. I don't like keeping things from her, but in this case, I get it."

"Thanks," I said.

"I ran a background check on Lawrence Finch. Nothing untoward. A few rumors about bribes being paid to planning departments early in his career—but show me a property developer who hasn't had allegations like that made against him. He has no obvious ties to Propaganda Tre or Raymond Chalmont, but we've been here before. Our checks on Philippe Duval also came back clear."

Mo-bot was referring to the former Interior Minister of Monaco, who had been part of Propaganda Tre and had been instrumental in luring Justine and me into a trap.

"I'll proceed with caution," I said.

"Wise," Mo-bot responded. "I pulled the property records for the warehouse. It's owned by Longshore Holdings, a shell company that has three other warehouses in Dublin. Ultimate ownership is obscure because there's a chain of corporations that leads offshore into some questionable jurisdictions."

"Can you look for anything that links Longshore Holdings to Raymond Chalmont?" I asked.

"Sure," Mo-bot said.

"And, Mo, I'd like you to move Justine to a new location. Find another hospital," I told her. She frowned before me on the screen. "Raymond Chalmont told me he would come for everyone who matters to me. You and Sci know how to take the proper precautions, but Jus is vulnerable."

Mo-bot nodded. "I'll get right on it."

"Tell no one where she goes," I said. "Not even me. That way I can't give her up if they get hold of me again."

"Okay," Mo-bot replied. "Try not to let that happen."

"I'll do my best," I assured her, and ended the call.

"Should I be afraid?" Andi asked me.

I looked at her somberly. "Raymond Chalmont and his associates kill without hesitation, and they have Private in their sights. We all need to be extremely careful."

CHAPTER 44

THAT NIGHT, I spoke to Justine in her new hospital room. She seemed bewildered by the move. Mo-bot had told her she'd have a better standard of care there and had forced through the transfer by sheer strength of will. She was known as Private's corporate mom for good reason, because when it came to pastoral care she was second to none. I knew Justine and I were particularly important to her.

"How are you feeling?" I asked Justine. "Apart from unsettled."

"A little better. I think the change of scene has stimulated me. I walked further today than I've done for a while," she replied with a proud smile.

"That's awesome," I said.

"What's up, Jack? You seem distracted."

"Just thinking about the investigation. I almost had Sam Farrell at Leopardstown. It's frustrating to have come so close and have nothing to show for it. I'm trying to figure out how we find him." It wasn't a lie, but I didn't tell her about the attack on me last night and the abduction, or the real reason why she'd been moved. Was it lying by omission? I didn't think so. There was nothing she could have done to help, and the greater good in this situation lay in her being left undisturbed and able to make a complete recovery.

"Try not to get too stressed by it," she said. "Our best breakthroughs often come during downtime, when we let the default mode network take over."

I took it as a good sign that she was using her profiling expertise to counsel me. It showed her injuries were no longer occupying her entire mind.

"I'll try," I assured her with a forced smile.

We chatted about nothing much and finally said our goodbyes a little before midnight in Dublin.

Justine had told me to get some rest, but I struggled to sleep that night and kept reliving that feeling of powerlessness, being cuffed and at the mercy of a man who wanted to kill me and those I loved. It was a terrible, impotent sensation and one I desired never to experience again. I had to be more careful. Now Raymond Chalmont had shown his face, there was no doubt Propaganda Tre was behind the attack, which meant our enemies were very well resourced.

I finally fell into a restless sleep near dawn and woke when my alarm sounded at 7:30 a.m.

Andi was already in the kitchen by the time I'd showered and dressed. I'd chosen a light blue suit and dark blue shirt.

"You still want to see Finch?" she asked, pouring me a coffee.

We'd discussed our plan of action over Chinese takeout the previous evening and I'd concluded an upfront return to Ballagh House was our best option until Mo-bot could develop the leads we'd given her. It seemed more likely Lawrence Finch was involved given that I'd been abducted from his property, and if he was, another visit might shake him into making a mistake. I have never been one to give in to fear and relished the prospect of returning to the place where I'd faced violence. It was as much an affirmation of my refusal to view myself as a victim as it was a confrontation.

After we'd finished our coffee, Andi drove us out to Ballagh and we were shown through the gates by security and directed to a large summerhouse by a member of Finch's close protection detail.

The summerhouse was warm and filled with tropical plants, creating a lush environment that felt vibrant and opulent. We found Finch swimming in a slate-tiled pool at the heart of the building.

He waved hello to us, completed his lap and hauled himself onto the poolside. He was a fit, muscular man who moved with assurance. He grabbed a towel from a lounger and dried himself, beckoning us to join him in a seating area.

"Would you like anything to drink?" he asked as he took a seat in a wicker chair.

Andi shook her head. "No, thanks."

"Not for me," I said. "Thanks."

"We had some excitement in the night," he revealed as Andi

and I sat down opposite him. "It seems someone broke into Sam Farrell's place. Looks like there was a struggle, but somehow whoever it was avoided being caught on the estate cameras. I wonder if Sam came back."

Finch finished drying his hair and hung the towel across the back of his chair. I scanned his body for signs of the distinctive Propaganda Tre tattoo, but there were no visible markings of any kind, which was a relief, though I couldn't relax entirely. There was no guarantee all members of Propaganda Tre carried the tattoo, but its absence was least a welcome indicator.

"That must be a headache," Andi said. "Having the police poking around."

"Ah, it's okay. My staff are dealing with it. Always happy to help the Garda."

He hesitated before he continued, saying, "Strange thing is, the police found a bag full of surveillance gear that I'm pretty sure wasn't there when we checked the place before. Certainly didn't belong to Sam."

For a second, I worried he was going to press us about the discovery, but he moved on.

"How can I help you both?" he asked.

"I wonder if you know a man called Raymond Chalmont?" I asked. "He ran the Chalmont Casino in Monaco."

Finch shook his head. "Never heard of the man. Sorry, Mr. Morgan. I wish I could say yes, but it's a no."

He looked me dead in the eye. His voice didn't waver, there were no sideways glances, no hesitation, nor upwards rolls of the eyes, which are all common traits in those spinning fiction.

I've interviewed hundreds of people in my career, and all my experience told me Lawrence Finch was being truthful. Which, given the fact I'd been abducted from one of his properties, meant that he was either a completely innocent man who was the victim of circumstances, or he was one of the most accomplished liars I'd ever met. Either way, this was a dead end. Lawrence Finch was giving us nothing. We'd have to wait and see what Mo-bot could uncover from the information we'd brought her.

CHAPTER 45

"WHAT NOW?" ANDI asked as I drove us back to Dublin.

I'd been considering the question as I steered the twisting country lanes that took us away from Finch's estate.

"They will realize the warehouse I escaped from has been compromised because I know its location," I replied. "But I doubt they will assume the other two warehouses have been identified because they won't expect me to have access to someone with Mo-bot's skills. I'm not sure there's anyone else quite like her."

"So, you want to find out what they're being used for?"

I nodded. "We take one each and stake it out. See if we can learn what they're up to."

Andi shook her head. "It's too risky. I don't want to find myself alone in a jam after what just happened to you, and I don't want you to take any undue risks either. We should work together. Pick one of the warehouses, set up a stakeout and keep watch in shifts, but with both of us on-site in case anything goes wrong."

I thought about disagreeing for a moment. Her approach had its own risks: we could both be captured, or we might choose the wrong warehouse to watch, but then I remembered how powerless I'd felt against those men last night, and I knew she was right. I didn't want to be in that situation again. Or at least I wanted to reduce the chances of it, and having a skilled operator like her at my side should do just that.

"Okay," I said. "Which one?"

She considered the question for a moment. "I don't know why, but my gut tells me the one on Manor Street to the north of the city."

I nodded. "Your guess is as good as mine. Let's do it."

I drove us back to the house in Fitzwilliam Square, taking a long, haphazard route to ensure we weren't followed from Ballagh House. Once there we changed into casual clothes, both opting for dark jeans and tops, and put together a surveillance pack of a mini-drone, camera and a night-vision scope. Losing the gear bag in Sam Farrell's house had given us limited options and these were all we had left of the supplies Andi had brought with her.

While I was packing food and drink, she checked Google Maps for overhead images of the warehouse, which was situated halfway along Manor Street in Dublin's Stoneybatter district, north of the River Liffey. The place was surrounded by businesses and other warehouses, which would hopefully ensure a steady stream of traffic and reduce the chances of us being noticed.

We planned to keep watch from the car, but Andi identified a couple of the surrounding rooftops as alternative locations if we felt the car was too exposed.

Satisfied we were ready, our gear and supplies prepared, we waited until sundown before beginning our journey. The drive took twenty minutes, and in that time we went from the upscale, immaculately restored historic buildings of Fitzwilliam Square through the historic heart of Dublin, past St Patrick's Cathedral and its high dressed-stone spire, along and over the river then through residential streets lined with rows of small Victorian terrace houses, before finally arriving at Manor Street, which turned out to be in a gritty commercial neighborhood.

We circled our target, a large redbrick warehouse set back from the road, and didn't see anything unusual. Andi spotted a space in the driveway of a vacant warehouse fifty meters along the street. It was the perfect spot because we were obscured to one side by the loading dock, which jutted out beside the driveway.

I parked nose-forward, facing the loading bay, meaning we also couldn't be seen from the front. The headrests made us difficult to spot from the street, so we were only really visible from the right, but we needed a clear view in that direction to keep watch on the building that was now the target of our investigation.

CHAPTER 46

I COULDN'T REMEMBER falling asleep, but at some point exhaustion swept over me like a tide, and as the adrenalin dissipated, fatigue carried me to a place of nightmares. I was back in the chair, staring down the barrel of Raymond Chalmont's gun. Only this time I didn't escape. He pulled the trigger and in the muzzle flash I was transported to the flaming wreckage of the Sea Knight helicopter I'd been piloting when it was shot down and many of my comrades had died. The nightmare seemed so real, I could have sworn I felt the heat of the flames on my face as I watched the chopper burn. But there was no crash and no chair, just the wild imaginings of my tormented mind trying to make sense of a life that had already seen too much horror and violence.

Andi saved me from the dreamscape when she shook me

awake, and for one bleary-eyed moment I struggled to recall why I was sleeping sitting up in the front seat of a car.

"There's something happening," she said, gesturing down the street.

It all came flooding back to me. My abduction by Raymond Chalmont, the three warehouses, our stakeout, Andi volunteering to take first watch.

I glanced at the dashboard and saw it was 3:42 a.m. I looked down the street to see a large truck parked in the yard outside of the warehouse owned by Longshore Holdings.

"We should take a closer look," Andi suggested.

I nodded and took the optical camera from the gear bag on the back seat. We opened the car doors quietly and crept out. We headed along the street, carefully hugging the building line and shadows.

When we reached the adjacent warehouse, Andi and I clambered over a high wall and dropped into the front yard, which was filled with a fleet of delivery vans belonging to an electrical components business. We crept across the paved area, trying to stay clear of the field of view of the security cameras mounted on the exterior walls of the warehouse.

Once on the other side of the yard, Andi and I climbed onto the roof of one of the delivery vans and peered over the high perimeter wall. The Longshore Holdings warehouse was an old Victorian building that looked as though it had been renovated and extended many times in its long history. There was no sign or business markings of any kind, and the windows were opaque. The truck outside was an unmarked late-model DAF 18-wheeler. Its rear doors were open toward the warehouse loading bay, and a team of six men were using pneumatic trolleys to unload boxes on pallets.

I took photographs and tried to get headshots of all six men and close ups of the boxes they were shifting.

"What is that?" Andi asked.

I lowered the camera and switched to playback to scroll through the images I'd taken. When I came to a clear one of a man pulling a pallet load of boxes, I zoomed in, and the word stamped on the side of the carton came into focus: Xylazine.

"What is it?" Andi asked when I showed her the photo.

She crouched behind the wall and used her phone to search for an answer.

"That's weird," she said. "It's a tranquilizer used on horses. Legal for veterinary use, but if it's legitimate, why are they moving it in the middle of the night?"

CHAPTER 47

WE WATCHED THE men unload the truck. When they were finished, two of them jumped in the cab and drove the large vehicle out of the yard. As it rumbled away from the warehouse into the distance, the other four went inside and rolled down the loading-bay shutter, obscuring our view of the interior. They soon emerged, locked the building, secured the gate, and got into a car parked on the street outside. I took photos of all of them, and of the car and its license plate as they drove away. I waited until the vehicle was out of sight, then turned my attention to the old warehouse.

"I think we should check it out," I said.

"Breaking and entering?" Andi responded.

"You can stay here if you feel uncomfortable," I suggested.

"No," she replied with a smile. "I just want to be clear what charges we'll face if we're caught."

I slung the camera over my shoulder and climbed the wall before dropping onto the concrete on the other side. Andi followed me, and we crept across the yard, keeping our eyes peeled for cameras. There were none, or at least none we could see. There were also none of the "building under surveillance signs" such as were posted on so many of the other warehouses in the neighborhood. I wondered if the people who owned and operated this place wanted to avoid any record of what went on here.

We moved quickly, jogging to a side door, where Andi produced a set of picks and went to work on the lock. She had the door open in under two minutes, and I shut it behind us once we were inside.

We stepped into a corridor that was flanked by offices, with a staff room to one side. There were stairs that led to an upper level and a door to the main warehouse on our left. I checked the inset window for danger, and, seeing the place was empty, I pulled the door open and went through. Andi followed, and we entered a 60 x 80 feet space filled with storage racks that towered almost to the ceiling. A mezzanine balcony wrapped around the space on three sides, and there was a row of forklifts and manual lifting gear positioned by the rear wall.

I went to one of the racks and saw cases of animal feed and veterinary supplements.

"Jack!" Andi called, and I turned to see her beckoning me toward the front of the warehouse.

The boxes we'd witnessed the men unload were stacked in the bay near the doors. I raised the camera to my eye and took some photos of the large quantity of sedatives, wondering what was going on, and what it had to do with Sam Farrell and Ray-mond Chalmont.

I heard the rumble of an engine and looked at Andi, who'd registered it too. The vehicle stopped outside, and I ran to the loading-bay door and looked through the envelope window to see a man jump down from the cab of a truck and unlock the warehouse gates. He pushed them open so the truck driver could steer the vehicle into the yard.

"Someone's coming," I said. "This way."

I led Andi to a rack of crates by one of the whitewashed brick columns that supported the mezzanine balcony, and we crouched there and listened to the large vehicle reversing into position outside of the loading bay.

Andi signaled at the inner door, suggesting we should make a run for it the way we'd come, but I shook my head. I wanted to find out what these people were doing.

"You get the door open. I'll unlock the wagon," a man said, and a few moments later, the roller shutter started to rise.

A heavy-set man in his early forties entered. He wore jeans and a plaid flannel shirt. He went to the back of the ware-house and grabbed a pneumatic loader, which he wheeled to the pallets of boxes we'd just witnessed being unloaded. I could hear his companion outside, preparing the truck.

A minute or so later, the second man entered and joined the guy in the plaid shirt. The second man wore a thick black jumper and jeans. He had the same brawny physique as his companion. I took photos of them through the mesh of the rack as they worked to get a pallet of painkillers onto the loader.

They wheeled it out of the bay and onto the truck, returning to repeat the process.

I nudged Andi and signaled the open truck.

She shook her head emphatically, but I started creeping around the rack and she followed reluctantly. We were quiet and the men were busy, so they didn't notice us as we made our way out of the warehouse and stepped inside the back of the truck.

"This is nuts," Andi whispered as we made our way to the cargo hold and crouched behind the first pallet of boxes.

"I have to know what they're doing," I replied. "And if there's a chance they might lead me to Sam Farrell or Raymond Chalmont, I must take it. You don't need to come with me."

Andi shook her head in reproof but she didn't leave. The two of us waited in silence until the men had finished loading the entire shipment into the truck. Finally, they closed the doors, consigning us to darkness.

CHAPTER 48

"THIS IS MAD," Andi said as we sat with our backs against the side of the truck.

We were in pitch darkness, trying to keep ourselves upright as the large vehicle bounced and rolled its way through Dublin.

"If you want out, I'll find a way to open the doors," I said, nodding in their direction even though I knew she couldn't see me.

"I don't want out," she replied. "I just want it noted on the record that I think this is mad."

"Duly noted," I said, and we spent the rest of the journey in silence. The stop-starts and sharp turns of the city gave way to long, uninterrupted runs and gentle curves, and I guessed we were on country roads. The rumble of the engine rose above the pounding thump of dance music coming from the cab, which helped mask our whispers and the sounds we made as we struggled to keep from sliding around on the metal floor.

"Do we fight if we're found?" Andi asked, as the vehicle slowed.

"We have to," I replied. "These people are dangerous."

There was a squeal of brakes and the truck shuddered as it went over a cattle grid. It accelerated briefly before coming to a halt a short while later.

The engine stopped and the radio fell silent.

"You get the lift and I'll open the wagon," one of the men said.

I heard the two of them jump from the cab and land on gravel. One set of footsteps moved away, while the other came along our side of the truck and went to the back.

A moment later, the rear door opened, letting in the gray light of dawn and a blast of cool, fresh air. Andi and I eased ourselves to our feet carefully as the man in the plaid shirt got busy opening the second rear door. We moved to the very back of the truck, behind the first pallet of boxes.

"Don't be such an eejit," the man at the doors said. "Here, I'll do it."

He hurried away to wherever his companion was, and I sensed an opportunity.

"Come on," I said, nudging Andi.

We crept to the mouth of the truck and I peered round the open door in the direction the man had gone. There was a large barn about thirty meters to our left. The double doors were open, and I could see industrial machinery standing idle inside.

To our right was an old redbrick watermill that looked as though it had been converted into a family home, although the twelve high-performance muscle cars in the driveway suggested either the occupants were having a party or there was more than one family living here.

"This way," Andi whispered, pointing at some lights that were on in one of the first-floor rooms of the converted mill.

I jumped out of the truck and followed her toward the three-story building, which still had a working waterwheel. The sound of the river rushing as it was forced through a narrow channel toward the wheel masked the noise of our advance. We moved along a gangway that ran alongside the house, around the wheel, and then behind the property.

There were more lights on at the back. We approached a low window and peered in to see that the old mill floor had been converted into a narcotics lab. Boxes of the sedative were being turned into a dry powder, and there was a chemical cooking bench where a suspension of the powder was being turned into something else.

"Synthetic opioid?" Andi suggested.

"Or a highly concentrated sedative. Plenty of demand for that on the street," I replied.

There was no sign of Sam Farrell or Raymond Chalmont, but I was in little doubt that this was the sort of enterprise our targets would be involved in.

I used the camera slung over my shoulder to take photos of the interior of the room, which contained four people in clinical gowns and protective N95 respirator masks. Identification would be difficult, but the photos would be useful as evidence to encourage the Garda to investigate this location.

"Hey, you!" a man's voice yelled. "Stop right there!"

I glanced at Andi, neither of us in any doubt that he was shouting at us.

"Run," she said, and we immediately started sprinting back the way we'd come.

CHAPTER 49

WE RAN TOWARD the waterwheel.

The man who'd shouted at us was on the other side of the concrete channel, an indistinct shape beyond the reach of the house lights. His silhouette was large and menacing, and I saw the shadow of a gun in his hands as I glanced back.

The first crack of gunfire echoed against the stone channel and the side of the house. The bullet ricocheted off the brick-work, chipping away flakes and sending dust into our faces.

He fired again, and this time he hit the waterwheel, with the noise of wood splintering to our right. Andi and I ran around the gangway, bringing us closer to the shooter. We couldn't have been any more than eighteen feet away.

He shot again, and this one zipped past my ear with a sharp rush of air that was unmistakable. We heard the projectile thud into the rear side panel of an Audi parked in the yard.

I saw shadows and movement in the house. Even with the noise of the waterwheel, the sound of gunfire would be audible inside. We needed an escape route and fast.

The shooter was running across a metal bridge that would bring him to our side of the river, and I had no doubt the occupants of the house would soon join him in trying to capture or kill us.

"Try the cars," I said to Andi, "and pray at least one driver is careless."

She nodded and we immediately ran along the row of parked vehicles trying to open the doors. The first two were locked, but the third was open.

Andi tried the push start button, but the car was unresponsive, so I ran to a black BMW M5 and did the same.

The engine roared to life as half a dozen men burst through the front door of the mill and yelled at us.

"Jump in," I shouted to Andi, who bolted to the passenger side.

The gunman rounded the waterwheel and started shooting.

"Hey! That's my car," one of the men by the front door yelled as bullets struck its bodywork.

The shooter stopped for a moment and Andi jumped into the passenger seat. I settled behind the wheel, flipped the paddles that controlled the semi-automatic gearbox into first. The engine growled as I stepped on the accelerator and the car shot forward, shooting gravel into the air behind us as we sped away.

CHAPTER 50

WE SHOT DOWN a bumpy country road, and the long grass growing in the middle whipped at the undercarriage of the fast car. We swung left and right as the engine delivered power to the rear wheels. I accelerated and felt the push against the sports seat at my back.

Behind us, lights and activity in the yard signaled that this wasn't going to be an easy getaway.

"I count two . . . no, three . . . vehicles coming after us," Andi said.

I nodded. "See if you can figure out where we are and find a way for us to lose them."

She produced her phone and opened a map application.

I swung the car around a tight left bend, into the glow of the rising sun. Light cast on the folds of the green valley deepened the patches of shadow in places. I followed the road round to the right, away from the direct sunlight, and swerved just in time because we'd come face to face with a large John Deere tractor. The green monster shuddered as the driver tried to stop, and I swung the BMW onto the verge, where the wheels chewed up the turf as they fought for traction. We shot past the giant machine and bounced back onto the road with a series of crunches and clanks that sent sparks flying up behind us.

I thanked the guardian angels watching over us when I saw the tractor was going to buy us some time. The three vehicles pursuing us, an Audi SUV, a silver Mercedes E-Class and a Range Rover, were all forced to a stop when they met the tractor at a narrow section of the road, where the dry-stone wall to either side was no more than a couple of feet from the tarmac. There was no way for the cars to get round, and the driver of the lead vehicle, the Range Rover, yelled at the man behind the wheel of the John Deere.

"Turn right," Andi said, pointing to the mouth of a tiny stone-chip trail no more than fifty meters ahead.

"Are you sure?" I asked.

It looked too insignificant to lead anywhere useful.

"Yes," she replied. "Take it."

I swung the wheel right and the car whipped round, propelling me toward Andi. She was flung against her door as we slewed into the mouth of the stone track. I glanced right and saw the three pursuing cars steering round the tractor, which had backed up and climbed onto the verge to give them space.

The BMW flung up dust and gravel as it raced along the

track. There were now stone walls just inches away from our wing mirrors, and if we hit a dead end we'd be trapped.

"Sharp bend left, about fifty meters ahead," Andi told me as she watched our progress on her phone.

"Got it," I replied, and shifted down into third to give me the power to push through the turn.

The BMW shimmied on loose stone but stayed true, and we growled round the bend at speed.

There was a rise ahead and the powerful vehicle accelerated toward it, catching clean air as we crested the summit.

The three cars following us had turned onto the stone track and were churning up dust and stone as they raced after us. We lost sight of them as the BMW landed and shot down the slope on the other side. As we rounded a bend, I saw why Andi had brought us this way.

Directly ahead, blocking the track, was a high gate, and beyond it a busy quarry where excavators and trucks shifted stone. Further on, past the site buildings, I saw a service road that led to what looked like a motorway.

"Nice work," I said, and pressed the accelerator, forcing the car to its limits.

The men behind us were becoming desperate. As the Range Rover jumped the summit, the man in the passenger seat leaned out of the window and tried to shoot out our rear tires. But he was a poor marksman and simply hit the road behind us.

We smashed through the gates and roared toward the site buildings.

Behind us, I saw the trio of vehicles slow to a halt. Maybe

they were afraid of being caught on site cameras? Or perhaps they couldn't afford to be seen by witnesses? Whatever the reason, they abandoned the pursuit, and we slowed as we drove through the site. We rolled past the buildings at the heart of the quarry and climbed the service road on the other side to join what proved to be a motorway, taking us back to Dublin.

CHAPTER 51

WE'D JOINED THE M3 near Garlow Cross and were on it with the first of the early-morning commuters as the sun rose over the horizon and brought color to the half-tones of night. I turned off the motorway just past Blanchardstown, and Andi directed me toward a neighborhood called Castleknock on the northern edge of Dublin. She took me to a residential street called Beechpark Avenue, and we left the BMW parked in front of a double-fronted redbrick house with white chimneys.

I could see Andi was on edge. She kept scanning our surroundings as we walked away from the stolen car, and I wasn't any more at ease.

"We'd know by now if they were following us," I said, trying to calm myself as much as her.

The pursuit had sent my adrenalin levels into overdrive, and my fight-or-flight response was on a hair trigger. I startled at an early-morning jogger who slammed her front door shut as she left home. Combat veterans know that fear is part of the experience of conflict. The key is to know how to manage it. Right now I just wanted all those stimulating hormones to dissipate so I could settle. I watched the jogger stride away and caught Andi's eye. She smiled awkwardly as we went north.

Walking helped to settle us. We moved quickly toward the junction with Navan Road, a major thoroughfare where we could catch a taxi. It was too early for schoolchildren and the roads weren't crowded. A few eager commuters steered their cars along the quiet street.

Andi and I reached a parade of stores that were set back from the road: a pharmacy, an estate agent, and a cafe, which was filling the air with the scent of bacon, coffee and freshly baked pastries.

I realized I was famished.

"Want some breakfast?" I asked, and Andi looked at me incredulously.

"Seriously? Now?" she asked.

"Why not?"

She opened her mouth as if to reply but thought better of it and shrugged.

"Why not?" she agreed.

We walked toward the cafe, which was at the northern end of the parade. There were a few outside tables beneath a black awning that advertised it as the Silver Spoon, but it was too cold to breakfast al fresco, so we headed inside where the air was thick with appetizing smells and warmth.

There were a couple of people ahead of us, so we joined the

line and placed an order for two farmhouse breakfasts with coffee. The friendly cashier told us to take our seats at one of the wooden tables for two. We chose one by the postcard rack, and Andi sat on a painted green bench while I took a wooden chair. We were too early for the morning rush and our fellow customers were taking their orders to go, so we watched a steady stream of people coming in for coffees, pastries and cakes while we waited for our food.

"Intense," I remarked.

Andi's eyes widened and she sighed. "Tell me about it. Good driving."

"Good navigating," I said.

"Who do I send my chiropractor's bill to?" she said with a smile, and I chuckled.

The waitress brought our orders with a cheerful greeting and a warm smile. The farmhouse breakfast turned out to be bacon, sausages, eggs, grilled tomato and something called black-and-white pudding, served with toast.

"What is black-and-white pudding?" I asked, staring down at a slice of something that looked like a square sausage.

"It's better you don't know," Andi replied. "Ignorance is bliss."

I tucked in and thought it reminded me of haggis, a spicy Scottish meat dish I'd once had. It was delicious.

"Good food," Andi said. "Good for the soul."

She took a swig of coffee.

"So, drugs?"

I nodded. "It gives us a new line of inquiry," I said between mouthfuls. "Can I borrow your phone?"

As she pulled her cell from her pocket and unlocked it, I made a mental note to buy myself a new one.

"What do you need?" she asked.

"Mo-bot," I replied. "Maureen Roth."

"Now?" she remarked.

"Mo keeps odd hours," I assured her.

She dialed the number before handing the phone across the table.

"Andi," Mo-bot said when she answered. "How's Jack?"

"He's okay," I replied.

"You get everywhere, Jack Morgan," Mo-bot scoffed. "What can I do for you?"

"We found what looked like a drugs lab tonight. Andi will send you the location. I'd like you to see if the property is connected to Noah Kearney, Lawrence Finch, Longshore Holdings or anyone else associated with the investigation so far," I replied. "I'd also like to know if Sam Farrell ever worked narcotics when he was a cop. See if he has any prior connection to the drugs trade. A lead we might be able to exploit."

"Sounds like things are getting heavy," Mo-bot remarked. "You need support on the ground?"

"No. We're okay. We're fast and nimble. An effective team." I looked across the table at Andi, who nodded as she took a bite of toast. "But if that changes, I'll let you know. For now, I want you with Justine."

"Got it," Mo-bot replied.

"And in any case, I'm planning to ask the cops to run

interference. As soon as I get off this call, I'm going to report the lab to the Garda," I told her.

"Well, what are you waiting for?" Mo-bot said. "I'll report back as soon as I've got anything."

She hung up.

"You really think you'll find a connection in Farrell's past cases?" Andi asked, as I used her phone to call the Garda.

"There might be something," I replied, before turning my attention to the call I'd placed. The operator asked me the nature of my emergency, and I told her, "I'd like to report a serious crime."

CHAPTER 52

WE TOOK A series of cabs to ensure we weren't tailed. The first delivered us to Bow Street, a cobblestone thoroughfare in the historic heart of Dublin, and we caught another outside of Jameson Distillery, which took us to Christ Church Cathedral. Tourists were already gathered to admire the magnificent Gothic building, founded in the eleventh century and one of the ancient landmarks of Ireland's rich past. Mingling with the tourists for a while to ensure we weren't being followed, Andi and I caught a final taxi outside of a tiny bistro. We got out a few blocks from Fitzwilliam Square and walked the final stretch. By the time we arrived at the townhouse, I was exhausted and in need of sleep.

"I'm going to lie down," I told Andi. "You should do the same."

She nodded, clearly weighed down with fatigue also. "I'll just make some tea to take up to bed."

She went into the kitchen while I climbed the stairs, entered my room, shut the door and flopped onto my bed. I didn't even bother kicking off my shoes.

I must have fallen asleep quickly. When I woke with a start, the sun was low in the sky and the day was beginning to dwindle.

I rose with a woolly-feeling head. I undressed and showered to revive myself and help shake off the blanket of fatigue.

I put on a pair of black pants and a pullover and went downstairs to find Andi at the dining table, which was now our operations center. She had put her portable printer to work and case files covered every surface. She was poring over material.

"Did you sleep?" I asked.

"I couldn't," she replied. She seemed more than a little wired. "My mind kept going back to that stud farm where we rescued the family. Kearney Stud. A place like that would be great cover for illicit horse tranquilizers. Maybe the reason they were threatening Noah and torturing his kids has something to do with those drugs?"

She'd printed out one of the photos I'd taken through the old mill window, showing the drugs lab, and held it up now.

"I reckon we go back out there and see if the family has returned. If they have, we pressure Noah Kearney about the connection," she suggested. "Now that we know more."

I thought about it for a moment. It was a reasonable idea. Kearney might talk if he knew we'd found out about the illegal activity another way and the information couldn't be tied back to him.

"Okay," I responded. "But you need sleep at some point."

"Yes, but for now I'll just have a shower," she said with an emphatic shake of her head. She seemed agitated, but I didn't want to push her to rest. I knew how elusive sleep could be when the mind was active, and she was more than capable of making her own decisions.

I used the time to write Justine a loving but suitably vague message. No need to worry her about what we were up against.

Ten minutes later, Andi came downstairs in jeans and a gray-and-black camo hoodie. We caught a cab to Manor Street where we found the Ford we'd abandoned outside of the vacant warehouse. I insisted on driving, and Andi navigated the route to Kearney Stud.

When we arrived, the gates were padlocked shut, so we checked there was no one around and climbed over the perimeter wall.

We made our way through the woods under the cover of darkness. There were a few horses grazing in surrounding fields, but the property itself was shut up and still. Wherever they'd gone that night, it seemed as though the Kearney family had not returned.

"Looks like there's no one home," I said.

Andi nodded. "We should search the place."

We gained entry through the kitchen door. There was plenty of evidence of our struggles against the home invaders, but no sign anyone else had been in the place since.

"You want to take upstairs?" Andi suggested. "I'll take down."

I nodded and started upstairs. I paused on the half-landing

when I saw something at my feet. It looked like a medicine box, and I stooped to pick it up. It was a box of Xylazine, the same tranquilizer we'd seen at the warehouse on Manor Street. I was sure it hadn't been here when I'd left the house on the night of the home invasion and attack on the Kearneys. I knew I would have noticed it.

As I stood studying the box, I heard the sound of glass shattering and a rush of air, before the familiar thud of a bullet slamming into the wall beside me. Someone was shooting through the full-length window behind me, and as I glanced over my shoulder and registered the faint glow of a sniper scope, I saw rapid muzzle flashes. The sniper knew he or she had been spotted and was sacrificing accuracy for volume.

The whole window shattered when the next volley hit, and I ducked and tumbled downstairs.

"Andi," I yelled, and she came running out of the living room. "We have to go."

The gunfire stopped, and in the eerie stillness that followed, we crept from the house and made our way through the forest. I took great care to keep cover between us and the sniper. By the time we reached the wall, my heart was racing with tension.

We'd be exposed as we climbed, and if we made it to the other side, there was a run across open ground to the car.

"On my count," I said to Andi, as we crouched by the trunk of an old oak tree.

"Three . . . two . . . one . . . go!"

We both sprinted to the wall. Andi reached the top first, and I wasn't far behind. The shots resumed when I rolled over the capstones, splinters and chips hitting my face as bullets strafed the stone wall inches from me.

I dropped to the ground on the other side and we raced to the car. Andi jumped in the driver's seat and I slid in beside her. She had the engine going and the car moving before I had the chance to slam the passenger door closed.

CHAPTER 53

"YIKES!" ANDI EXCLAIMED as we shot along a dark, narrow country lane, the high hedges zipping past us in a blur. "They must have been watching for the Kearneys to come back."

I nodded. "We were lucky."

It felt as though electricity was coursing through my veins and it was all I could do to stop myself from shaking with the power of the adrenalin rush I was experiencing. I forced myself to breathe, to try and take the edge off my body's potent response to danger.

"You're probably right about them using the stud as a cover," I said, trying to direct my mind toward something other than an all-consuming flight from death. "If they were helping bring in the medicines, Noah and Mary Kearney must have done something to make their business partners mad."

"But taking shots at us?" she remarked. "This goes beyond an internal drug feud."

"I think it proves the Kearneys are linked to whatever Propaganda Tre is doing with the drugs. Why else would you station a shooter at their house? Takes a lot of manpower to keep a constant watch on a place like that," I replied.

"But why target us?" Andi asked.

"We're on their list," I said. "That was no random shooter waiting for the Kearneys. That was someone connected to the investigation who knows who we are. They must also know that the higher-ups want us dead."

She glanced in the rear-view mirror. "I don't think we're being followed."

I checked and nodded, and she took her foot off the gas.

As the car slowed, I said, "Can I borrow your phone?"

She slipped it out of her pocket and handed it to me.

I called the Garda and reported seeing a man with a gun in the vicinity of Kearney Stud. It was unlikely to yield anything as the shooter would be long gone, but it was the right thing to do; a police presence might help protect the Kearneys and their children if they ever came home.

"What now?" Andi asked when I handed back her phone.

"Head for Fitzwilliam Square," I replied. "Try to get some rest and regroup."

I sensed she had something on her mind.

"You don't agree?"

"I do," she replied. "God knows, I'm exhausted. I was just thinking about our possible leads and I realized we're running thin."

"I know," I conceded.

"I think we should pay Lawrence Finch another visit," she said. "If Kearney is involved in the drugs trade, then a racing supremo like Finch might have heard rumors. And if we've missed something and Finch really is part of Propaganda Tre, then he's probably involved himself and it won't hurt us to give the tree another shake."

I wasn't sure about the advisability of returning to see Finch when we were still unsure about him, but Andi's logic was reasonable. "We'll go first thing tomorrow," I told her.

CHAPTER 54

THE FOLLOWING MORNING, I woke feeling more rested than I had at any point since arriving in Dublin. I went downstairs to find an email from Justine waiting for me. It was a loving message and ended with an instruction to call her whenever I woke. It was a little after 8 a.m. in Dublin, so it would be after midnight in Los Angeles. Not a terrible time to call, and she might have something important to say. I used my laptop to place a video call, and she answered almost immediately.

"Jack," she said dreamily. She looked as though she was on the verge of sleep. "I miss you."

"I miss you too," I replied. "How are you feeling?"

"Getting there," she said. "Much better. Moving around on my own more. The pain is manageable. Less shortness of breath."

"Good," I said, relieved.

"How's the investigation?" she asked.

"We're working our leads," I told her. I wasn't lying, but I wasn't being completely open either, which bothered me.

"You okay?" she asked.

I nodded. "Just missing you."

"Me too."

Andi entered the dining room wearing a red summer dress. "Ready?" she asked, without registering I was on a call. "Oh, sorry."

"Is that Andi?" Justine asked.

"Yes," she replied, leaning into the frame to wave. "Sorry for interrupting. I'll leave you guys in peace."

She stepped out of the room.

"How are you getting along?" Justine asked, and I wondered if I imagined an edge to her voice.

"She's a smart detective," I replied.

"That's good." Justine's neutral tone sounded slightly forced. We'd had issues like this before when she'd been worried I was growing too close to Dinara Orlova on an investigation in Moscow.

"We're working well together," I assured her. "That's all."

"I understand. I'm just feeling lonely and vulnerable, Jack," she said.

"I'm sorry, Jus. I want to get this done quickly so I can get right back to LA and be with you," I told her.

"Then go do it," she responded.

I hesitated.

"Go," she said. "I'm fine. I just need to get some sleep. 'Night, Jack. Love you."

"Love you too," I replied, before she disconnected.

I found Andi in the hallway by the front door.

"All good?" she asked, and I wondered whether she'd heard the tail end of the conversation.

"All good," I said. "Ready?"

She held up the car key in reply, and two minutes later, we were in the Ford heading west.

Andi phoned Lawrence Finch on our way out to Ballagh House, and his executive assistant told us to go to the training facility located ten miles west of his grand estate.

Lugh Stud, according to the research I did during the drive, was named after one of the Tuatha Dé Danann. These were the pre-Christian Gaelic deities who formed a pantheon of gods and heroes similar to those worshipped by the Ancient Greeks. Lugh is said to have invented horse racing, and the training facility that bore his name was worthy of this divine association. About a mile west of the village of Carbury, onyx pillars set either side of silver gates marked the start of the property, set in beautiful rolling countryside.

Andi turned off the road, and we drove a couple of miles along a tarmac track that cut through woodland and fallow fields. Beyond them lay hundreds of acres of pasture, meadows and paddocks. Lawrence Finch had a vast, modern training facility and at the heart of the complex lay a network of modern buildings in black-stained cedar, with panoramic smoked-glass windows and solar panels. The horses' accommodations looked better than most human homes.

Our car was checked at a second gate near the stables, and

we were directed to the visitors' car park and told we'd find Finch in Stable B.

Andi pulled into a space, and we got out and followed discreet signs that marked out key buildings.

Lawrence Finch was in the paddock outside, talking with the trainer about a horse they were watching being exercised by a groom. I could see them both pointing to different aspects of the animal's action and discussing it somberly.

Finch caught sight of me and Andi and excused himself before sauntering over. We met him by the fence.

"Good morning, Mr. Morgan, Ms. Harris. Any news?" he said, offering us a warm smile.

"We found evidence Sam Farrell might be linked to a narcotics operation," I replied.

"Oh dear." His smile fell. "Drugs are a terrible scourge. I sincerely hope you're wrong. I can't bear the thought of having had someone like that working for me."

"We wondered whether you'd ever heard anything about Noah Kearney being involved in anything like that?" Andi asked. "Illegally importing medicines or anything?"

"Jesus," Finch responded, before falling silent. He thought for a moment. "No, sorry. Any breeder who got mixed up in that sort of thing would be risking their reputation, livelihood and freedom. If he was doing anything shady, he'd keep it quieter than the grave. I haven't heard a thing about it. I'm sorry I can't be of more help. As far as I know, Noah Kearney is a reputable breeder and trainer, and a decent, law-abiding man. I've never heard a bad word spoken of him."

Andi and I were crestfallen. She looked particularly disappointed, and I guessed it was because this had been her idea.

Lawrence Finch took advantage of our silence. "I wish I could give you something that would help crack this case, but I can't. If there's nothing else . . ." He trailed off and gestured to the racehorse behind him.

"Thank you, Mr. Finch," I said.

"No—thank you," he responded. "Now if you'll excuse me? We're in the middle of race preparations here."

With that, he left us and returned to his beautiful thoroughbred.

CHAPTER 55

ANDI DROVE US away from Lugh Stud. Our visit had left us none the wiser.

"What now?" she asked as she steered the Ford along a narrow country road, zipping past stone cottages and fields of barley and oilseed rape.

"I don't know," I replied with a sigh. "Looks like we need to review everything we have again. See if we can't develop a few new leads."

"So, we need some thinking time?" Andi asked with more than a hint of mischief in her voice.

I nodded uncertainly.

"In that case, I know the perfect place for us," she said, before taking the next right off the road to Dublin.

"Where are we going?" I asked, as she steered us down a narrow single-track lane.

She winked at me but said no more. I grinned in bemusement and turned my attention to the hedgerows and expansive green fields that lined our route.

Cows and sheep grazed here and there, and wildflowers flourished on the verges. It felt like the very edge of civilization because we didn't see another person or vehicle for twenty minutes. When we crested each rise, a new snapshot of Ireland impressed the country's beauty upon me.

My question about our destination was answered a little over thirty minutes later when we pulled into the car park of a pub called Roches. Located on a quiet country road, the single-story building initially looked underwhelming. It might have been a simple farm cottage once but had been extended over the years and its walls painted cream with bright red trim. If I'd been alone, I'd probably have driven straight past and looked for something architecturally more pleasing, but as we searched for a space in the overflowing car park and I looked at the packed beer garden, I realized that would have been a mistake.

"Looks like lots of people need to do some thinking," I said to Andi, gesturing at the busy pub.

"They do," she replied. "Thinking and eating and drinking. The place is known for it. They say Einstein came up with the Theory of Relativity here."

"I thought that was Bern in Switzerland," I said.

"No. That's fake news," she said as she stopped the engine. "Why in the world would an Irishman have an idea like that in Bern?"

"Einstein was Irish?" I scoffed.

"Of course. All the best people are," Andi said with a wry smile. "And after the food and drink in this place, you'll be sworn Irish too, Jack Morgan."

I laughed, and we got out of the car and went into the pub, which was even more crowded than the beer garden. Servers hurried to and fro, ferrying plates of delicious-looking food to busy tables and clearing away empty dishes. I thought we might struggle to find a table, but Andi spoke to a barman who directed us to one that had just become vacant outside. It was a beautiful spot with a view over the open country to the rear of the pub.

I had a Guinness and some fish and chips, and Andi had Bulmers cider and a crispy chicken baguette. The food was excellent. We cleared our plates.

"Sign me up," I said.

"So, you're Irish now?" Andi asked with a grin.

"In all seriousness, I do have some Irish blood in me," I revealed, "and places like this make it all the more potent."

She chuckled before her attention was drawn to her phone, which had started to ring.

"It's Maureen," she said, handing it to me. "I'm guessing it's you she wants."

"Thanks," I replied, before answering the call. "Go ahead, Mo."

"Jack, I was looking through Sam Farrell's case assignments with the Garda and digging into his life when the strangest thing happened. I discovered his personal email was already in the Private system."

"What?" I asked. "How?"

"He applied for a job at Private London six months ago," Mo-bot revealed. "The man who put Justine in hospital tried to come and work for you, Jack."

CHAPTER 56

MY MIND REELED at the idea Sam Farrell had tried to get a job at Private. That couldn't have been a coincidence. Had he been planning this far ahead to get close enough to kill me? Or was there some other play in progress here? And why hadn't he succeeded in his job application?

"Let me call you back," I said to Mo.

"Sure," she replied.

I ended the call and found Emily Knighton's number in Andi's phonebook.

"What is it?" she asked as I dialed.

"One second," I replied. The call went through.

"Andi," Emily said when she answered.

"No, it's Jack," I responded. "Did a guy called Sam Farrell interview with you for a job a few months ago?"

"Sam Farrell?" Emily repeated, and I saw Andi's eyes widen as she registered the significance of what I was asking. She looked at me in disbelief.

"Yes, I remember him. Garda officer, wanted to move to London," Emily said. "Why?"

"He's the guy who shot Justine," I said.

"No!" Emily responded. "I have a good memory for faces and names, I should have—"

I cut her off. "Don't beat yourself up. It was a short meeting six months ago. Why would you have remembered? Could have happened to anyone."

"But we're not supposed to be just anyone," Emily countered, sounding glum. "I should have done better."

"I'm serious," I said. "There's no point. You can't undo the past. If you want to help, send Mo-bot everything you can remember about the guy. Every detail of your interactions with him and the interview, no matter how small."

"I record all my interviews," she said. "I'll have the footage stored somewhere on the system. I'll send that too."

"Thanks," I replied. "And I want you to run a background check on everyone hired in the London office in the past two years."

"What?" Emily asked. "Why?"

"Sam Farrell didn't come to us by accident. I think Propaganda Tre was trying to get someone on the inside of Private."

"Damn," Emily remarked.

"Yep," I concurred.

"I was hired within the last two years," Andi remarked. "Does that mean I'm under suspicion?"

"Of course not," I replied, when in truth I couldn't be certain of anyone now. Not beyond my core team of legacy hires. "We're merely checking everyone as a formality."

"Doesn't feel like a formality when you're the one being checked," Andi said.

"I'll get right on it," Emily cut in.

"Thanks," I said before hanging up.

"You really think Propaganda Tre tried to get someone inside Private?" Andi asked. "No offence, but it's a detective agency. Hardly MI6."

"Why not? Someone felt enough hatred for me to kill five innocent people and put many more in hospital when they came after Justine and me. They could have been trying to find out about us earlier or else looking at our case files to see what we know about Propaganda Tre."

Andi nodded and took a sip of her cider. "Good point."

"We need to get back to the city," I said. "I want to take a look at the case notes through the lens of Farrell having a longer history with us."

"I'm going to settle up," Andi responded. "Finish your drink and I'll meet you at the car."

"I don't suppose there's any point in me arguing over the check," I said.

"None whatsoever," she replied quickly. "I'm going to expense it, so you're picking up the tab either way."

She broke into a broad smile as she stood up and walked inside. I shook my head at her impish humor, but part of me couldn't help but wonder whether I could truly trust her.

CHAPTER 57

WE DIDN'T SPEAK much during the drive back to Dublin. I wondered if Andi felt awkward now she was under review. Despite what I'd said about it being a formality, a good investigator would know that wasn't true. The new hires would have to be re-vetted, their lives and references examined anew, and this time we'd specifically be looking for anything that linked them to Propaganda Tre, the Dark Fates, or any of the principal players: Lawrence Finch, the billionaire racehorse owner, Sam Farrell, the former cop turned assassin, and Joe McGee, the street dealer who'd brutalized Noah and Mary Kearney.

But maybe she wasn't the one causing this new constraint between us. Maybe the conversation had dwindled because I was killing it. Maybe I was afraid of speaking freely until I knew if she was truly friend or foe.

As we made our way into the inner city, passing the

boarded-up, derelict stores in Dolphin's Barn, I revisited the investigation. If Andi was compromised, then her lines of inquiry were too, and everything she'd suggested was suspect. Instead of an ally, I might have a threat sitting in the car with me, which meant not only did I have to be on my guard constantly, but I also had to look again at everything about this investigation from the very beginning. Starting with the arrest of Joe McGee, the ketamine dealer linked to the Dark Fates, who we'd followed to Kearney Stud.

As Andi parked in Fitzwilliam Square, I stretched to ease away the effects of the long drive.

"I'm going to get some milk," I said. "See if I can buy a phone."

"I can do that," Andi replied as she stopped the engine and opened the driver's door.

"It's alright. I want to stretch my legs," I said.

"I can come with—" she began, but I cut her off.

"I'll be a while getting a new phone. And if they sell me one with some charge, I'll call Justine."

She smiled wryly and her head drooped. "Formality," she said quietly.

There wasn't anything I could say to make her feel better.

"I shouldn't be more than an hour or so," I said, and didn't wait for a reply as I got out the car and walked away.

I went into Mobile123, a phone shop on Mespil Road near the canal, where I bought a phone in less than fifteen minutes. The pay-as-you-go device had sufficient charge for a few calls, so I tried Mo-bot, knowing she'd probably be awake even though it was very early in Los Angeles.

"Hello?" she said.

"Mo, make a note of this number. It's my new phone," I replied. "I want you to dig into Andrea 'Andi' Harris. Tell Emily she's a priority for review. If she's dirty, I want to know ASAP. If she's clean, I also need to know so there's no distance between us."

"I'm on it," Mo-bot told me. "Anything else?"

"The pub where Joe McGee was arrested. It should be in the case files. I need the name."

I heard Mo-bot typing. "It was the Night Watch," she said after a short while.

"Thanks," I replied. "I'll call you later."

I used my new phone to find the Night Watch, which was a thirty-minute walk to my east on Irishtown Road. I hurried across the city, passing Lansdowne Road stadium and crossing the River Dodder on a small stone bridge.

The Night Watch was one of Dublin's oldest pubs, set back from the road at the mouth of a narrow cobblestone yard. It was as if the place was a gateway to the city's history. The two-story building was painted black, with gold lettering, and the sign hanging over the door depicted a group of men in hoods searching for something by the golden glow of a lantern. The place was busy despite it only being late afternoon on a weekday, and from the look of the folks inside, this wasn't a pub for tourists.

Men with hard faces, some of them with broken noses or mouths shy of a full set of teeth, eyed me openly as I entered. But I wasn't intimidated and went to the bar, where I jostled my way to the barkeeper's notice and ordered a pint of stout. Once I'd got my drink, I moved to a quieter section of the pub and leaned against a wall while I studied the customers.

I was looking for anyone dealing or using drugs, because the chances were they would know Joe McGee. If I got really lucky, I might spot the man himself.

After an hour nursing my now-warm pint, something caught my eye, and I moved across the pub to check it out.

A large man in jeans and a T-shirt was pushing his way across the saloon toward a corridor at the rear of the pub. A sign above the doorway read "Toilets," but there was another door further along from the restrooms, which brought the corridor to a premature end. When I got closer to the guy, I was able to get a better look at the thing that had caught my eye—a tattoo on his upper arm, just above the elbow. It was the mark of Propaganda Tre. This was one of Joe McGee's fellow foot soldiers.

The man went into the corridor and I put my pint glass on a nearby table and followed him. I saw him enter the room at the end. Two bouncers standing either side of the open doorway eyed me closely as I approached.

"Can we help you, sir?" the one on the right asked.

The guy on the left leaned in and closed the door, but not before I'd had the chance to peer into the busy function room and see a couple dozen men, maybe more, drinking and talking in small groups.

"I'm looking for the men's room," I said, playing up my American accent.

"Right behind you, pal," my guide told me.

I looked over my shoulder and made a play of registering the sign for the men's toilet.

"Sorry," I said. "Head's a little fuzzy for some reason. I might have had too much of your black stuff."

I made a show of being drunk and staggered when I turned away. I walked along the corridor and into the men's room where I waited patiently until, about five minutes later, I heard a cacophony of voices and the thud of many footsteps. The meeting had broken up and the men were leaving. I left it another minute or so before I slipped out and followed them.

CHAPTER 58

THEY DIDN'T DISPERSE outside of the pub, which surprised me. Instead, the large group turned right, into the mouth of a dark cobblestone alleyway. They didn't talk much and for the most part moved in silence, which was disconcerting. It was rare to see this many people so purposeful and somber except at a funeral, yet they were not dressed for that. They wore casual clothes: jeans, T-shirts, sweatshirts, boots, trainers. Most walked with a pronounced swagger.

I followed about thirty paces back, checking my phone nonchalantly, as though messaging a friend, while I was in fact studying the map as we turned right onto Bath Street, a residential neighborhood of small terrace houses. There were no front yards and the houses pressed in on the narrow street, making it seem even more claustrophobic. Cars had to slow to avoid the group of men, the left flank of whom had spilled off the sidewalk, but there were no protests either from the drivers or from the men, which made me wonder whether these guys were known locally.

We continued walking until we reached an intersection. Beyond the lights stood a vacant former car showroom that was showing signs of disrepair, but light spilled from an open door at one side and two large men flanked it. The group crossed the street, hopped a low wall into the empty parking lot, and picked up speed as they approached the open door.

I continued along Beach Road, watching the group as they were nodded inside by the bouncers. Was this a speakeasy or some sort of private club? It didn't feel like somewhere people went to have fun.

I went south until I was beyond the vacant retail unit. When I couldn't be seen by the men on the door, I jumped the low wall and ran back across the parking lot and down the blind side of the unit where I would not be observed, into an alleyway separating it from the neighboring abandoned office block. I came to a rear yard that was full of rusting and rotting office furniture, shelving units, metal containers and trash. I picked my way through this, past all the detritus, and went to a single-story extension unit. Here I hauled myself onto the flat roof, taking great care to test each step before trusting it with my full weight. I made slow progress to the main building and a run of small reinforced windows, most of which had been broken long ago. I could hear the hubbub of conversation coming from inside and reached beyond the remaining shards of glass to unlock a catch and open one of the windows.

I carefully clambered into a damp corridor that led to offices along the other side of the building. I followed it until the voices grew louder and went through a fire exit that was missing a door. I was on a gantry that linked the offices with some fire stairs running down to the main showroom that would once have been full of cars. This was where the group of men from the pub had gathered.

The windows had been covered with blackout material, which explained why it had looked dark from the main road. The showroom had been converted into an auditorium and the men I'd followed were seated in rows in front of a small make-shift stage. There were six men in suits on the stage, all of them hard-faced, with the haircuts, toned bodies and ramrod posture of military men. One of them, who had a face like a forty-fight pugilist, was addressing the group from the center of the stage.

"We've struck a blow before, and it made the national news. We need these invaders to know they're not welcome and that they should stay in their own countries or choose somewhere other than here.," he said. "Leave Ireland for the Irish!"

The group yelled as one, "Ireland for the Irish!"

"Let's strike another blow for the motherland," the speaker said, and the other men in suits lifted holdalls from behind the stage and started distributing their contents to the audience.

They filed up to receive ski masks and weapons like machetes, clubs, batons, and a few handguns.

I heard vehicles pull up out front and started to make my way out of the building, returning the way I'd come.

I knew the Dark Fates were the street arm of Propaganda Tre, the muscle that did the dirty work. But this looked like a polit-ical far-right paramilitary group rather than organized crime, which meant Propaganda Tre's mission to seek power through the chaos of hatred and division was very much a part of its street operations too. We'd underestimated the Dark Fates by classifying them as a purely criminal gang of thugs and hoodlums.

As I picked my way through the yard full of trash, I used my phone to call the Garda.

"What's the nature of your emergency?" the operator asked.

"I think there's going to be trouble," I replied.

CHAPTER 59

THE EMERGENCY OPERATOR didn't take me seriously, and I couldn't blame her. I told her what I'd seen, but there was no crime in progress to report, just some concerning words and the distribution of weapons. I impressed upon her the fact that I'd seen guns, but she asked how I could be certain and whether they might have been something else. If, in fact, I had seen more than two dozen men being armed in this way, it would require a major police mobilization, and that was something she wasn't prepared to request on the hunch of an anonymous caller. She said she would send a patrol car to my location, but as I made my way along the alley between the retail unit and the office block, I realized any such response from a single police vehicle would be too late.

There were three white vans parked outside of the retail unit, and the men I'd followed were streaming out of the building and getting into the waiting vehicles. I glanced right and saw the yellow-and-blue roof signage of a taxi making its way north along Beach Road.

When the vans pulled out of the lot and turned left, I ran across the open space to the street, where I hailed the cab.

The driver, a rosy-cheeked man in his fifties, smiled and said, "Hello, nice evening," as I climbed into the back.

"I don't know about nice, but it's interesting," I replied. "I'm going to need you to follow those vans." I pointed at the trio of white vehicles that were heading north.

He did a double-take, glancing from them back to me. "You're serious?"

I produced my billfold and peeled off five 20-euro notes. "Just for the hire. Add the fare on top and there's another hundred for you if we find out where they're going," I said.

"Right you are," he replied cheerfully, putting his Toyota Avensis in drive and pulling away.

As we went past the retail unit, I saw the two bouncers go inside and lock the front doors behind them.

"My name's Jimmy," the cab driver said as we went north onto Bath Street.

"Nice to meet you, Jimmy," I replied. "Jack."

He didn't say anything for a moment, but I saw him sizing me up in the rear-view mirror.

"So, are you a cop then, Jack?"

"Private detective," I told him.

"One of the good guys?"

"I try to be," I replied.

He nodded toward the vans, which were passing the mouth of the cobblestone alleyway near the Night Watch pub.

"And are those the bad guys?"

"Definitely. Very bad," I assured him.

"Good," he said. "I like to know how things stand. It's easier taking money from a righteous hand."

He didn't say anything else as we drove north through Dublin, following the vans as they took the Samuel Beckett Bridge across the River Liffey. I called Andi. I felt I had to trust her a little, since I couldn't convince the Garda to respond to my warning.

"Hello?" she answered.

"Andi, it's Jack. Don't ask me why, but I'm following about thirty men in three vans. We're on Guild Street, heading north, just beyond the river. I think they're planning serious trouble. They're heavily armed."

I saw Jimmy flash me a concerned look.

"Don't get too close," I told him.

"Jack, you're not serious, are you?" Andi asked.

"I am," I replied. "I'll text you my location. Tell your Garda friend to have a couple of units ready to respond."

"Of course, Jack. I'll get straight on it," she replied.

"Thanks. I appreciate it," I said, before hanging up.

I sent her a pin of my current location and continued doing this as we travelled further north. We went over another bridge, through a commercial district, then on into a residential neighborhood and over another bridge, before the vans took a left onto Richmond Road. We drove beside a canal for a while before buildings sprang up to our left.

Up ahead, the vans finally pulled to a halt in front of a residential apartment block on the south side of Richmond Road. The building looked to be in a state of disrepair and was surrounded by a high fence on all sides. Jimmy stopped a block away and we watched the gang of men stream from the vehicles. They were now wearing masks and brandishing their weapons, and four of them carried glass bottles filled with fluid, necks stuffed with rag fuses—the unmistakable Molotov cocktail. There was no doubt these men were intent on serious violence.

"Where are they going?" Jimmy asked, and we watched them approach the building with the high chain-link fence.

Six stories high, the place looked like some sort of institution, and sure enough, my eyes soon settled on a sign beside the main gate, which read "Richmond Refugee Centre."

"Jeez," Jimmy remarked, when he registered the sign. "These lads mean to cause real trouble."

The gang used heavy bolt cutters to force open the gate, and as the metal barrier swung wide they surged forward, running into the grounds and spreading out. The four men with petrol bombs lit the fuses and the evil orange flames signaled the start of mayhem.

"Call the Garda," I said to Jimmy as I got out of the cab.

"Way ahead of you," he replied, and I heard the ringing tone on his car's Bluetooth system.

The first petrol bomb arced through the air and hit the side of the building, spreading fire over four floors. The other three Molotov cocktails quickly followed.

As I ran along the street, I saw the fire quickly take hold while the rioting men banged their weapons against the ground and yelled, "Born here. Belong here. Ireland for the Irish!"

When the first occupants came to their windows and saw the hostile force awaiting them and the building ablaze, the screams started.

CHAPTER 60

I'D EXPERIENCED THE violence of war. I'd seen horror up close. The anguish of a mother holding a dying baby, a husband lamenting the loss of his wife, soldiers weeping for their fallen comrades. I'd seen that same look in their eyes, desperately pleading, searching for an answer to a troubling question: How can I go on living in a world capable of inflicting such cruelty?

The hurt so profound and severe it would never truly be healed. The pain so deep it could cause unexpected anguish even years later. I still carried the psychological scars of combat. I'd lost comrades and witnessed atrocities and the suffering of others, but had come through unscathed myself. At least physically.

These men, these cruel men with their masks and weapons and chemicals, were bringing horror into the lives of people whose only crime was to have fled violence or persecution elsewhere. They had sought sanctuary somewhere they thought was safe and supposedly welcoming. On one level, I couldn't understand civilians who would unleash such violence onto their own streets, who wanted to cause strife in an otherwise peaceful city, and who brought conflict and pain into their communities. On another level, I understood it all too well. These men had been radicalized into believing the poor families in the refugee center were their enemies, and as such they had to take matters into their own hands.

Misinformation, misdirected anger and mob mentality made radicalization a relatively simple matter in the age of social media, and it was easy to see the groupthink at work.

The masked men had gathered around the main entrance and were banging and brandishing their weapons, chanting racist slogans while flames spread throughout the building.

They cast a red glow on the masked thugs, making them look utterly demonic, and I watched as the first refugees tried to flee the building.

A man, his wife and their two young children, all dressed in pajamas, all terrified, were beaten back inside the main entrance by the vile thugs. They weren't just here to cause trouble. It looked as though they wanted to murder. The children cried and the husband and wife begged for mercy as the thugs chained and padlocked the front doors from the outside. The desperation in the refugees' eyes reminded me of the people I'd encountered in Sanctuary City, the temporary encampment in Temescal Canyon. Refugee outsider or impoverished citizen, these people were hated when they should have been helped in their time of need.

Every fiber in me wanted to run and help that family, but I knew I was seriously outnumbered. I needed a smarter solution.

I went through the gate and stayed close to the fence, skirting the perimeter of the property, until I was to one side of the block. I raced along the concrete yard until I hit a lawned area at the rear of the building. There was a small picnic area and playground, and it pained me to wonder how many young children were trapped inside the burning building.

I saw two masked members of the gang standing by the glazed rear fire door, holding clubs, waiting for anyone trying to escape. I knew I had no time to waste, and I was too angry for caution. I charged at the smaller of the pair, and as he turned and raised his club, I tackled him and sent him tumbling back. I wrested the club from him as he fell and turned to parry a blow from his associate. I rolled clear of the fallen man and brought the club down on the aggressor's head, knocking him senseless.

His associate came at me, but he was poorly trained and my blood was up. I parried a couple of ineffectual blows before thrusting the tip of the club into the man's chin. As he staggered back, I swung at him hard, catching the side of his head and knocking him out.

I ran to the back door and thumped on it as loudly as I could. After a minute of frenzied banging by me it was opened.

The man who'd been trying to flee with his family stuck his head outside cautiously. He saw the two masked thugs lying unconscious behind me.

"This way," I said. "It's safe."

He nodded.

"Tell the other residents," I said.

He ushered his wife and children out and ran back inside to yell something up the stairwell in Arabic. I guessed he was relaying my instructions.

When he returned, I pointed to one of the picnic tables.

"Let's move this to the wall. You can use it to climb over," I instructed.

He nodded again, and we ran over to it and each grabbed an end. We carried it over to the high wall at the side of the property, and as we positioned it, the back yard filled with people fleeing the flaming building.

"This way," I said, when we'd set the table flush against the wall.

I helped the first people onto the table and over the obstacle.

"My name is Adel," the father told me. "I will help get the people up."

"Thank you, Adel," I said.

He nodded and clambered to the top of the wall, where he set himself so he could help the other less capable residents up. Soon others were doing the same, and the crowd of people on my side quickly shrank. As they fled to safety, I wondered how many of these people were lamenting what had become of their supposed sanctuary.

"Oi!" a man yelled, and I turned to see one of the masked gang members peering down the alley at the side of the building.

He shone a flashlight in my direction and caught sight of the last stragglers fleeing over the wall.

"Get them to safety," I told Adel. "I'll hold the gang for as long as I can."

"Don't do it," Adel responded as he helped the last refugee, an elderly woman, over. "They are dangerous. Come."

I shook my head. "No. You need time to get these people away."

I jumped down from the table, picked up the two clubs I'd discarded and prepared to intercept four men who were now running down the side of the building toward me. I wondered how many of them I could hurt before they took me down.

CHAPTER 61

AS THE FOUR masked men ran at me, I saw two were carrying clubs, one had an ax and the fourth held a machete. They saw their fallen comrades near the fire exit, and I could feel their anger surge.

"You . . ." the axman yelled, so angry he never finished his curse.

He sprinted ahead of the others and I raised both clubs as I prepared to face him. He didn't hesitate but took a swipe straight at my head. The ax is a poor weapon in untrained hands because the heavy head keeps traveling if a target is missed, which is exactly what happened in this instance.

The wild swing forced him off balance and I took advantage of his misjudgment by striking his right knee with the club in my left hand, cracking it. As he buckled and dropped the ax so he could soothe his injured knee, I smacked him on the ear with the other club, and he went crashing to the ground, out cold.

The two men with clubs came at me and I parried their blows at furious speed, but one caught me with a vicious strike to my left shoulder. That side of my body exploded with pain, but I've had experience of shoulder injuries, which are often sharp and debilitating but pass quickly. The club in my left hand dropped automatically. I rolled to the side and grabbed it as the searing pain in my shoulder subsided.

I stamped on the taller man's foot. As he stepped back, I caught him with a club to the ribs, winding him. His accomplice swung at me with his weapon, but I stepped forward, moving between the two men. I grabbed the injured man and thrust him into the path of his angry companion as he came for me again with his club. The blow connected and the accomplice stepped back in shock as he realized he'd knocked out his friend.

Exploiting his surprise, I swung with my left club. He recovered enough to partially block the blow, but I caught him on his shoulder, and as he was dealing with the pain, freed him from it entirely by cracking his head with the club in my right hand. He fell to the ground unconscious.

I sensed movement behind me and ducked and rolled. As I came up and looked around, I saw machete man rushing me, swinging his blade wildly.

I tried to parry a blow and the razor-sharp edge of the blade lopped the tip off of the wooden club.

Machete man paused, and in the momentary silence I heard a voice yell, "Hey!"

I looked beyond my assailant to see one of his masked accomplices who'd been at the front of the building register the mayhem at the back. More men started to come around the corner until there was a large group of them.

"He helped them escape," machete man yelled to the group that had started toward us.

"Let's get him!" the leader shouted, and ran forward, followed by the entire gang, roaring and jeering as they came.

I couldn't see machete man's mouth, but I could tell from his eyes that he was smiling.

I thought about turning and running for the picnic table, but my opponent would slice my back open as soon as I showed it to him, so I squared up to him and the approaching mob and prepared to go down fighting.

CHAPTER 62

MY HEART THUNDERED with fear and adrenalin as the masked horde approached, brandishing weapons. I'd rarely faced such poor odds and felt strangely calm as I realized these were likely to be my last moments. I was heartbroken at the prospect of losing Justine, and the pain of impending loss filled me with sorrow. It was goodbye to Mo-bot and Sci too, and all the other people I considered my friends. But there was no panic, just the clarity and peace of knowing I would face the end on my own terms.

Sorrow turned to relief when I heard sirens close by, and the klaxons of the emergency services.

I glanced behind me to see twin beams of light. There were two Irish police officers, leaning over the top of the wall, shining their flashlights toward me. I had no idea what they were standing on. It could have been air for all I cared. They were joined by Adel, who pointed at me.

"That's him," he said. "That's the man who saved us, and those are the men who tried to kill us."

Machete man hesitated. Behind him, the advance of the baying mob slowed to a halt.

"Stand where you are!" one of the Gardai commanded.

Machete man dropped his blade and turned and ran. The whole gang of masked men did likewise, fleeing as emergency vehicles flooded the scene.

I watched the gangsters sprint away and jogged after them, to see them surging through the gate and scattering into the night. Police cars and fire engines pulled up and the three vans were surrounded, but from what I saw, most of the men got away, running into adjacent properties or down side streets and alleyways, lost to the shadows and the night. The Gardai and firefighters had a more urgent issue to address: the blaze that was rapidly consuming the building. I watched for a moment as firefighters prepared themselves and their gear to combat the flames, and then I hurried out through the gate to the perimeter where the chain-link fence adjoined the high side wall. As I ran alongside it, into an empty lot, I saw the refugees huddled together in a large group, and found Adel being interviewed by the two Gardai who'd parked their patrol car by the wall. The trio fell silent as I approached.

"You saved my life," I said, nodding to the two officers. "You all did," I added, acknowledging Adel.

"Then we are even," he replied. "My family are safe because of you. You got us out of there."

He nodded toward the burning buildings, which had turned the night sky a hellish orange color.

"Jack Morgan."

I recognized the voice and turned to see Conor Roche emerging from an unmarked vehicle he'd driven into the vacant lot. The passenger door opened and Andi got out and hurried over.

"I managed to convince him the threat was serious," she said.

"Trouble seems to follow you around," Conor remarked, eyeing the flames engulfing the refugee center.

"We are alive because of him," Adel said.

"I'm sure," Conor replied. "You've done good work here, Mr. Morgan."

"You said you were going for a new phone and a pint of milk," Andi challenged me.

I brandished my cell. "I got the phone, but not the milk."

"How did you end up here?" she asked. "I know you don't trust me, and I understand why, Jack, but this is too dangerous to tackle alone."

I wasn't going to apologize, but I knew she was right. This was too dangerous for one person to take on, but without a team behind me that I could completely trust, I didn't see any other way.

"I want to get him home," Andi told Conor. "It's not safe for him here."

"Understood," Conor replied. "But my colleagues will want a

statement. Won't you, fellas?" he asked the two Gardai who had resumed taking Adel's account of events.

"Yes, we'll need his statement," one of the cops replied.

"Fine with me," I said.

"Okay," Andi conceded. "But I want it done quickly, and when it's over we're going home."

CHAPTER 63

I GAVE MY statement to the Gardai and watched the firefighters struggle to bring the blaze under control.

Once I was finished, Conor released me from the scene. He was coordinating the operation and the nascent investigation. From snippets I heard of his conversations with uniformed officers, they hadn't captured a single member of the gang responsible.

Adel and his family had been taken away to temporary accommodation along with the other occupants of the center. He and his wife and children had reiterated their thanks before they'd left. Much as I appreciated their generosity of spirit, they should never have been put in a situation where they were called upon to show gratitude merely for surviving. I couldn't understand the hatred in men's hearts that could compel them to visit such atrocities on innocents. Understanding and love might be powerful, but my experience had taught me that hate would always come more easily to some people. Still, I wondered whether those men ever held up a mirror to themselves. Did they question how they'd reached the point of throwing a firebomb at a building full of children? Did they ever ask where their lives had gone so wrong? What had damaged their moral compass so badly?

By the time Conor cleared me, the firefighters had got the worst of the blaze contained and were working on isolated hot spots here and there. The building had been gutted, and if it could be repaired rather than demolished, there would be months of restoration work involved. The rudimentary temporary home these poor refugees had had here was gone, and all their belongings likely destroyed. They now faced further hardship and uncertainty in their already uncertain lives.

"Are you okay?" Andi asked me during the cab ride back to Fitzwilliam Square.

I nodded, but I think I might have been in shock. The fire had triggered some of my own traumatic memories of the Sea Knight crash and the inferno in which my comrades had perished all those years ago.

"You don't look okay," Andi responded. "What happened, Jack? What did you discover?"

I still didn't know if I could trust her, so I was evasive. "I can't talk about this now. I'm exhausted. Let's discuss it in the morning."

She nodded, but I could see she was hurt.

"Have you spoken to Maureen or Justine?" she asked. "You need to talk to someone. You can't bottle these things up."

"I'm okay," I told her. "At least, I will be."

She didn't press me any further.

We had the driver drop us off a few blocks from the house, and when we reached our temporary home, I gave Andi a perfunctory goodnight and went upstairs to my room.

I was eager to wash away the grime of the fire, and showered to try and cleanse myself.

When I came out of the bathroom, I found my phone ringing and recognized the caller's number immediately.

"Justine," I said when I answered.

"Jack," she responded. "What's going on? Where have you been?"

"Just following up a lead," I told her, though inside my heart was breaking because I couldn't tell her about the experience that had shaken me so profoundly. Her recovery must come first. "I miss you."

"I miss you too," she said. "Mo gave me your new number."

I was so glad. I'd been thinking about calling Justine but hadn't wanted to risk my distress being apparent in my voice and giving her any cause for concern. Her timing could not have been more perfect. The shower and some time and space away from the recent horror had stopped my mood from spiraling, and the sound of Justine's voice brought me joy and relief.

We talked for over thirty minutes. I focused on her recovery, asking her what the doctors had said, which was all positive, what she'd been watching on TV, trash, and what she'd been eating—bland, nutritious hospital food. I told her about the visit to Lawrence Finch's training facility and the pub lunch I'd had with Andi, both of which seemed so distant now, but I left out the latter half of the day and the aspects of this Ireland trip that would cause her grave concern.

When I heard fatigue seep into her voice, we said our loving goodbyes and I hung up, feeling more myself.

I put my phone on the bedside table, lay down and quickly fell asleep.

CHAPTER 64

I WOKE SUDDENLY, my heart racing, certain I'd heard some-thing. My ears strained against the silence of the early hours and my entire body was alert, even though it took my mind a beat to orientate itself.

I was in my bedroom in the house in Fitzwilliam Square, and the absence of light around the edges of the heavy drapes sug-gested it was still night. I checked my phone and saw that it was 3:06 a.m.

I listened carefully and heard another sound: the scraping of metal on metal. I rolled out of bed, crept to my wardrobe and slid on a pair of jeans and a black pullover. I picked up a pair of boots and some socks and carried them as I moved silently to the door.

I pressed my ear against the painted surface and listened closely. Hearing nothing, I opened the door slowly and crept across the landing to the stairs.

I heard the unmistakable sound of a lock turning and realized it was coming from the kitchen. Almost certainly the back door. There was a shift in the silence, a change of air pressure, as the back door opened. I could have sworn I heard a whisper then, but pitched so low I couldn't be certain. One thing I was sure of was that we had intruders.

I moved away from the stairs and went along the landing to the next flight. I climbed carefully and heard more clearly defined sounds coming from the first floor. I moved silently across the top floor and opened the door to Andi's bedroom.

I crept to her bed and placed my hand over her mouth, which was enough to wake her while stifling her instinctive cry. I raised a finger to my lips to signal her to be silent.

"Downstairs," I whispered. "Moving up. They must have followed us from the fire."

She nodded and rolled out of bed, grabbing some clothes from a pile on an armchair.

I signaled toward the low inset window, and she nodded again. I crept over to it while she pulled on her clothes. I lifted the catch and opened the window as a floorboard creaked directly beneath us. The intruders were on the floor below.

I climbed through onto a stone ledge and helped Andi out. My stomach lurched at the sight of the sidewalk so far away. I made myself look up, rather than down at the doom that awaited if we fell. We edged our way around the gable window and slid down the sloping roof to the flat section below, and from there moved toward a large stone chimney.

We settled behind it just in time. I peered around one side

to see a man climb out on the sloping roof and look around him, scanning for any sign of us. He wore a ski mask and carried a pistol. I tensed, ready to fight if he came toward us, but seeing nothing, he retreated, and I heard him climb back into Andi's room.

She glanced at me, her relief obvious, and I signaled for us to move. She nodded and I led her across the roofs of the adjacent townhouses on that side of the square to the house at the very end of the block. This had been converted into offices and was fitted with a fire escape at the rear. We crept down them, and when we reached the bottom, hurried across the small back yard, clambered over the brick wall, and dropped onto the sidewalk of Fitzwilliam Street.

Our safehouse had been compromised and we had to assume they would keep watch on the place. We could never go back.

We hurried to the Ford, which was parked in the square. I had the key in my pocket and unlocked the doors as we approached. Andi climbed in the passenger seat and I got behind the wheel, started the engine, and quickly drove us out of Fitzwilliam Square to avoid being spotted.

CHAPTER 65

I DROVE THROUGH Dublin, my mind racing. I'd been knocked off balance by the attack on the refugee center and hadn't been as careful as I should have been to ensure we weren't followed from the scene. With hindsight, it was easy to see that I should have taken more precautions on the way back from the fire, and I realized how simple it would have been for the Dark Fates on the ground to put a man or two on our tail. They could have watched me being interviewed by the Gardai and afterward followed me and Andi, identifying our safehouse and making a move at their leisure.

I hit the steering wheel in frustration, and Andi jumped.

"Sorry," I said.

"No, I'm sorry," she replied. "I should have been paying more attention on our way back."

"I was thinking exactly the same thing," I confessed. "About myself, of course."

She smiled wistfully. "A couple of high achievers blaming themselves for a perceived failing they probably could have done very little to prevent," she remarked.

I wasn't sure where I was heading, but we were on Morehampton Road, heading south, and had just passed the intersection with Herbert Park when my phone rang. I hadn't saved any contact details yet, but I knew this number by heart.

"Mo," I said when I answered.

"Jack, where are you?" she asked.

"In the car. We had to evacuate in a hurry. Some unwanted guests came to visit."

"Jeez, Jack. Are you okay?"

"Yes," I replied. "Apart from a bruised ego."

"Is Andi with you?" she asked, and something about her tone made my hackles rise.

"Yes," I replied, glancing at Andi, who smiled.

"But she can't hear me?"

"No," I said, glad I hadn't connected my phone to the car's Bluetooth system.

Mo hesitated for a moment.

"Jack, I went through Sam Farrell's narcotics cases. His biggest was a joint operation between the Gardai and the Metropolitan Police in London," she revealed, and my stomach lurched in anticipation of what was coming. "His Met liaison was Andrea Harris."

I looked sidelong at Andi and tried to conceal my dismay as the implications of this revelation hit me.

"They worked together for six months, Jack," Mo-bot continued. "She knows him. She knows him well."

"Thanks for that," I replied, trying to maintain my composure. "Follow up and let me know what else you find."

"I will, Jack, but please be careful," Mo-bot cautioned. "She's dangerous."

"I hear you," I replied. "You don't need to worry. I'll be in touch."

I hung up and pocketed my phone. I felt sick but forced myself to look at Andi. I was horrified when I saw her reach into her pocket and produce a small .38 revolver, which she rested on her lap. She wrapped her fingers around the gun, its muzzle pointing straight at me.

"I knew it was only a matter of time," she said, and my whole body flushed with rage as I realized I'd been outsmarted by a traitor.

CHAPTER 66

"KEEP YOUR HANDS on the wheel," Andi told me, brandishing the pistol.

I stared ahead, partly because I couldn't bear to look at her, but also seeking out an opportunity to escape.

We were on Donnybrook Road now, a broad commercial thoroughfare lined with offices, shops and bars, heading south toward University College. The traffic was not heavy at this time of the morning before the first light of day brightened the purple night. We were still in darkness, with few pedestrians or vehicles to be seen.

"Why?" I asked.

"Why Propaganda Tre?" she responded. "Or why Private?"

"Both," I replied, very conscious of the gun between us.

"Work enough years as a cop and you see the world differently. You realize the softly-softly approach doesn't work. That the criminals you locked up as a rookie cop are back on the street committing worse offenses. Do-gooders have taken us into a world where the just are shackled by procedure and policy, and evil has free reign. Propaganda Tre redresses the balance."

"By setting refugee centers on fire?" I seethed.

"If that's what it takes to show people the way," Andi replied nonchalantly, as if her conscience was completely untroubled by the horrific crime. "If that's what's needed to build a strong nation. A strong nation starts with strong borders. European countries have never been melting pots. The UK and Ireland are not like America. But for many it's easy gratification, quick-fix ideas, that get traction. Our politicians imported the alien concept of the melting pot of mass migration, when it was never previously part of our way of life."

"The melting pot policy made America the most powerful nation on earth," I countered this argument. "And every successful empire before it."

She jeered at this. "Empires conquered people, they didn't assimilate them. But you tell yourself whatever comforting stories you need to."

She paused before continuing. In the quiet, I tried to decide my next move.

"As for Private," she said, "we needed to know what you know. Who you've spoken to about us. We needed access to the Monaco and Rome case files, which meant getting someone inside."

"And the shooting in LA?" I asked.

"When Chalmont discovered I was working in the London office, he asked me for your schedule, so . . ." she trailed off with a shrug.

"You gave us up?" I remarked coldly. "Justine is in hospital because of you."

"She's in hospital because Sam Farrell failed to do his job," Andi replied angrily, and I was shocked to hear her lament the fact the man hadn't killed us.

"You could have finished it for him any time," I said.

"And given myself away? I'm still going through the files, and the higher-ups have realized how much of an asset Private can be to us. You know so many secrets about the rich and powerful. It'll be no surprise if one of our friends buys the business from your estate."

I tried not to react to her callousness, but failed.

"Don't look so shocked, Jack. This only ends one way," she said.

"Who are the higher-ups?" I asked, playing for time.

"Don't trouble yourself with questions like that," she replied. "It's the end of the road for you, Jack. You don't come out of this one alive."

Outwardly, I stayed cool. Inside, I was burning with rage, my blood boiling, aflame with anger and disappointment in her.

"You're planning on killing me yourself, are you?" I asked.

She waved the gun and shrugged, but her eyes told me I'd asked a stupid question.

I resolved never to give her the opportunity. We went through the intersection with Eglinton Terrace, and I saw a lamppost beside the gates to a soccer stadium. As we approached, I mounted the sidewalk to my left, and the obstacle taken at speed threw Andi forward against the dash. The pistol discharged and the sound of the shot set my ears ringing. I ducked instinctively as the bullet tore through the roof.

"What are you . . ." Andi began, but was silenced by a second impact.

The Ford hit a lamppost on her side at around forty miles per hour and stopped dead. The lamppost collapsed against the gray concrete stadium wall, showering it with sparks, and the airbags deployed as Andi and I were flung forward. I let myself go limp but was ready for action the moment the car settled.

I made to grab the pistol, which had fallen into the passenger footwell, but Andi came to her senses and elbowed me in the face, knocking me back in my seat as she leaned forward to scrabble for the gun.

I popped my seatbelt, flung my door open and sprinted toward the stadium wall just as Andi used the pistol to smash the passenger window. She started shooting as I hauled myself up and over the concrete. The capstones were chipped by a volley of bullets as I dropped into the car park on the other side.

I didn't skip a beat when I landed but started sprinting toward the grandstand to my right.

CHAPTER 67

I RACED TO the rectangular stand and hid behind the metal screen that separated it from the parking lot. I didn't waste time looking to see if Andi would try to follow me. I knew that she would but hoped I'd made it to the bleachers before she'd seen me. This would mean she couldn't be certain I hadn't made a run for the clubhouse, a long low building on the other side of the parking lot.

I hurried along the stand, sprinting the length of the front row of seats until I reached the wall of aluminum siding at the other end. As I rounded the structure, I glanced back to see Andi in the parking lot, brandishing the pistol as she searched around the clubhouse. I ducked down behind the side of the stand and hauled myself over the wall further along Donnybrook Road.

By the time I dropped onto the sidewalk on the other side, I was drenched in sweat thanks to a combination of nerves and exertion, and must have looked wild-eyed. Thankfully, there were no pedestrians and only a handful of pre-dawn commuters besides some cab and delivery drivers.

I jogged south until I reached a wide, tree-lined avenue that was flanked by grand terraces, villas and apartment blocks. Further on, by a large monument to a former Lord Mayor of Dublin, I went left again and kept running until I found a series of high-end apartment buildings that overlooked a large city park.

I went into the expansive green space, which was almost empty except for a couple of very early-morning joggers, and kept going until I reached a bench by the lake at the heart of the park. Here I sat down and put my head in my hands.

I knew self-pity was counterproductive, but couldn't help feeling defeated and beleaguered. Private, the organization I had worked so hard to build, had been compromised by one of the most formidable criminal entities I'd ever encountered. Nothing I thought I knew about my people would ever be the same again. I had no idea who I could trust outside my core group. We'd welcomed Andi into the Private family and she'd conspired to have me and Justine killed. I was devastated by the realization that someone who I'd thought I could trust was capable of such evil and deceit.

My phone rang and I recognized Mo-bot's number.

"Jack," she said the moment I answered. "Are you okay?"

"I'm alive," I told her. "But I'm not sure I'm okay. Andi tried to kill me just now. She collaborated with Raymond Chalmont to murder me and Justine."

"I'm sorry, Jack," Mo-bot responded, and I could sense her heartbreak. She was a key part of the Private family and would feel Andi's betrayal too. "Are you safe?"

I looked around the park and saw no sign of pursuit in the dim light. "For now. I managed to escape. But she'll be looking for me. She has friends in the Garda, and the Dark Fates have a lot of bodies on the street."

"We need to get you off it in that case. Let me start to work on that," Mo-bot said.

"Mo, where there's one rat, there are usually more. We need every country office to do in-depth background checks of every new hire. Look for connections to any key players in this investigation, including Andi."

"I'll send out an alert to all office heads," Mo-bot told me. "Stay safe until I get back to you with a place to lie low."

"Thanks, Mo," I replied.

She could have no idea just how grateful I was at that moment to have someone in my life I could trust, completely and unequivocally.

CHAPTER 68

MO-BOT PHONED ME back thirty minutes later.

I was on my feet, exhausted but determined not to be caught, and keeping moving seemed to be the most sensible option. I'd left the park and was on a wide street called Serpentine Avenue, which had pretty two-story terrace houses on one side and impressive new commercial buildings on the other. The road was busy with traffic and the sidewalks were crowded with a steady stream of workers on their way to Meta's Dublin head- quarters. It was easy to be anonymous here and blend in as just another face in the crowd. I stepped out of the flow of pedestri- ans and paused beneath a tree when my phone rang.

"Jack, I've got you a safe place. Last-minute rental under one of our gray names. Key-box entry, so you don't even need to see anyone to check in. It's ready now. I'll message you the address. It's near the river."

"Thank you," I said with a sense of tremendous relief. I felt tired and vulnerable and needed sanctuary. "I'm going to get right over there and then I want to talk if you and Sci are still up."

"He's at the hospital with Justine, but I can patch him in. Are you sure you don't want to rest first?" she asked.

"This is very personal, Mo. They planted someone inside my business and used her to try and kill us. I'm going to do whatever it takes to ensure the entire Propaganda Tre organization answers for this."

"I understand," she responded. "And I feel the same way. I'll wait for your call and tell Sci to stand by."

I hung up and checked my messages for the address, which was on Pigeon House Road. I checked Google Maps and saw the property was located on the bank of the river, opposite Dublin Port.

To make sure I wasn't followed, I took three different taxis to reach the rental house and walked the last mile. I took a circuitous route, stopping in a cafe for an espresso and a cream breakfast cake, a local treat recommended to me by the cashier.

I finally reached Pigeon House Road shortly before 9 a.m. and found a long terrace of tiny single-story homes that looked out over a highway with beyond it the estuary and busy port on the far bank of the river. The key-box was beside the front door of the small white-rendered house with black trim located halfway along the terrace. I used the code Mo-bot had sent me to open it. I took out the key, unlocked the front door and went inside the two-bedroomed home.

It was decorated on a nautical theme, with boats, anchors, seashells and depictions of mermaids everywhere. I went into the kitchen, which overlooked a small yard, and took a seat at the table. I was worried a more comfortable chair would entice me to sleep.

I phoned Mo-bot, who answered immediately.

"Let me loop in Sci," she told me, and the line went silent for a moment.

"Jack," he said when he joined the call. "How are you? Mo says you've run into trouble and she told me about Andrea Harris. Turncoat!"

"It's been rough," I responded. "Does Justine know anything?"

"I don't agree with keeping secrets, but I understand about not wanting her to be worried right now," he said. "She's sleeping, but she's been pushing herself hard to get out of here. Too hard maybe. Sometimes I see the pain and fatigue on her face when she thinks no one is watching."

It distressed me to hear about Justine soldiering on like that, being made to suffer through no fault of her own. I wondered if she was pushing herself so hard because she was desperate to be useful again. I hoped not.

I briefed Mo-bot and Sci on the events that had led to me escaping from Andi, and when I was through, Sci spoke first.

"Wow."

"Yeah," Mo-bot agreed. "Wow."

"I know," I said.

"This might seem outside my comfort zone but one of my specialist lecture topics is forensic accounting and data analysis.

I'm not just fingerprint dust and fibers," Sci said. "I suggested to Mo that she look for any links between Andi and all the key players."

"He did," Mo-bot chimed in. "Much as it pains me to admit his brilliance, credit where it's due."

"And?" I asked, knowing neither would have raised a dead end in these circumstances.

"I didn't find a link to a major player, but I did discover a connection to a minor one," Mo-bot revealed. "Remember the warehouse you escaped from? It's owned by Longshore Holdings. The law firm that incorporated Longshore Holdings is a small corporate outfit with offices in London and Dublin called Byrne and Fitzgerald. It's the same firm that negotiated Andrea Harris's employment contract when she joined Private."

CHAPTER 69

I SLEPT FITFULLY. While the world was awake, working, studying and playing, I was lying in a darkened converted attic in the tiny riverside home. I had nothing but the clothes I'd hurriedly gathered when I'd fled the house in Fitzwilliam Square. I'd abandoned the rest, my computer and passport there, and could not risk a return.

I had nightmares when sleep overtook me. Images of fallen comrades, colleagues, victims of crime. Their faces filled my mind, which made the horrifying dreams so vivid they would wake me, and then I'd spend a while listening to the steady flow of traffic on the highway outside. I couldn't stop wondering how someone as seemingly intelligent as Andi could support such violence against innocent people. I was deeply troubled by the memory of Adel and his family at the refugee center, how close they had come to burning to death. Surely no one with the slightest shred of decency in them could sanction such persecution. I was also distressed to reflect upon how normal Andi had seemed to me while we'd worked together. I wished I could believe she wasn't in her right mind when she acted as she did and could rationalize her treachery that way. But instead, she'd seemed proud when Mo-bot had exposed her treachery, portraying it as somehow justified in pursuit of the greater good.

Eventually the drone of cars going by would lull me to sleep and I'd fall right back into nightmares until the next fitful episode of waking.

Finally, at 5:13 p.m., I knew I wouldn't be able to sleep anymore. Even if my mind didn't feel at peace, I knew that my body had been partially restored. I showered again, eager to wash away troubling memories, and once dry, I put on yesterday's jeans and top, which felt slick with sweat and grime.

I left the house and walked along the riverside to a long bridge, crossing it to reach the docklands leisure center, office and shopping development on the other side. I found a men's clothing store and brightened the shop assistant's day twenty minutes before closing by purchasing a whole new wardrobe.

I returned to the cottage on Pigeon House Road to deposit my purchases and change into fresh clothes. After that I felt much better and left the house for Featherblade, a steakhouse near the National Gallery that was reputed to serve the best burgers in Dublin. I wanted to avoid crowds, so I placed a click and collect takeout order and ate the burger while sitting on the wall of College Park, watching people go by.

Justine tried calling, but I didn't want to talk to her when my mind was so unsettled and I knew a conversation would likely involve overt lying, which I wasn't prepared to do.

She sent me a message asking if I was okay, and I replied saying I was fine but that I was tied up with something. I knew she wouldn't want me out here alone, facing impossible odds. After what she'd been through, she knew at first hand exactly how dangerous these people were.

As I ate, I studied the satellite map, which showed the streets around the Byrne and Fitzgerald building, and Street View images that allowed me to see the detail of the block itself. I finished my burger, which was excellent though I found little joy in it, got to my feet and headed for Harcourt Street, near St Stephen's Green, where Byrne and Fitzgerald's Dublin office was located.

After a twenty-minute walk, I arrived in the bustling business district. One side of the street was taken up by tramlines, and the sidewalks were crowded with people heading home or on their way to more entertaining parts of the city. Here unbroken four-story redbrick terraces lined the streets. The beautiful, historic buildings in excellent condition were home to the law and accountancy firms that dominated the neighborhood.

Byrne and Fitzgerald was in a contemporary office complex that had been constructed at the end of a more traditional terrace. The law firm was located on the fourth floor of the six-story building. There was a security guard at the desk in the main reception and I had no desire to risk being caught, so I walked the block and found a ramp to an underground parking lot beneath the building. A metal grille blocked the entrance, but I found a fire escape nearby and watched and waited until a car approached from inside. It was driven by a weary-looking man in a crumpled shirt. He paused the car while he swiped his keycard over a reader, which prompted the grille to rise.

I pressed back into the shadows of the fire escape as the car passed and then quickly hurried down the ramp, ducking to avoid the grille as it closed.

I turned my head away from the security camera mounted on the wall, which was pointed toward the keycard-reader, and continued into the underground car park.

I prayed the security guard wasn't particularly attentive as I passed another camera on my way to the elevators. I called one, but when it arrived, saw I needed a keycard to make it rise. The fire stairs were secured the same way, so I returned to the elevator and climbed through the escape hatch in the roof.

I used the elevator shaft service ladder to get to the fourth floor and arrived, breathless and sweating. I located the emergency release for the elevator doors and managed to force them open. I stepped out into a wood-paneled lobby. Behind an impressive, sweeping reception desk a wall-hung sign confirmed that this was Byrne and Fitzgerald.

I pulled out my phone and called Mo-bot, who answered immediately.

"I'm in," I said.

"Good," she replied. "They have no remote server access, which is very unusual. So, they will have an on-site server room. Find it."

I went through the double doors that led to the main office

and found an open-plan space with corridors that linked to private offices and common areas with kitchens, coffee stations and meeting rooms. It took me a few minutes to locate the server room, which was locked, but I was able to force the door with my shoulder.

"I've found it," I told Mo-bot.

"Sounded noisy," she responded. "Are you sure you're alone?"

"For now," I said. "So let's be quick."

"Can you see a terminal?" she asked.

"Yes," I replied, going to a bank of four machines. "Let me put you on camera."

I positioned my phone so she could see the screen and she talked me through the security protocols once she understood the nature of the system. It was a privilege to work with some of the best law-enforcement personnel in the world, but Sci and Mo-bot were in a league of their own, recognized as leaders within their respective fields.

Mo-bot demonstrated her capabilities now, getting me past the server security measures and into the law firm's database.

I soon found the billing system, which had been Sci's suggestion. He said crooked lawyers sometimes covered up document trails to conceal the identity of the principal issuing instructions, but they would always record client billing. I looked up the Longshore Holdings incorporation work and discovered it had been paid by Carrington International. While I dug around for the bills in relation to the purchase of the three Dublin warehouses by Longshore Holdings, Mo-bot went to work on Carrington International.

"It's domiciled in Gibraltar," she said.

"It also paid for the property deals on the warehouses," I revealed, and started to search the system for the bills for work on Andi's employment contract with Private.

"And it paid for Andi's legal work," I told Mo-bot.

"Carrington International is owned by Carrington Construction Limited, which is domiciled in Malta, which is in turn owned by King Finch Financial, a company based in England," she said. "According to Companies House, the ultimate beneficial owner of King Finch is Lawrence Finch."

CHAPTER 70

I WASN'T ENTIRELY surprised at the revelation Finch was involved. Part of me wondered whether I might have discerned the truth sooner if Andi hadn't been at my side, running interference. I thought back to every twist and turn I'd experienced since arriving in Dublin and realized that, in small ways and in large, Andi had been subtly steering me away from the truth, steering me away from Lawrence Finch.

And there was the attack at Kearney Stud, when the sniper had been trying to shoot me and I'd assumed Noah and Mary Kearney had been the true targets. Now I understood it was more likely Andi had summoned the shooter there and walked me into a trap, to have me killed by someone else and sustain her own cover. And the time she'd suggested we shake the tree by returning to see Lawrence Finch . . . had she taken me there so we could be followed as we left? The same was true of the house invasion at Fitzwilliam Square. She must have set that up.

Her influence throughout had been pernicious. Chance was not involved in any of this. She'd volunteered for the assignment when Emily Knighton had asked for someone from the London office to be my guide in Dublin.

"You okay, Jack?" Mo-bot asked.

"Yeah," I said. "Just getting to grips with it."

"I hear you," she replied. "But you need to move fast. Find a drive and copy anything and everything related to Longshore Holdings."

I did as instructed and found a solid-state drive in a nearby supply closet. I hooked it up to the machine I'd been using and copied across everything I found on Longshore Holdings.

A few minutes later, I climbed down the way I'd come. I couldn't open the grille over the car-park entrance. Instead, I found a fire exit and stepped out, not caring about the loud alarm I triggered before running into the night.

"I'm away," I told Mo-bot. "I'll send the files as soon as I have access to a computer."

"I'll see what I can dig up in the meantime," she replied. "Based on what we already know. Then get some rest, Jack."

"Will do," I assured her. "Thank you, Mo. For everything."

We said our goodbyes and she hung up. I pocketed my phone and walked back to the place on Pigeon House Road, which took me forty minutes.

I showered yet again and settled into bed. Lawrence Finch

was the key. Through him, I could reach Andi, Sam Farrell and Raymond Chalmont. Through him, I could find justice.

I woke to find a message from Justine, saying she was worried about me, and realized I hadn't sent her anything before going to sleep.

Call me the moment you see this. No matter when, her message said.

My phone told me it was 7:06 a.m., which meant it was just after 11 p.m. in LA, a reasonable if late time for a call.

"Jack, please tell me you're okay," she said the moment she answered.

"I'm okay," I replied. Then hesitated. I couldn't lie to her anymore, whether by omission or overtly as I'd just done. "Actually, scratch that. I'm not okay, Jus. Andi Harris is a member of Propaganda Tre. She's been working against us all along."

Justine hesitated.

"Did she hurt you?" she asked at last.

"She tried. I had to move. I found out Lawrence Finch is in on it too."

""Jack—" she began, but I cut her off.

"I know what you're going to say. You want me to come home and to—"

It was her turn to interrupt me. "Actually, no, I wasn't going to say anything of the kind. I was going to tell you that I never want us to be in this situation again. Caught off guard by evil. These people won't stop coming for us until we stop them for good."

I was surprised, but I shouldn't have been. I loved Justine for many reasons and, right now, she was showing that her resolve was one of them.

"I don't want you doing this alone, Jack," she went on. "You have Sci and Mo-bot in your corner. And you have me. I might not be at full capacity physically, but my mind is as sharp as ever. You don't have to treat me with kid gloves."

"I love you," I replied.

"I love you too, Jack, but right now, it's all about work. It's about putting a stop to these people so we can get our lives back," she said. "Tell me what you know about what's going on and let me figure out a way I might be able to help."

I'd known what I wanted to do since the previous night, but Justine's inspiring words made me more determined than ever.

"I want to get Lawrence Finch," I told her.

CHAPTER 71

JUSTINE AND I talked for an hour, and it felt good finally to be entirely open and honest with her, to re-establish our connection. I should never have doubted her ability to see the right course of action or her reserves of strength to discuss ideas and theories about Lawrence, Andi, Sam Farrell and Raymond Chalmont. In fact, she seemed to come alive as we spoke, as if memories of past investigations and her personal drive for justice were infusing her with energy.

In the end, though, she conceded defeat to the lateness of the hour and her fatigue, and we said our goodbyes.

"Be careful," she told me.

"Always," I replied. "Thank you."

"What for? You're the one out there risking everything."

"For being you," I said. "I love you."

"Love you too. And I was being serious about being careful. These people are very dangerous, Jack."

"I know. Get some sleep."

I hung up and put on a new black suit. Fifteen minutes later, I was in the back of a taxi I'd hailed a safe distance from my new accommodation.

"Where to?" the driver asked.

"Curragh Racecourse," I replied, and he smiled.

He couldn't have been more than twenty-five and he had a glint in his eye.

"If it's losing money you're after, I'm quite happy to take it off you."

"I don't normally lose," I replied coolly, and his impish smile fell for a moment before it returned, this time with a degree of uncertainty.

He put on some music and the rest of our journey took place to the soundtrack of "Good Luck, Babe!" on repeat. I called Mo-bot.

"Jack," she said when she answered.

"Has Justine spoken to you?" I asked.

"Yes, we're all good here," she told me.

"That's all I needed to know," I replied. "I'm on my way."

"Good luck."

I pocketed my phone and settled back to watch the city roll by as we headed west. When we neared the Curragh, the traffic started to build. Today was the Airlie Stud Stakes. Trainers and owners used the day to prepare for the Derby, and I had no doubt Lawrence Finch would be here to watch his horses.

The roads surrounding the course were busier than I'd experienced at Leopardstown. Dating back to the eighteenth century, the Curragh Racecourse is built around a large grandstand and has capacity for up to 30,000 fans. Judging by the crowds thronging toward the complex, today would be a test of the upper limit. With more than 1,500 acres of course and training facilities, the Curragh hosts some of the most iconic Irish racing fixtures.

The cab driver dropped me off near the main stand, and I bought a pass from a tout who sold me a winners' enclosure lanyard for an exorbitant sum. They weren't strictly available for sale, but touts managed to get hold of them somehow and charged high prices for those who wanted to buy access to the rarified parts of the course. I didn't care about money. I needed to get to Lawrence Finch.

I joined the throng of well-heeled, knowledgeable racegoers making their way into the course. After a moment's doubt over whether my pass was a fake, I was waved through by the steward, who told me I could use the VIP entrance in future.

I walked through the course, past the hospitality buildings, listening to the groundswell of a crowd full of excited anticipation. Jeers, cries and shouts were coming at me in waves from every direction.

I made my way to the winners' enclosure and went into the building beyond it, where I found Finch in the private bar. He was holding court, surrounded by about twenty smartly dressed men and women and three members of his close protection detail.

Justine had given me her assessment of the man's psychological profile based on publicly available interviews, news articles, and my accounts of meeting him. She had told me that if I succeeded in reaching him, the first thing he was likely to do was smile.

As he did now: a broad genial grin, calculated to disarm.

I pushed my way through the crowd paying court to him, barely registering their hostile expressions. Were they all members of Propaganda Tre? Or just entitled high-hats who objected to being pushed around? The bodyguard closest to me stepped forward, but Lawrence waved him back.

"How long have you run the organization?" I tried.

"What organization, Mr. Morgan? I'm under no obligation to answer your questions," said Finch. "Though I will say, I admire your tenacity, first in Rome, then Monaco and now here. Terrible shame about Ms. Smith though."

I bridled visibly at the jibe, and his bodyguard stepped forward again.

"It's okay," Lawrence told him. "Mr. Morgan just came here to flex his muscles."

"I came here to tell you that no man, not even a king, is above the law. You will face justice for what you've done."

"Justice is an artificial concept, created by the strong to make the weak believe there is a rationale for robbing a person of life or liberty. It is an illusion designed to make those without power believe the world is fair." He leaned close to me and spoke in a low, menacing tone. "If you want to come for me, I won't need fairytale excuses to do whatever needs to be done."

I stared at him. He held my gaze.

"Whenever you're ready, Mr. Morgan," he said.

I glanced at his security detail and the group of people gathered around us, most of whom would be loyal to him. I was outnumbered. I'd come here to give him a message and rattle him. As tempting as it was to deliver a painful lesson, it would be counterproductive to the aims I'd clarified with Justine.

"Tell Raymond Chalmont I'm coming for him too," I said, and for the first time saw a flash of uncertainty cross Finch's face.

He recovered his composure quickly and smiled again, but it wasn't the same comfortable grin he had greeted me with.

Satisfied I'd achieved my objective, I pushed him out of my way and headed for the exit.

CHAPTER 72

THE TWO MEN from his close protection detail were easy to spot. They followed me through the crowds gathered between the main grandstand and the winners' enclosure. The first race was underway and the clamor was deafening. I weaved around groups of excited racing enthusiasts, some of whom were holding betting slips, others with drinks in their hands. Some racegoers were cheering the leading horse, which, according to the commentary being broadcast over the public address system, was called Graham's Legend. Others were booing.

My two pursuers, a tall blond man with a closely shaved head, and a thick-set muscular man with a crop of dark wavy hair, were pushing their way through the throng of people, suit jackets flapping wide to reveal flashes of the holsters they carried at their sides. They couldn't have guns, could they?

Lawrence Finch wouldn't be so reckless or so bold, would he? Sidearms weren't legal for private security in Ireland.

I couldn't run the risk of finding out when I wasn't fully in control of the situation, so I veered toward the main grandstand and went through the nearest entrance, joining the crush of people heading for the concessions, bars and bookies.

I slipped into a corridor to my left, heading for a door marked "Toilets," and when I went through it, found myself in another corridor. There was a line for the ladies', but the men's room had no wait. I loitered behind the door I'd just come through and the moment it opened, and my two pursuers stepped through, I attacked them. The women immediately around us scattered, looking bewildered as I drove the squat man's head against the opposite wall and knocked him senseless. The taller, blond guy reached into his jacket, but I grabbed his arm and swung him back into the wall. The women in the line retreated and cried out. One started calling for help as the tall man and I fell over his accomplice's motionless body and tumbled to the floor, rolling over and grappling together.

I scissored my legs and pulled him into a rear triangle choke-hold to stop him struggling. I kept the pressure up until he fell limp. When he was unconscious, I reached into his jacket and freed a Beretta M9 pistol from its holster. These men were armed.

"Make sure the cops find their guns," I told the three women who hadn't fled into the ladies' room.

I pushed the pistol toward them and it skidded across the

floor. I got to my feet and left through the main door, joining the crowds of people in the corridor beyond. I peeled off once I was on the main thoroughfare and headed for an exit.

Outside, I caught a cab and used it to take me near the cottage on Pigeon House Road. I took every precaution to ensure I wasn't followed and opened the front door with a sense of relief.

Lawrence Finch would act soon to neutralize the threat I posed, and with Mo-bot and her team tracking his comms, he was sure to make a mistake we could exploit. All I had to do was wait, and I intended to do so with a cup of coffee in my hand.

I walked into the kitchen and stopped in my tracks, my heart suddenly thundering in my chest.

There, sitting at the kitchen table, was Andi Harris, and she was pointing a Walther PDP pistol at me.

"Sit down, Jack," she said nonchalantly. "And keep your hands where I can see them."

I had no choice but to comply.

CHAPTER 73

"HOW DID YOU find me?" I asked as I settled into my seat.

"Maureen Roth is the epicenter of all things digital, but she's not as invincible as everyone thinks," Andi replied.

"Key logger?" I guessed. "Spyware?"

These were two basic methods for tracking someone else's computer use and stealing data.

She didn't reply. She didn't need to. It didn't matter how she'd done it. The simple fact was she'd managed to compromise our technology lead without Mo-bot realizing, and she'd done it by being inside our organization.

"What now?" I asked.

"Raymond Chalmont is on his way," she replied, indicating her phone which was on the table between us. "I messaged him when you put your key in the door. He isn't very far away."

I had no doubt the man was on his way to kill me.

"They know what you are," I said. "My team know you're a traitor."

"I'd guessed you wouldn't keep that to yourself. It doesn't matter anymore."

"It does," I replied. "If something happens to me, they won't rest until you're behind bars."

She laughed. "You think the threat of prison scares me? You felt our reach in Rome and Monaco. I'd never see the inside of a cell. Not for a single day. We have friends everywhere."

The silence of the kitchen pressed in for a moment.

"No," she went on. "You should worry about your team. What will happen to them once you're gone."

I bridled at the threat but tried to control the fury rising within me. The wrong move would get me killed instantly.

"Doesn't it bother you?" I asked. "Breaking the law you once swore to uphold? Four innocent people died at that screening. Many more were injured."

"Innocent," she scoffed. "There's no such thing. Morality is a question of perspective. You know that from your many years at this work, surely?"

I didn't respond.

"Everyone believes they're the good guy. Even when they're doing bad things. So, we're either all good or all bad." She sat forward. "Or maybe morality is just a story we tell ourselves to ease our journey through a world that is actually about power."

"I've heard the same rationale before. From people looking to justify evil," I replied. "Tell me, when you gave Raymond Chalmont the details of the screening, how did it feel knowing he would use that information to kill us? Did you feel glee? Shame? Either answer tells you more about yourself than I ever could."

She pondered my words for a moment. "I felt nothing," she said at last. "Except perhaps a little pride that I was succeeding in my mission."

CHAPTER 74

I STARED AT Andi, wondering at the layers of pretense and deception that had enabled her to pass for a trusted member of the team, at the way in which she had endeared herself to me, the meals we'd shared, the time we'd spent together. How could anyone be so callous and deceiving?

She was about to say something else when her phone rang.

"Yes," she answered. "Yes. Still here. Waiting for you."

She hung up and looked at me. "That was Raymond. He's five minutes out and eager to see you."

"You're going to let them kill me?" I asked.

Her expression hardened. "Who knows? I might be the one to pull the trigger."

I was about to respond when I was startled by the sound of a crash and splintering wood. Then came the tramp of footsteps and cries of, "Garda! Armed police! Armed police!"

The kitchen was invaded by a squad of armed Gardai from the force's tactical unit in full body armor. The four men trained their pistols on Andi, who put her weapon on the table and raised her hands.

Two of the officers moved quickly to restrain her, pushing her head onto the table and snapping cuffs around her wrists.

"Andi, Andi, Andi," Conor Roche said as he sauntered into the room. "I never thought I'd have to do this."

The two tactical officers hauled her to her feet and turned her to face Roche.

"It's a crying shame," he went on, "but thanks to Mr. Morgan and his colleagues we've caught another rotten apple."

She glanced at me, her expression full of anger.

"How?" she asked.

I pulled my phone from my pocket. "I never hung up. It's been on the whole time, recording everything. My colleagues have been monitoring my movements and interactions to ensure I'm safe." I hadn't ended my call with Mo-bot before I arrived at the Curragh and had just slipped my phone into my pocket, so she could listen to and record everything that followed my confrontation with Lawrence Finch. I spoke into my phone now. "Thanks for saving my bacon."

"Anytime," Mo-bot replied. "Make sure they lock her up somewhere nice and tight."

"You sound irritated," I remarked.

"No one installs surveillance on my machines," Mo-bot replied. "I take that very personally."

I smiled. "Let me finish up here and I'll call you back."

I hung up and turned to Conor Roche. "I'll make sure you get a copy of the recording of what she said today."

Andi glared at me.

"Thanks, Mr. Morgan," he replied. "We'll need a statement too."

"Can we do that tomorrow?" I asked. "I've got somewhere to be."

"Of course," he said. "There's no rush. She won't be going anywhere except prison."

Andi's eyes flashed with hatred.

"Come by headquarters in the morning," Conor told me.

"Will do," I said, easing myself past him and the two tactical officers who had helped secure the room.

"He's clear to exit," Conor yelled, and the uniformed officers in the hallway allowed me to pass.

I stepped into the early-afternoon sunshine and jogged away from the cottage. I got out just in time to duck behind a parked car as a Range Rover turned onto the street and crawled slowly past. I didn't recognize the men seated in front, but in the back were Raymond Chalmont and Sam Farrell.

When the occupants saw the police and realized what had happened, the car accelerated quickly as it passed the burgeoning crime scene and the Gardai bringing Andi out of the property. I couldn't understand why Roche hadn't mobilized his unit to intercept Raymond Chalmont. Mo would surely have relayed what she'd heard. Experience had taught me some police officers were slow to respond to a live situation and struggled with rapid deployment. I knew it would be up to me to bring these men in.

The Range Rover made a right at the end of the street. I cast around for a cab or some other means of following them, and saw a silver unmarked police car parked haphazardly in a space near my cottage. The red-and-blue dash lights were still flashing, and the engine was running. I recognized it as Conor Roche's car from when Andi and I had been to see him at Garda Headquarters. As I slipped behind the wheel, I hoped he wouldn't mind me borrowing it in pursuit of justice.

CHAPTER 75

I SET OFF after the men who had come to murder me.

I killed the emergency lights, turning the car back into a standard BMW 3-Series, and tracked the Range Rover through the city, staying three or four cars back, taking streets that ran parallel when I saw them turn ahead of me. They had no reason to suspect they were being followed and the silver BMW was a sufficiently common model not to draw attention.

When we drove out of the city and headed west, I had a suspicion about where they were heading, but I needed to be certain. Following them was made easier by my surmise, because all I had to do was catch a fleeting glimpse of the Range Rover in the distance to know it was still on its predicted route and I was on its tail.

We left the M4 motorway thirty miles west of Dublin and took winding country lanes to the village of Ballagh, leaving me in little doubt about where Chalmont and Farrell were headed.

I stayed well back now, satisfying myself with a distant view of the black Range Rover's roof as it sped along country lanes, rising and falling with the folds of the landscape. Finally, I watched the big car turn off the road through the gates of Ballagh House. These men were under the protection of the king himself. I now had confirmation they were all working together, and the seeds of an idea started to grow, filling my mind with a plan for the way I might be able to bring them all down.

I pulled over before I reached the gates and executed a U-turn to take me back into Dublin. I retraced my journey as far as the outskirts and went east. I used my phone to find a hostel on Eustace Street in the heart of the city.

The hostel was a three-story redbrick building next to a pizzeria, and Eustace Street turned out to be a narrow cobblestone alley that linked busy Dame Street with lively Essex Street.

I left the BMW in an underground parking lot on Trinity Street, a couple of blocks from the hostel, and pocketed the key. I had no luggage and was once again reduced to a phone and the clothes on my back, but if that fazed the guy at reception, he didn't show it. He was grateful for a week's rent in advance for one of their superior rooms and insisted on showing me my new accommodation himself. He was all eager bows, smiles and friendly chit-chat until he put the key in the lock and opened the door to my room with a "*Voilà!*"

The superior room made me never want to see a standard one in this place. The bedclothes were threadbare and stained, the carpet too dark to be sure what lingered there, and the furniture—a single bed, chest of drawers and solitary empty bookshelf—was chipped veneer. The bathroom looked as though it had been installed in 1970 and had not been cleaned properly since. The avocado-green ceramic fittings were stained with grime and rust.

"Grand, so?" the receptionist asked.

"It will suit me fine," I replied, slipping him a 5-euro tip.

He looked at the money in disbelief. "Thanks very much," he said before leaving.

I shut the door behind him and took my phone from my pocket to call home.

CHAPTER 76

"WE'RE MONITORING LAWRENCE Finch's phones and emails," Mo-bot said. "At least, the numbers and accounts we know about. Even an illegal move will leave a legal trace if he makes it using one of these means."

I knew this to be true from my years of investigative experience. Finch's connection to the Dark Fates warehouses was a case in point. Few criminals are ever willing to totally relinquish control to someone else. Having absolutely no link to or control over a criminal enterprise requires a level of trust in associates who, by virtue of their occupation, are untrustworthy. So, most high-ranking criminals have a legal entity somewhere, acting as a front, to enable them to exert ultimate power or control over their operations. Finch might have made it difficult to trace the true ownership, but I'd found the link between him and the warehouses eventually.

"He'll do something," Justine said. "He won't want you at large posing a risk to their entire enterprise."

She and Mo-bot were in the new hospital room, which looked comfortable and bright with the California sun streaming through a large panoramic window. It seemed they were somewhere on LA's west side, but I couldn't see enough of the city skyline to be sure, which was exactly how I wanted it.

"If I can persuade the Garda to let me talk to Andi, I might be able to convince her to—" I was interrupted by another call coming in from a local number I didn't recognize.

"I have to take this. Be right back with you," I said to Justine and Mo-bot before hanging up.

I answered the incoming number. "Hello."

"Mr. Morgan, it's Conor Roche."

The moment he announced himself, a question formed in my mind.

"I've got bad news," he said. "Andi Harris has been released. The higher-ups said we don't have enough cause to hold her. Where are you? Maybe there's some information you can give me to help us re-arrest her."

It didn't sound right. Andi was caught pointing a gun at me. How could they release her? My internal alarm bells were ringing and the question that played on my mind the most was how he'd got my new number. Only four people in the world had it: Justine, Mo-bot, Sci and Andi.

"I'm busy today," I replied. "Can we stick to our plan? I'll be at Garda headquarters first thing."

He hesitated and I could sense him trying to think of a way to press me on the issue.

"It would be helpful if—" he began, but I cut him off.

"I really can't," I said. "I'll see you first thing tomorrow."

I didn't give him a chance to reply and hung up.

I immediately video-called Justine and Mo-bot.

"Well?" Mo-bot asked.

"The cops released Andi," I replied. "Did you give anyone from the Garda my new number?"

Mo-bot shook her head. "Why would I?"

"That's what I thought," I said. "I just got a call from Andi's Garda friend, Conor Roche, on a number he shouldn't have. He told me he was pressured by higher-ups into releasing her."

"Sounds off," Justine remarked.

I nodded. "It confirms our suspicion that we can't trust the police here. We know Propaganda Tre has compromised law enforcement agencies before and they have almost certainly done it here if Sam Farrell is anything to go by."

"So, what's the plan?" Mo-bot asked.

"We can't wait for them to make a move. I need to leave immediately in case they made the call to locate me," I replied. "And I need to find out what Propaganda Tre is up to here in Ireland and get conclusive evidence against Lawrence Finch."

CHAPTER 77

I LEFT MY phone on the bedside table and abandoned the hostel immediately. It was early evening and a light drizzle was falling as I made my way to the parking lot on Trinity Street.

I was taking a risk using a stolen police car, but I could not hire one without a fake ID and if Conor Roche was dirty, there was every chance he wouldn't report the theft.

I drove through slick streets that reflected the lights of cars and streetlamps beneath ominous clouds. The rain was light but persistent and the dark sky threatened a downpour at any moment.

I went to the George's Street Arcade, a shopping mall a few blocks away, and bought another phone and some tools that would be necessary for what I was about to do next.

When I returned to the car, I used the new phone to send messages to Sci, Mo-bot and Justine, using my safe phrase so they would know it was me giving them my new number. I received messages back from all of them wishing me luck, and an extra one from Justine who told me she loved me and asked me not to do anything too dangerous.

I hadn't bothered with new clothes. My black suit would suffice for the work ahead.

I took the BMW on a run out to Ballagh House and parked it behind a copse of trees, so it was well hidden from the road.

With the car concealed, I made my way on foot to the perimeter wall that surrounded the vast estate and went to the nearest security camera as it rotated away from me. I climbed the wall and clambered up the camera post. With the small can of black spray paint I had ready in my pocket, I coated the lens. A blank screen was more likely to result in the dispatch of a maintenance team than to raise a full-scale alarm, but I didn't care too much either way. I planned to be in and out before anyone could review the last footage and see my hand and the spray can.

I clambered down the post and dropped onto Finch's property, immediately setting off through the ravine and the woods that stretched toward the house.

As I crept through the trees, I caught glimpses of the palatial home beyond the meadows and lawns. I heard movement some distance ahead and froze. A moment later, I saw a uniformed security guard shine a flashlight into the forest. I ducked behind a tree and pressed myself against the trunk as the light danced around me. After what seemed like an age, it moved on and I resumed my cautious journey to the house.

The paddocks and gardens were the most dangerous sections

and involved a few sprints across open ground. My lungs were burning by the time I slowed to a walk on reaching the paved terrace to the rear of the east wing. I crept to the large windows and saw a library illuminated by the gentle glow of night lights, which burnished the gilt tooling on the spines of some of the ancient books. Beyond the shelves, through a double-width doorway, I saw an office with a large partners' desk covered in papers. On the far side of the desk was a laptop. My target.

I went to some French doors opening into a dining room next to the library. I took a small chisel from my pocket, checked the frame and catch for signs of an alarm and found none. I pushed the implement between the double doors and forced it deep, so I could use it as a lever to snap the lock through the frame.

"I wouldn't do that. These particular doors are two hundred years old," Lawrence Finch said, and I turned to find him standing close behind me.

Sam Farrell, Andi Harris and Raymond Chalmont accompanied him along with two bodyguards and Jackson Kyle, Finch's head of security, plus the uniformed guard I'd seen in the woods.

The guard shone his flashlight in my eyes, dazzling me.

"You've reached the end of your race, Mr. Morgan," Finch said. "And you're not even going to show in the results."

He nodded and Jackson Kyle covered me with a pistol while the two bodyguards stepped forward and took my arms.

CHAPTER 78

THEY LOCATED MY new phone and smashed it against the paving before hauling me away from the house, slapping and punching me if they felt I was stepping out of line. They marched me along the broad path that led to the old stables. No one said anything, the two bodyguards just pulled me along, inflicting small cruelties as we followed Finch, Andi and Chalmont. Sam followed me a few paces back and Jackson stalked behind us all, eyeing me closely. The uniformed guard went back to his patrol duties.

They took me to the yard outside Sam Farrell's quarters and I knew it would be pointless trying to call for help. This was the domain of Finch's private army and the men and women in the homes around the yard would be more likely to lend a hand in my murder than to try and save me.

"Let's end this now," Chalmont said, producing a pistol from inside his jacket and leveling it at me as he approached.

"No," Finch responded angrily, grabbing him by the shoulder. He yanked the other man back and forced Chalmont to face him. "How dare you? Not here in my home. Not on my land."

"What does it matter?" Chalmont countered.

Andi and Sam Farrell shrank back, clearly uncomfortable with the conflict between their leaders.

"It matters because I say it matters," Lawrence Finch replied. "It matters because this is my home. It matters because you have risked everything for a personal vendetta. I would never have sanctioned what you all tried in Los Angeles. And for you to use one of my men as the instrument of your vengeance . . ." He trailed off and glared at Sam. "I say no."

"And I say yes," Chalmont challenged him angrily.

Finch struck him across the face. The slap startled Andi and Sam, but I'd seen the fury building in Finch's eyes.

"Your anger and incompetence have led Private here," he said. "You have brought his people into our world and now they represent more of a threat to us than if you'd left Morgan alone. Kill him here and there may come a time when we have to answer for his death to someone we can't buy, kill or control. Morgan has powerful friends and I don't want any of them at my door looking for his body."

Chalmont looked at him defiantly.

"Don't let hurt pride jeopardize everything we've built," Lawrence told him. "One day you may stand in my place, but not if you fail to curb this reckless streak."

Chalmont wrestled with his emotions and finally tucked his pistol into his waistband. "Then we will take him and do it somewhere else."

"I have no problem with that," Finch replied. "But make sure it's somewhere that isn't connected to any of us."

And with that, the king of Propaganda Tre had sanctioned my execution.

CHAPTER 79

SAM FARRELL APPROACHED me and said, "Hold him."

The two bodyguards tightened their grip on me and Sam slugged me in the gut, knocking the wind from me.

"I'm going to do what I should have done in LA," he said, and nodded at my captors.

At his signal, they dragged me out of the courtyard to a small parking lot located behind the old stables. There were eight cars and a couple of unmarked vans.

Sam climbed behind the wheel of a silver Ford Transit and as the bodyguards manhandled me into the cargo compartment, I saw Andi get behind the wheel of a black Mercedes GLS, and Raymond Chalmont take the passenger's place beside her.

The larger of the two bodyguards pulled the side door shut

and Sam started the engine. The second bodyguard pushed me onto one of the bench seats. He and his companion sat either side of me and pressed close as Sam drove us out of Finch's estate. Through the windows in the rear doors, I could see Andi and Raymond following in the Mercedes.

The headlights of the van illuminated the narrow lane, thick with shadows from the trees overhanging it on both sides. Ominous clouds hung on the horizon, still with the weight of an impending storm, crowding the light from the night sky. I couldn't help but feel a sense of desperation as these evil and twisted men drove me to my fate.

We emerged from the lane and came to an intersection where we turned onto a main road cutting between hills and fields that remained indistinct under the dark skies. The van gathered speed on the deserted road, and I realized I might not have a better chance than this.

I moved suddenly, catching the larger of my captors with a vicious headbutt on his temple, using my skull to inflict as much pain as possible. He crumpled to one side, clutching his head, giving me the space to lean over and bring my elbow into the nose of the startled smaller man. As his hands went up to protect his face, I reached round and punched him in the stomach. I stood to unleash a furious volley of further punches and kicks to the men.

While I delivered the frenzied assault, fighting for my life, I sensed the van slow and turned to see Farrell braking hard, while reaching for something in his waistband. I rushed toward him, and he tried to fend me off with one hand as he kept the other on the steering wheel.

I punched him, grabbed the wheel and yanked it as hard as I could. The van veered onto two wheels with the sharp turn. Momentum fought gravity, and I braced myself as best I could as the vehicle rolled over onto its side.

CHAPTER 80

THE VAN FLIPPED and tumbled. I was tossed around the cab as metal crashed and ground against hard asphalt. I banged my head against the front passenger seat but fought the pain and black edges to my vision. I leaned into the surging adrenalin that coursed through my veins, so that when the vehicle came to a grinding halt, I was alert and ready.

The van was on its roof, Sam Farrell dazed but conscious. The two men in the back were out cold, their bodies twisted in ways that spoke of broken bones and hospital beds.

I popped Sam's seatbelt. When he fell out of his seat, I leaned over him and opened the driver's door. I pushed him out of the cab and found a pistol in his waistband as I hauled him to his feet. He could stand but wasn't lucid, mumbling incoherently.

I held him in front of me as Andi and Chalmont stepped from the Mercedes, which had stopped a short distance away.

They walked into the dazzling headlights and became silhouettes. The glare made it difficult to look at them for long periods of time.

"Let him go," Andi said. "And put the gun down."

"Give me your keys," I countered. "And I'll let him go."

"You think you can escape again, Mr. Morgan?" Chalmont asked.

"Give me the keys to the Mercedes," I yelled.

I alternated between pointing the gun at Sam's head and aiming it in their direction.

"That's not going to happen, Mr. Morgan," Chalmont said. "You destroyed my life. Ruined me." His voice was jagged with anger. "There is no escape for you. You will die here tonight, Jack Morgan."

The sound of the gunshot startled me, and I felt the bullet hit Sam Farrell in the chest. He groaned and went heavy. Then came the second and third shots, cutting the stillness of the night like thundercracks.

Andi cried out as the fourth shot hit Sam in the gut and he slumped forward, dead.

I couldn't hold him up. His body fell onto the road.

Raymond Chalmont stepped out of the blinding light, his gun raised and aimed at my head. Behind him, I heard Andi start to sob.

"Nothing will save you, Mr. Morgan," he said. "Nothing."

CHAPTER 81

"SAM?" ANDI WHISPERED between shuddering sobs. "Sam!"

She ran to the dead man's side and fell to her knees a couple of meters from me. She took his head in her hands and stared down at his glassy eyes, sobbing.

"Sam," she repeated, wiping her face. She looked at Chalmont, her expression hardening. "You killed him."

"He was in my way," Chalmont said.

Andi was on her knees between us, obscuring part of me, but when he uttered those words, she wiped away the last of her tears and stood up to face him defiantly.

"And what about me?" she asked. "Am I in your way too?"

Chalmont waved his gun at her. "Move aside."

Andi stayed where she was, directly in front of me. "Sam was one of us," she said. "He was loyal to the cause. He was true to his oath. He was a friend."

"Step aside, Andi," Chalmont told her.

Still she didn't move.

"Step aside." He was more insistent now.

"What does it all mean?" she asked, her tone hollow. "What does any of it mean? You tell us we have to keep the faith. That we are the true custodians of order and righteousness. That our day will come. That we're making the world a better place."

She hesitated and looked down at Sam's body.

"But you just murdered him," she said. "This wasn't about making the world a better place. This was about *you*. What you want. You shot him as though he was worthless."

I stayed perfectly still. I sensed the enormity of this moment for Andi, and knew if I said anything, I risked sending her back toward the beliefs that had twisted her mind. Sam Farrell's death had made her see clearly that for all their talk about righteousness and honor, Propaganda Tre were only interested in themselves and in the power they could obtain through manipulating others. I think Raymond Chalmont also sensed the importance of the moment and recognized his loss of control over the mind of a previously faithful follower.

He raised his gun, and for a moment there was no sound except for the wind stirring the leaves and the creak of swaying branches.

"What is this, Raymond?" Andi asked. "What am I really part of?"

She glanced at me, and I saw nothing but regret in her eyes. Tears welled up in them.

"Get out of the way," Chalmont commanded, aiming his gun directly at her.

Andi wiped her eyes, and her entire demeanor suddenly changed. Her posture stiffened and she raised her gun and shot him without warning.

The bullet hit him in the shoulder, knocking him back. He pulled the trigger instinctively and Andi cried out as the shot hit her in the stomach. She fell beside Sam Farrell and her pistol clattered along the road.

I raced to grab it and turned it on Chalmont, but he had already made it to the Mercedes and slid behind the wheel. He threw the car into gear and reversed away at speed. I tried to shoot out the tires, but my shots went wide. He killed the headlights and then spun the vehicle around, before racing away into the darkness.

As the sound of his engine faded, I heard a moan and turned and ran to Andi's side.

CHAPTER 82

I CROUCHED BESIDE her, but I knew her wound would be bad even before I'd examined it. Her skin had turned pallid, gray-looking in the darkness. Her breathing was rapid and shallow, and her expression full of shock and fear. I was familiar with that look, having seen it before on the faces of others who were realizing the dividing line between life and death was wafer-thin.

"Jack," she gasped. "Jack, please don't let me die."

I ignored the irony of this conspirator in my attempted murder pleading with me to save her, and the fact that like Justine she had suffered a stomach wound. I lifted her shirt to find dark blood oozing from the bullet hole. It looked like an oil slick spreading across her pale skin.

"Jack," she said faintly. "Please."

I found her phone and used her thumb to unlock it before

calling the emergency services. I gave the operator our location and stressed the urgency of the situation. I could patch up an arm or leg, but a gunshot wound to the stomach would almost certainly require surgery, which was well beyond my field medicine skills.

"Jack, will you hold my hand?" she asked, her voice weak, her breathing growing shallow.

I wrapped my fingers around her cold, delicate hand and squeezed gently.

She smiled. "Thank you. I don't want to make this journey alone."

"You're not going anywhere," I told her, but my words sounded false even as I uttered them. It's always a struggle for me to lie convincingly

Her smile faltered and her eyes brimmed as she winced with pain. She took a series of rapid breaths and recovered something like composure.

"After Monaco, we lost the Chalmont Casino," she said. She was gasping for air now, trying to hold enough life within her to pass on the information she knew I was seeking. "We needed a way to launder funds, so Lawrence has been coercing other racehorse owners into manipulating results so we can launder cash from our illegal operations through gambling. He runs a network of online accounts through the many proxies we have working for us overseas."

It suddenly made sense. The intimidation of the Kearneys was about getting them to throw races. I reflected on my role in causing this by shutting down the Monaco operation and forcing Propaganda Tre to establish another means of cleaning the money it made from its illegal operations, selling drugs on the streets of Dublin and quite probably across all of Europe. Billions were gambled on Irish racing each year and it was an international concern with massive online betting markets. It would be easy to conceal huge sums in illegal gains within the sea of legitimate stakes.

"The cash is used to fund our political objectives," Andi said between gasps. "We want an end to liberalism—to bring about cultural and political disintegration. Then we can step in and establish a new order, a return to traditional values, where people stay where they belong."

I shook my head slowly, wondering how someone so smart could become so twisted by hate.

"I'm sorry. I was a fool. It's only now I see the truth," she said, before her breathing became very labored. "Help me, Jack. Please," she cried before she began to shudder. Her eyes filled with terror, and the breath rasped in her throat with an ugly choking sound. "Jack . . ."

She fell still and I felt the life leave her. Her eyes glazed over and stared beyond me at the dark sky above.

Andi was dead.

CHAPTER 83

THE VAN WAS on its roof and Raymond Chalmont had taken the only other vehicle, so I was stranded.

I used Andi's thumb to unlock her phone again and changed her security ID to a six-digit PIN so I could access her phone independently. I left her body where it lay near Sam Farrell's and set off on foot, using Google Maps to guide me cross-country.

I avoided roads in case Chalmont returned to the scene to finish me off, so I found myself traipsing on foot over heavy, damp earth between high trees that reached toward the brooding sky. The drizzle was growing heavier and I had no doubt a storm was coming. I was heading west toward the village of Rathcoffey, moving as fast as I could, hoping I could avoid the worst of the downpour and find some sort of transportation there.

I used Andi's phone to call Mo-bot.

"Hello," she said hesitantly.

"It's me," I replied.

"Jack," she said, and then, to the people she was with, she remarked, "It's Jack."

I heard indistinct expressions of relief in the background.

"Is Justine there?" I asked.

"Yes," Mo replied. "And Sci. Let me put you on speaker."

The acoustics changed a moment later.

"Jack, thank God!" Justine said.

"You okay?" Sci asked.

"Yes," I replied. "Sam Farrell and Andi Harris are dead. Raymond Chalmont shot them both."

"Jeez," Sci said.

"But you're okay?" Justine asked.

"I'm fine," I replied. "Seriously. Before she died, Andi told me Propaganda Tre is using Irish horse racing fixtures to launder money from its street operations. She said they had to make the change after we shut things down in Monaco."

"You need to take this to the cops," Sci insisted. "No amount of political clout is going to get them off two murders."

"I can't," I replied. "We know Andi was released after someone intervened. Whether it was Conor Roche himself or someone higher up, it's clear Propaganda Tre is well protected. If I take this information to the wrong person, they'll just bury it and me alongside it."

"You need to be careful, Jack," Mo-bot responded. "Andi's phone ties you to the scene of the murders and might be used to track you."

"It's all I've got right now," I told her. "My only means of navigation and communication."

She gave a disgruntled murmur but didn't say any more.

"So, what's your plan?" Justine asked.

"Confront Lawrence Finch in a way he can't escape from," I replied. "Force him to give up his network. Get him to reveal some information we can give to people we trust."

"Eli Carver?" Justine suggested.

"Why not? He has a personal interest in all of this," I replied. Carver had been the target of the Propaganda Tre assassination attempt in Monaco. "He will have people in the FBI who will listen to him. There's no way an operation like this doesn't touch the United States in some way, and if Lawrence Finch really is the head of Propaganda Tre, then he sanctioned the attempted hit on the Secretary of Defense."

"He's got horses running tomorrow," Mo-bot said. "Including one in the Irish Derby, the largest of the five Classics."

"Perfect. Then I know exactly where he'll be," I responded. "And how to get him to rise to the bait."

CHAPTER 84

I MANAGED TO call a taxi to collect me from Rathcoffey and asked the driver to take me back to Dublin, where I found a hotel on Mercer Street. The receptionist was too well trained to ask any questions about my odd check-in time or lack of luggage, and when I went up to my room, I showered and lay on the bed, falling into a deep sleep around 3 a.m. after my racing mind finally settled.

I dreamed about Andi, lying in the road, breathing her last, and even in the unreal realm of memory and the surreal landscape of dreams, I felt the tragedy of a bright soul wasted on corrupt ideology. I pitied her even though she'd played a key role in my attempted murder.

I woke at 7:52 a.m. to the sound of my phone, or more accurately Andi's phone. Feeling groggy and exhausted, I rolled over to grab it from the nightstand.

"Hello," I said when I answered.

"Mr. Morgan, it's Conor Roche here. Have you seen the news?"

I put the phone on speaker and switched to the internet browser.

"No," I replied, as I found the *Irish Times* website. "Why?"

"We'd like to ask you some questions about where you were last night."

The moment the newspaper's home page loaded, I knew exactly why he was calling. The lead story was the murders of two former police officers, and I featured prominently as the chief suspect in the investigation.

"I'd like to know how you ended up with Andrea Harris's phone," Roche said, and I looked at the device in my hand with a growing sense of resignation.

Mo-bot had warned me it tied me to the murders and that it could be used to trace my location. My refusal to dispose of it hadn't purely been due to my lack of any other communication device. I wanted Mo to examine it for evidence on Propaganda Tre and would only have been parted from it reluctantly. However, as I realized the threat it now posed, I started to question that decision.

"I've got plans today," I replied.

"It's not a request anymore, Mr. Morgan," Conor Roche told me. "You're now a wanted man."

"Can I ask you a question, Conor?" I said.

"Sure," he replied. "Knock yourself out."

"How long have you been a member of Propaganda Tre?"

There was a long silence.

"This isn't helping you, Mr. Morgan," he replied at last. "Your pursuit of wild conspiracies and shadows has led you to cross the line into serious crime."

I suspected this call was being recorded.

"Can't be honest because the line is tapped?" I tried.

"Tapped and traced," he replied. "Knock, knock, Mr. Morgan."

He hung up and I heard the tramp of boots outside my room. Then came the thunder of fists knocking against the hotel's flimsy door, and I knew Conor and his people were already here.

CHAPTER 85

I WENT TO my door and opened it a crack, with the chain firmly in place. I saw Conor Roche and a squad of Gardai in tactical gear clustered outside of a room at the far end of the corridor.

One of the officers rapped on the door again and yelled, "Garda! Open up."

She glanced at Roche, who nodded and an officer who'd been concealed by the squad stepped into view holding a heavy metal ram. He slammed it into the door and the lock split from the frame with a loud crack.

As they rushed inside, I slipped out of my room, heading straight for the fire stairs. I headed up, climbing toward the roof, and after I'd gone a few flights, my phone rang again.

"Didn't find what you were looking for?" I remarked.

"Very clever, Mr. Morgan," Roche replied.

It had been Mo-bot's idea to spoof Andi's phone to a device

on the same floor as me, and to change the hotel's reservation system to match the location of the other phone. I felt bad for the innocent person we had marked as me but gambled on their innocence being protection enough.

"I'm not on my official line anymore," Conor Roche went on, "so I can tell you that we're coming for you, no matter what tricks you play."

"How long have you done Lawrence Finch's dirty work for him?" I asked. "How long have you been in Propaganda Tre?"

"You think I don't know you're recording this?" he countered. "Besides, I've no idea what you're talking about."

"You know," I said. "How else could you be sure I was even at the scene of the murders last night?"

He hesitated.

"Only the real killer knew I was there," I told him. "There were no cameras, and my presence was under duress since I'd been abducted. Nobody but Raymond Chalmont and his accomplices knew I was there, and the newspaper report says the police only found two dead bodies at the scene. No arrests. No witnesses. So how did *you* hear about it, Conor? When they examine the chain of evidence, what will they find linking me to the scene—other than your report?"

"It doesn't matter," he responded angrily. "Even if people knew, do you think they could touch me? I've been in the organization long enough to understand its reach, Mr. Morgan, and we will find you wherever you go."

I could have cried out with relief. He'd just confessed to being part of a criminal conspiracy.

"I look forward to it," I told him as I reached the roof.

I hung up and opened the access door. The flat roof was linked to other buildings on the terrace, and as I started across to the neighboring one, I made a call.

Mo-bot answered after two rings. "He's not very smart, is he?"

"Smart enough to have got this far," I replied. "Did you get it?"

"Yes," she said.

Conor Roche was right; Mo-bot had been monitoring and recording all calls to Andi's phone. He'd been sufficiently cunning to avoid saying anything incriminating during the initial call, but anger at having lost me and the evidence of his own corruption being laid in front of him had made him reveal enough to put him behind bars.

"We've got him," Mo-bot said.

"Good," I replied. "Get the audio to Carver's people. They can alert the Garda that there's at least one other rotten apple still serving in the force."

"On it," Mo-bot said. "What about you?"

"I'm going to go topple a king," I replied as I forced open a roof-access door and entered the stairwell of the building at the other end of the terrace.

CHAPTER 86

THE IRISH DERBY is one of the world's most popular racing fixtures. People travel there from all over the globe and they like to dress up for the event. I joined them, filing into the Curragh after purchasing a new suit and shoes from a menswear store near the hotel. I couldn't afford to look out of place and needed to pass unnoticed now my photograph was all over the news.

The sky had cleared after the storms of the previous night and the sun was bright and high, so I completed my look with a pair of oversized black sunglasses that matched my suit and shoes. The shades concealed much of my face, and only an astute observer would recognize me.

I hoped the throng of people would prevent police and security guards from identifying me, and expected the sport's enthusiasts to be so enthralled by the day's racing they wouldn't notice an alleged murderer in their midst.

"Are you still there?" I asked, speaking for the benefit of the mic in my Bluetooth earpiece.

It wasn't the most sophisticated wire, but it was adequate in the circumstances. I'd purchased a new phone and headset when I'd bought the suit and was on an open call with Mo-bot, who was monitoring my location and recording audio.

"I can hear you loud and clear," she replied. "Sounds like a fun place."

"On any other day, I might enjoy a pint, some Irish hospitality and the ponies, but not today," I replied.

The Curragh looked magnificent in the sunshine, and the crowds for the Derby easily surpassed those for the Airlie Stud Stakes. I was swept along until I reached the main grandstand, where I found a tout who sold me a general pass for five times face value.

My heart jumped a gear when I thought I saw recognition in the steward's eye, but he waved me through the gate without hesitation and I filed onto the course, on my way to the grandstand.

"I'm in," I said for Mo-bot's benefit.

"I know," she replied. "I can see your phone."

"We're watching the key exchanges," Sci chimed in. He was referring to online bookies and spread betting exchanges.

Mo-bot had used an artificial intelligence program to identify betting patterns at the 1000 and 2000 Guineas and zero in on sites used by Lawrence Finch to launder Propaganda Tre money. Apparently, these were easy to spot once she knew what to look for.

"Are we ready to make bets?" I asked.

"Everything is set to go," Sci replied.

We'd set up accounts on the key exchanges, and Private had put up a total of half a million dollars in stake money.

"We'll start placing bets as soon as we see Finch's people make their moves," Mo-bot said.

I went into the main grandstand, which was heaving. All the men were in suits and the women wore fine dresses, and most of them were loud and rowdy, which was perfect because it meant no one paid attention to me as I scanned the owners' boxes for Lawrence Finch.

I finally spotted him with Jackson Kyle at his side. Finch was surrounded by a group of twenty or so people, many of whom I recognized from my confrontation with him in the winners' enclosure bar. They were all standing on a terrace above the main grandstand, laughing, chatting and enjoying drinks from the private bar in Finch's box.

I settled into my seat near the very front of the grandstand, which allowed me to keep watch on him as I waited for racing to start.

CHAPTER 87

THERE IS SOMETHING unique about horse racing in Ireland. Similar cheering, clamoring crowds can be found at other race-tracks around the world, as well as the thunder of hooves on turf, the thrill of a wager on a runner with a meaningful name, free-flowing alcohol, party atmosphere, beautiful surroundings . . . these are all replicated elsewhere. However, as I stood watching the Derby Day scene at the Curragh, listening to Mo-bot and Sci follow the action of Lawrence Finch's clandestine syndicate and place bets of their own that followed Propaganda Tre's flow of dirty money, I realized that the quality that makes Irish racing so special is its magic.

I'd noted that Ireland was a special place when I'd first seen it from the air, and it was brought home to me again as I watched beautiful, gleaming thoroughbreds come charging down the final straight. Somehow the Irish still keep wonder and mystery at the heart of their everyday life and I think that is part of what makes them such a hospitable people. They want to share the magic they've discovered. They want to welcome strangers to their beautiful corner of the world and showcase the wonder of it. And that ethos means every Irish endeavor is doubly celebrated, not just for the joy of the pursuit itself, but for the fact that it is an expression of that wonder. There is a unique quality to this country that everyone can feel, but few can describe, and in that magic lies much of what makes Ireland so special. At least that's how it seemed to me as I absorbed the Derby Day atmosphere.

Lawrence Finch rarely bet on his own horses, but one of his was victorious in the race before the Derby, the 3:25 challenge for horses over three years old. The winner was a five-year-old gelding called King Finch. I watched Finch and his entourage cheer the win and saw him leave his box.

That was my cue to make my own way out of the grandstand. I navigated the throng of racegoers, many of whom were now cheerfully unsteady on their feet, making my way to the winners' enclosure, where I stood beside the gate and watched people coming and going.

I waited until I saw a particularly drunk man staggering away from the enclosure with his arms around a woman in a peach-colored summer dress. I started toward them and deliberately bumped into him. When we collided, I apologized profusely and snapped off his lanyard without him noticing. Mollified by my display of remorse, he and the woman went on their way, and I tied the lanyard around my own neck before heading to the gate.

It was thronged as people were changing stations between races, and everyone wanted to be in their chosen spot before the Derby started. The hustle and bustle helped me because the steward gave my pass only the most cursory of glances before waving me through.

I found Lawrence Finch in the winners' circle awaiting the return of King Finch. He was surrounded by people who were congratulating him and celebrating his moment of triumph. He spotted me as the horses were led in, and this time he didn't smile. In fact, his mood turned instantly sour. His eyes blazed with anger and he nudged Jackson Kyle, who immediately started toward me.

I was in no mood to deal with underlings and followed the white-painted railing around the enclosure, pressing through the assembled crowd as though it wasn't there. I didn't break stride as I encountered Jackson but slugged him in the mouth before he had the chance to open it. He fell hard, and the people around us gasped and backed away.

Someone shouted for security, but I was in front of Lawrence Finch before anyone could stop me.

He flinched and took a step back.

"Don't worry, Mr. Finch. I promise I'm not here to hurt you," I said. "I've come to finish you."

CHAPTER 88

"THIS MAN IS deranged and has been harassing me," Finch told the onlookers. "He's wanted for questioning in relation to two murders."

"Murders your associate committed," I fired back as loudly as I could.

I saw security guards pushing their way toward us and was conscious I didn't have much time.

"My name is Jack Morgan, and last week my colleague and I were shot at after a screening at the Motion Picture Academy in Los Angeles. Some of you might have seen it on the news," I said as loudly as possible, so people at the very back of the crowd could hear me. I was pleased to see some already had their phones out.

"Don't listen to him," Finch countered, but his tone betrayed uncertainty and a degree of weakness.

"The gunman was an employee of Mr. Finch's, a man called Sam Farrell, one of the victims in yesterday's shooting."

I saw the security guards slow their advance and eye Lawrence Finch sidelong, willing to listen to the rest of my tale. There were police at the scene now too, making their way through the rear of the crowd.

"I followed Sam Farrell to Ireland," I said, "where I discovered his connection to Mr. Finch."

More people were filming me now, including a couple of journalists with press badges, who had turned their DSLR cameras and shotgun microphones in my direction.

"He's lying," Finch yelled. 'The man's making this up—can't you tell?"

"Then you can sue me for libel," I responded quickly. "Except truth is a defense and I have proof of everything I'm saying. I can prove your connection to another corrupt Garda officer called Conor Roche, who tried to frame me for last night's murders. I can prove the group you lead, which was behind murders in Rome and Monaco, was responsible for the firebombing of the Richmond Refugee Centre here in Dublin. I can also prove you've been financing these illegal activities by rigging horse races after intimidating local owners, trainers and breeders to collude in fixing results."

There was a collective intake of breath. While the other crimes were horrific, this was relevant and immediate to many of the racegoers around Lawrence Finch, some of whom would have torn up betting slips for races he'd rigged. After a short pause there were mutterings and hisses. Then came the boos. Finch didn't know how to react, which was precisely what I'd wanted. I knew being accused of race-fixing on the day of the biggest fixture in Ireland's calendar would cause a major scandal—something that would be anathema to a self-made man like Finch.

"In fact," I continued, "by following your syndicate, Mr. Finch, and placing the same bets as they did, I've been able to turn half a million dollars into twenty-five million in a single day."

Lawrence Finch realized the severity of his predicament at the very moment the Gardai appeared at his shoulder. The crowd had turned sullen and hostile, calling him a liar and cheat and other words I couldn't quite make out, though the angry tone in which they were spoken was clear enough.

"He's lying," Finch protested again, but his denials sounded thin and pathetic now. "He's crazy."

"I don't think these good folks are happy with you," I told him. "Many of them will have lost money on the results you fixed. Most of them will have seen the fire you set in the heart of Dublin and despise you for bringing hatred to this beautiful, friendly city."

My words were on point. The whole crowd seemed to bristle. Desperate by now, Finch tried to flee under the railing of the parade ring, but I grabbed him and pushed him back toward the Gardai.

"And if the authorities deem it legal for me to keep today's winnings, I will be donating the money to the refugee center, to help with its rebuild, and offering financial support to the affected families, with any remaining balance going to anti-racism charities."

Lawrence Finch fixed me with a defiant glare as one of the police officers took his wrists and put the first manacle on him.

"I'll be out before sundown," he said.

"Not this time," I replied. "All the evidence we've gathered has gone to the American and Irish governments. People with real power, well above your grubby ability to corrupt and influence. People who will see justice done impartially."

I watched the defiance ebb away and his spirit crumble.

"I keep my promises, Mr. Finch," I told him. "You and your rotten organization are finished."

CHAPTER 89

MO-BOT, SCI AND our LA team sent the evidence we'd accu-mulated to Eli Carver, who referred it to Marie Silver, Deputy Assistant Attorney General in the Criminal Division of the Just-ice Department. From there the FBI got involved and coordinated the effort with the Garda, who wanted to interview me. I refused, saying I didn't feel they could guarantee my safety.

I'd used the sensation of Lawrence Finch's arrest to slip away from the Curragh, and had booked myself a room in a new hotel in the city, from where I'd asked Mo-bot and Sci to com-municate with the Irish authorities and inform them that I was only willing to give my statement on neutral ground, to senior representatives of Irish law enforcement, government and the judiciary, and that these had to be people with reputations that were beyond reproach.

We suggested Kearney Stud as the meeting place, and Noah

and Mary were only too happy to host. I felt safe with them because I knew they'd made an enemy of Lawrence Finch before I'd been drawn into this case. They felt they owed their lives to me and were eager to do whatever they could to repay their perceived debt.

The Irish government agreed to my terms and sent the Secretary General of the Department of Justice, a serving judge, and the detective chief superintendent in charge of the Garda National Drugs and Organised Crime Bureau, to take my deposition.

And so, two days after Lawrence Finch's arrest, I found myself in Noah and Mary's dining room being served coddle, a delicious sausage and bacon stew, alongside Mary's homemade soda bread, sharing what I knew with Judge Nessa Boland, Department of Justice Secretary General Helen Higgins, and Detective Chief Superintendent Kieran McQuinn.

"Lawrence Finch has many enemies," Helen said. As a senior civil servant she had seen a succession of politicians come and go, and probably knew more than most about Ireland's rich and powerful. "I wouldn't worry about him evading justice. Not this time. The people he has acted against will ensure he is held to account. And his friends won't want to be tainted by scandal. I bet not a man in Dublin will admit to knowing him tonight."

"Will you cut a deal with him, to get him to give up the membership of Propaganda Tre?" I asked, after I finished the last mouthfuls of the delicious coddle.

"We can certainly try," Judge Boland said. She was thoughtful and severe, and I could easily imagine her intimidating criminals. Even someone as arrogant and entitled as Lawrence Finch would shrink in her presence. "We have legal arrangements that enable us to reduce time served in exchange for cooperation."

"Would you like some more, Mr. Morgan?" Mary asked, offering me the serving dish.

I nodded. "Only to be greedy. It's delicious. Thank you."

"You'll never have to thank us," Noah said, and Mary smiled and nodded. "And you'll always have a home here in Ireland. We owe you a debt we can never repay. You've freed our family from those cruel men. Saved us."

"We all owe you a debt," Detective Chief Superintendent Kieran McQuinn added. "These people were a blight on our country."

"I just want to see them stopped, so I don't have to keep looking over my shoulder for the rest of my life," I said.

"We'll do our very best," Helen assured me.

"What about Raymond Chalmont?" I asked.

There had been no sign of him since he'd fled the scene of Andi and Sam's murders, and it worried me that the man with the vendetta that had started this investigation was still at large.

"He's gone to ground," Kieran said. "But we want to assure you we're doing everything possible to find him."

It was no reflection on the Irish authorities, but I couldn't trust our futures to that assurance. Mary's food lost some of its flavor as my unease deepened. For so long as Raymond Chalmont was free, my life and Justine's would always be in danger.

CHAPTER 90

EVER CAUTIOUS, I stayed in the hotel the following day, leaving my room only to buy a new cellphone, which I did first thing. Mo-bot, Sci, Justine and Emily Knighton were the only people I sent the new number to, so I knew it was one of them calling when the phone rang at 10:15 a.m.

"Jack, it's Emily," she said, when I answered. "I've got good news. Our London legal adviser has been liaising with the Irish authorities and they've cleared you to go home. They've said they have all they need from you for now and can do any follow-up remotely."

My heart soared at the prospect of going back to LA and being reunited with Justine. "That's great news. Thanks for letting me know."

"It's the least I can do to make up for . . ." she hesitated. "I'm sorry."

"What for?" I asked.

"For failing to spot Andi was a bad apple."

"There's only so much we can do to discover what evil lies in people's hearts," I said. "You have nothing to apologize for."

"Thank you," she replied with relief. "We're turning our attention to Raymond Chalmont next and doing everything we can to track him down."

"I appreciate it," I said. "I'm going to try to get over to London before the end of the year, so maybe we can catch up properly then."

"Look forward to it," she replied.

We said our farewells and she wished me safe travels, and the instant I hung up I booked a ticket on the Aer Lingus flight that was due to leave Dublin for Los Angeles at 3:25 p.m.

I sent messages to Sci, Mo-bot and Justine giving them my flight details, and after a quick check-in and a short stay in the departure lounge, I settled into my business-class seat for take-off. As the plane reached cruising altitude, the cabin crew went through drinks and meal service before setting the lights low so people could sleep, but I was too excited and full of anticipation. My mind whirred, working through what had happened, turning over aspects of the investigation and the Rome and Monaco cases to see if I'd missed anything that might offer a clue to Chalmont's current whereabouts.

I was frustrated by the lack of a breakthrough and exhausted by the time the wheels finally touched the runway at LAX, but adrenalin kept me going. I showed no signs of fatigue when I met Sci in the Arrivals hall.

"It's so good to see you," he said, pulling me into a warm embrace.

"You too," I replied. "It's good to be home."

We talked about the investigation on the way from the airport to the hospital, but I didn't absorb much of what Sci was saying. My mind was abuzz with excitement and most of my responses were brief and automatic.

We met Mo-bot in the corridor on the third floor of UCLA Medical Center in Santa Monica, where she'd set up a little workstation outside of Justine's private room.

"Jack," she said, putting her laptop aside and rising the moment she saw me.

"Mo," I replied as we embraced. "I can't tell you how good it is to see you in person."

"I'm glad you made it back in one piece," she said. "Listen, we can talk properly and be all hugs and kisses some other time, but I know you're not here to see me." She glanced pointedly at the door. "I think she's resting, but she won't mind being woken for this."

I smiled, and my heart thundered with exhilaration as I entered Justine's room.

Mo-bot was right. Justine was asleep in bed, her face lit by the gentle glow of the Californian sunlight edging through the blinds.

As I approached, Justine stirred, rubbed her eyes, and then gave the broadest smile when she saw me.

I beamed right back.

CHAPTER 91

EIGHT DAYS LATER, on the second Tuesday in July, Justine was discharged from hospital. I walked alongside her as she was wheeled to the lobby—a formal requirement apparently—and held her hand as she thanked the orderly and stood up.

"I can't tell you how good this feels," she said, as we walked into the late-afternoon sunshine.

"I have an idea," I replied. "And it's almost as good as it feels to be taking you home."

She smiled and we walked to the car parked in the hospital lot. I knew Mo-bot and Sci had wanted to be here too, but they had the sensitivity to realize Justine might be overwhelmed and easily tired. So they were at the office, busying themselves with the aftermath of the Dublin investigation. We'd arranged a cele-bratory meal at Geoffrey's in Malibu on Saturday if Justine's rehab and recovery saw her well enough. Judging by the walk to the car, I was confident we'd be dining beside the Pacific Ocean that weekend.

I drove her to my place in Pacific Palisades and we smiled at each other as I steered my Mercedes through the automatic gates. We usually lived separately, but I wanted her with me for the next couple of weeks at the very least.

"Are you sure about this?" she asked. "I'm well enough to go home. I don't want to intrude."

"You're not intruding. I've cleared the decks to help look after you," I replied as I parked in my driveway. "Anyway, it was about time we did something like this."

She leaned over and kissed me.

"I don't want you being alone until I know you're safe," I told her.

"You worried I might melt?" she asked.

"I just want to be sure," I replied. In fact, I knew I had reason for caution beyond any lingering worry for Justine's health. Raymond Chalmont was still out there, and he was almost certainly going to try again. I didn't want to drive the point home now though because I didn't want Justine to feel even more vulnerable than her injuries had already made her. "It will be nice. We'll watch movies, eat well, hang out."

"Works for me," she said before getting out of the car.

We made good on my plan and cuddled on the couch while we watched the latest *Dune* movie. Later, I ordered Thai food, which we ate on the terrace overlooking the ocean, enjoying the gentle breeze and dying embers of what had been a perfect sunset.

"Life doesn't get any better than this," I remarked. I was so happy to see her well and on her way to a full recovery.

"I can think of a way to improve it," she said suggestively.

"Really?" I asked. "I didn't want to . . ."

"We can just take it slowly," she replied, and led me inside and upstairs to my bedroom.

We'd just crossed the threshold when my phone vibrated in my pocket. I knew exactly what the alert meant.

"Sorry," I said, stepping back from Justine. "I have to take this."

When I glanced at the screen, I saw footage coming from one of the motion-activated cameras in the garden. A gang of masked men were making their way toward the house.

"What is it?" Justine asked, sensing my sudden concern.

"You need to get to the panic room now," I said, leading her out into the hallway and to the secure secret room installed behind a false wall in the second bedroom.

"Don't come out," I told her. "No matter what happens."

CHAPTER 92

THE PANIC ROOM was accessed through a concealed panel in the wall, which retracted from the corner of the room.

"Come in with me," Justine pleaded. "Let's call the cops."

"I know what I'm doing," I replied, ushering her into the tiny, secure space. "Please trust me. I need you to do that. Remember: don't come out. No matter what."

"Jack, you're scaring me," she said.

"There's nothing to be afraid of," I told her, and leaned in for a kiss. "Trust me."

She nodded reluctantly, and I watched her move to the console where the home-security system was displaying footage of the interior of my house, recording everything that happened. She pressed the button that shut and locked the armored panel, and I stepped away, satisfied she was safe.

I crept across the hallway and went to my bedroom. I had a

gun-safe in my closet where I kept my personal arsenal, but I didn't need to waste any time. I'd prepared for this eventuality and had a pistol ready in the top drawer of my dresser. I grabbed it and held it ready as I went downstairs, slowly and silently.

I heard movement by the French doors that opened onto the terrace and went toward the sound. A masked man with a pistol in his hand came into view, creeping along the terrace and heading for the open doors.

I ducked behind the wall quickly, confident the sound of the ocean would mask my footsteps. If he'd heard me, he showed no sign but came through the door oblivious to my presence.

"Freeze," I whispered, and the man turned, startled.

I clocked him in the face with my pistol, catching him on the ear. As he doubled over in pain and waved his gun in my direction, I swung mine down and hit the back of his head, knocking him senseless.

He fell in a heap. At the same time I heard the shattering of glass and went to the kitchen, where I peered round the doorway to see a masked man unlocking a window he'd broken. As he clambered inside, I felt something hard and cold press against my temple and realized someone had pressed a gun to my head. One of his accomplices had got the jump on me.

"Don't move," the man beside me said.

I turned and tried to bring my pistol up toward him, but he blocked the move and knocked the gun out of my hand. He lashed out with his own weapon, but I ducked and rolled and reached my hand beside a kitchen cabinet, where I kept a baseball bat as a last line of home defense.

I swung it at the gunman and knocked the pistol from his hand before driving the thick end into his nose and knocking him cold.

Before I could reach for my pistol, the second man grabbed me, and we fell into a grapple against one of the counters. I used the bat to knock the gun out of his hand, but he reached for a butcher's knife and lunged for me.

I parried with the bat and rolled clear of the next attack. I swung and caught his forearm, causing him to drop the blade, which landed with a clatter. I didn't waste a moment in pressing my advantage.

As he stepped back and tried to find another weapon, I kicked his right knee, caught him on the shoulder with a heavy blow from the bat, and swung the pommel into his face, dazing him. I followed this combination with a headbutt that knocked him flat.

The front door caved in with a crack and crash of wood splintering, and I grabbed my gun and ran into the hallway to see three more masked men enter my home.

The first rushed me, and we wrestled for control of my gun. I pulled the trigger and the sound of two gunshots deafened me, but neither of us relinquished our hold. His accomplices joined the fray, trying to pull me off the weapon. I knew if I let go, I was a dead man, so I clung to the gun and wrenched it clear, but the momentum was too great and I lost my hold on it. The pistol spun clear across the room and hit the far wall

The trio pushed me clear of their scrum and the nearest tried to shoot me, but I ducked and drove my fist into his groin. The crack of the gunshot was so loud it stung in my ears, but I didn't miss a beat. As he doubled over in pain, I swung my elbow up into his face, breaking his nose and knocking him cold.

I pushed past him as he fell and squared up to his two accomplices, who trained their pistols on me. I wasn't afraid but rushed at them and threw my fists at the taller of the two. I sidestepped his shot and moved between the men. I drove my elbow into the taller one's face and punched his accomplice in the jaw. Both dazed, they staggered back clutching their heads. I didn't hesitate, knocking them down with a furious combination of punches.

Their bodies fell with heavy thuds. In the stillness that followed, I heard nothing but the roll and crash of the ocean.

Then came footsteps and the voice I'd been expecting all along.

"Impressive, Mr. Morgan," Raymond Chalmont said. "But it will do you no good."

I turned to see the Frenchman standing on the terrace, pointing a machine pistol at me through the open doors.

CHAPTER 93

"DON'T MOVE," SAID Chalmont. "Did you really think you could walk away from what you've done?" he asked, stepping closer. "Did you think you could simply resume your old life after crossing my path, Mr. Morgan?"

I didn't answer but instead kept my eyes focused on the gun, preparing for the shot I was certain would come. I hadn't been expecting to be the one staring down the barrel of a gun, and looked longingly across the room at the spot where my own pistol had fallen.

"You have wounded our organization, but for as long as I'm free it will never die. Lawrence designated me his successor. I know where our money is hidden, who our members are all around the world," Chalmont told me. "Under my leadership we will regroup and return stronger than ever."

"You will face justice for your past crimes and for what's happened tonight," I replied. "You will rot in prison."

He smiled. "You mean your surveillance system? My people and I will raze to the ground this house, your video footage, and the panic room where you have stashed your girlfriend." He paused to let his words sink in. "Yes, I know about that, Mr. Morgan."

I glared at him but said nothing.

"I want you to understand the pain I'm going to inflict on everyone you care about. I want you to consider that before you die."

Then I heard the sound I'd been dreading: locks opening upstairs and the noise of the concealed panel retracting.

"She doesn't want to sit in that little coffin and watch you die," Raymond said. "It seems she is eager to join you."

I heard Justine's footsteps upstairs as she crossed the landing. She must have been watching the exchange on the house surveillance system and known there was no point staying hidden because Chalmont was aware of her location.

I couldn't risk him hurting Justine so I lunged for him. The suddenness of my movement startled him and we wrestled for control of his machine pistol.

He kicked me and I swung for him but missed. As he stepped back and ducked, he snatched the pistol away from me.

We stood there for a moment, me glaring at him from the wrong end of the barrel of his gun. I saw his finger tighten around the trigger and knew my end had come.

"Jack!" Justine cried, and I turned to see her enter the room with my gun raised in our direction.

She didn't hesitate, but shot him once in the leg and a second time in his side.

CHAPTER 94

CHALMONT CRIED OUT as he was knocked backward and fell to the floor moaning in agony.

"Jack!" Justine yelled, running over to me.

We embraced and I kissed her before taking back my gun.

I aimed my pistol at the wounded man, who glared at me through his pain.

"Our friends in US Intelligence have been monitoring the border, watching for your entry," I said.

Eli Carver had offered whatever support was necessary to apprehend the remnants of the Monaco conspirators, the last of the men who'd tried to kill him.

"You came in through Dallas," I told Raymond. "I'm guessing because you thought it wouldn't be as likely to be watched as some of the other airports. And you arrived by private jet to further minimize risk, traveling under a false identity, which was the first of your many crimes on US soil."

Few people had any real idea of America's true surveillance capabilities at its borders. I don't know whether it was Homeland Security, the NSA or both, but an official body's facial-recognition software had flagged Raymond Chalmont the moment he'd entered the terminal building.

"You were followed from the airport to Los Angeles and the rental house where you met with the other men who came here tonight to kill us. We needed to catch you in the commission of a serious crime in the United States to avoid legal wrangling over extradition, and since I knew you'd come for me, I agreed to act as bait. I hadn't expected to be facing you unarmed."

Justine elbowed me. "We're going to have to talk about your communication issues."

"Sorry," I said to her. "I didn't want to worry you."

"You'll never—" Raymond began, but I cut him off.

"Yes, we will. You came here to commit murder. Every aspect of your trip has been recorded, including your actions tonight." I nodded at a camera mounted in the corner of the room. "You're going away for a very long time."

"Hello?" a voice called through the broken front door.

I turned to see Mo-bot and Sci leading a group of FBI agents and LAPD officers into the house.

"Good to see you both," I said.

Salvatore Mattera and his captain, Linda Brooks, were among those who followed them in. Sal had his arm in a sling.

"So you're the asshole who sent that assassin?" he asked Chalmont, who groaned in agony and clutched at his wounds. "Conspired to kill a cop?"

"He needs an ambulance," I said.

"Oh, we'll make sure he lives," Brooks replied before turning to the prisoner. "I can't wait to see you in court," she said. "Judge is going to love hearing all about you." She turned to a couple of uniformed LAPD officers at her side. "Cuff him and book him."

They stepped forward, hauled Chalmont roughly to his feet and took him into custody.

I lowered my gun as FBI agents and other LAPD officers moved through the house arresting Chalmont's fallen accomplices.

"I think it's over," Justine said.

I smiled at her. "I think it finally is."

CHAPTER 95

THE HUBBUB OF conversation, chime of cutlery against dishes, and tinkle of glasses meeting in toasts rose above the sound of the Pacific waves rolling against the Malibu sands.

Geoffrey's was busy, and Sci, Mo-bot, Justine and I had a table for four on the terrace near the low glass barrier that fronted the water. Every other table was occupied by Tinseltown folk or well-heeled locals, a few of whom I recognized from the silver screen, small screen or gossip sites.

"Nerves of steel," Sci remarked, tucking into his steak. "That's what you've got, Jack."

"Takes guts to face down people like Lawrence Finch and Raymond Chalmont," Mo-bot agreed. "Zealots with money are so dangerous."

A server poured Justine another half-glass of champagne, and she raised it in salute. "To bravery."

"To recovery," I added, lifting my own glass.

"To bravery and recovery," Mo-bot and Sci said, and we all drank to those sentiments.

My phone rang. I would normally have ignored it during a meal, but so much had happened in the past few weeks, I couldn't afford to miss anything important.

"Excuse me," I said, taking my cell from my jacket pocket.

I was glad I had because I saw the call was from Secretary of Defense Eli Carver.

"Eli," I said. "What can I do for you?"

"Nothing, Jack," he replied. "You've already done more than enough. I wanted to let you know Raymond Chalmont is trying to cut a deal with the Justice Department. He'll name every member of Propaganda Tre and give us the details of their money flows and power structure, in exchange for a reduced sentence in a medium-security federal prison. Minimum of twenty-five years. I just wanted to run it past you, Jack. After what he did to you and Justine."

"Twenty-five years, medium-security," I said to Justine. "In exchange for giving up the whole organization."

"Twenty-five years is still hard time, wherever it's served," Justine responded. "And if it means we can sleep easily, I'm all for it."

I nodded.

"It's fine with us," I told Carver.

"Lawrence Finch is trying to cut something similar in Ireland, so we'll be able to cross-check what they tell us and play one off against the other, to ensure we get the whole picture," Carver said.

"That works," I remarked.

"Thanks, Jack," he said. "I have a personal interest in seeing the demise of this group."

"I can understand that," I told him. "Let me know if there's anything you need from Private, Mr. Secretary."

"Don't start that again, Jack. It's Eli to you," he insisted. "Look me up when you're next in DC. And give my thanks to your people. You all did an amazing job again."

"I will, Eli," I assured him. "On both counts."

We said our goodbyes, and I hung up.

"Sounds like that's the end of Propaganda Tre," Mo-bot said.

I nodded. "He said you all did a great job and to send his thanks."

"Hush now," Sci replied. "You'll make me blush."

"Speak for yourself," Mo-bot said. "I live for praise."

I smiled and raised my glass again. "To justice," I said.

They lifted their own glasses and responded in unison. "To justice."

ACKNOWLEDGMENTS

We'd like to thank Rachel Imrie, Claire Simmonds, Lynn Curtis, Laurie Ip Fung Chun and the team at Penguin for their excellent work on this book. We'd also like to thank you, the reader, for joining Jack Morgan and the Private team on another adventure, and hope you'll return for the next one.

Adam would like to thank James Patterson for his continued collaboration. Thanks too to his wife, Amy, and their children, Maya, Elliot and Thomas, for their love and support. He'd also like to express his gratitude to his agent, Nicola Barr. Thanks too to Jean-Benoît and Clare Berty for their unwavering friendship over the years.

ABOUT THE AUTHORS

JAMES PATTERSON is one of the best-known and biggest-selling writers of all time. Among his creations are some of the world's most popular series, including Alex Cross, the Women's Murder Club, Michael Bennett and the Private novels. He has written many other number one bestsellers including collaborations with President Bill Clinton and Dolly Parton, stand-alone thrillers and non-fiction. James has donated millions in grants to independent bookshops and has been the most borrowed adult author in UK libraries for the past fourteen years in a row. He lives in Florida with his family.

ADAM HAMDY is a bestselling author and screenwriter. His novel, *The Other Side of Night,* has been described as ingenious, constantly surprising and deeply moving. He is the author of the Scott Pearce series of contemporary espionage thrillers, *Black 13*, *Red Wolves* and *White Fire*, and the Pendulum series. Keep up to date with his latest books and news at www.adamhamdy.com.

Have you read them all?

PRIVATE
(with Maxine Paetro)

Jack Morgan is head of Private, the world's largest investigation company with branches around the globe. When his best friend's wife is murdered, he sets out to track down her killer. But be warned: Jack doesn't play by the rules.

PRIVATE LONDON
(with Mark Pearson)

Hannah Shapiro, a young American student, has fled her country, but can't flee her past. Can Private save Hannah from the terror that has followed her to London?

PRIVATE GAMES
(with Mark Sullivan)

It's July 2012 and excitement is sky high for the Olympic Games in London. But when one of the organisers is found brutally murdered, it soon becomes clear to Private London that everyone involved is under threat.

PRIVATE: NO. 1 SUSPECT
(with Maxine Paetro)

When Jack Morgan's former lover is found murdered in his bed, Jack is instantly the number one suspect, and he quickly realises he is facing his toughest challenge yet.

PRIVATE BERLIN
(with Mark Sullivan)

Mattie Engel, one of Private Berlin's rising stars, is horrified when her former fiancé, Chris, is murdered. Even more so when she realises that the killer is picking off Chris's friends. Will Mattie be next?

PRIVATE DOWN UNDER
(with Michael White)

Private Sydney's glamorous launch party is cut short by a shocking discovery – the murdered son of one of Australia's richest men. Meanwhile, someone is killing the wealthy wives of the Eastern Suburbs, and the next victim could be someone close to Private.

PRIVATE L.A.
(with Mark Sullivan)

A killer is holding L.A. to ransom. On top of this, Hollywood's golden couple have been kidnapped. Can Private prove themselves once again?

PRIVATE INDIA
(with Ashwin Sanghi)

In Mumbai, someone is murdering seemingly unconnected women in a chilling ritual. As the Private team race to find the killer, an even greater threat emerges . . .

PRIVATE VEGAS
(with Maxine Paetro)

Jack Morgan's client has just confessed to murdering his wife, and his best friend is being held on a trumped-up charge that could see him locked away for a very long time. With Jack pushed to the limit, all bets are off.

PRIVATE SYDNEY
(with Kathryn Fox)

Private Sydney are investigating the disappearance of the CEO of a high-profile research company. He shouldn't be difficult to find, but why has every trace of evidence he ever existed vanished too?

PRIVATE PARIS
(with Mark Sullivan)

When several members of Paris's cultural elite are found dead, the French police turn to the Private Paris team for help tackling one of the biggest threats the city has ever faced.

THE GAMES
(with Mark Sullivan)

The eyes of the world are on Rio for the Olympic Games, and Jack is in Brazil's beautiful capital. But it's not long before he uncovers terrifying evidence that the Games could be the setting for the worst atrocity the world has ever seen.

PRIVATE DELHI
(with Ashwin Sanghi)

Private have opened a new office in Delhi, and it's not long before the agency takes on a case that could make or break them. Human remains have been found in the basement of a house in South Delhi. But this isn't just any house, this property belongs to the state government.

PRIVATE PRINCESS
(with Rees Jones)

Jack Morgan has been invited to meet Princess Caroline, third in line to the British throne, who needs his skills (and discretion) to help find her missing friend. Jack knows there is more to this case than he is being told. What is the Princess hiding?

PRIVATE MOSCOW
(with Adam Hamdy)

Jack Morgan is investigating a murder at the New York Stock Exchange and identifies another killing in Moscow that appears to be linked. So he heads to Russia, and begins to uncover a conspiracy that could have global consequences.

PRIVATE ROGUE
(with Adam Hamdy)

A wealthy businessman approaches Jack Morgan with a desperate plea to track down his daughter and grandchildren, who have disappeared without a trace. As Jack investigates the disappearances, the trail leads towards Afghanistan – where Jack's career as a US Marine ended in catastrophe . . .

PRIVATE BEIJING
(with Adam Hamdy)

After an attack on the Beijing office leaves three agents dead and the head of the team missing, Jack Morgan immediately gets on a plane from LA to investigate. But it's not long before another Private office is attacked and it's clear that the entire organisation is under threat . . .

PRIVATE ROME
(with Adam Hamdy)

A priest is murdered and a Private agent is the number one suspect. But as Jack Morgan strives to prove the man's innocence, he uncovers a much deadlier conspiracy . . .

PRIVATE MONACO
(with Adam Hamdy)

Jack Morgan's luxurious vacation on the Monaco coast is quickly cut short when his partner, Justine, is abducted. The kidnappers send Jack clear instructions – if he wants to see the woman he loves again, he must take a life in exchange for hers . . .

Also By James Patterson

ALEX CROSS NOVELS

Along Came a Spider • Kiss the Girls • Jack and Jill • Cat and Mouse • Pop Goes the Weasel • Roses Are Red • Violets Are Blue • Four Blind Mice • The Big Bad Wolf • London Bridges • Mary, Mary • Cross • Double Cross • Cross Country • Alex Cross's Trial (*with Richard DiLallo*) • I, Alex Cross • Cross Fire • Kill Alex Cross • Merry Christmas, Alex Cross • Alex Cross, Run • Cross My Heart • Hope to Die • Cross Justice • Cross the Line • The People vs. Alex Cross • Target: Alex Cross • Criss Cross • Deadly Cross • Fear No Evil • Triple Cross • Alex Cross Must Die • The House of Cross

THE WOMEN'S MURDER CLUB SERIES

1st to Die (*with Andrew Gross*) • 2nd Chance (*with Andrew Gross*) • 3rd Degree (*with Andrew Gross*) • 4th of July (*with Maxine Paetro*) • The 5th Horseman (*with Maxine Paetro*) • The 6th Target (*with Maxine Paetro*) • 7th Heaven (*with Maxine Paetro*) • 8th Confession (*with Maxine Paetro*) • 9th Judgement (*with Maxine Paetro*) • 10th Anniversary (*with Maxine Paetro*) • 11th Hour (*with Maxine Paetro*) • 12th of Never (*with Maxine Paetro*) • Unlucky 13 (*with Maxine Paetro*) • 14th Deadly Sin (*with Maxine Paetro*) • 15th Affair (*with Maxine Paetro*) • 16th Seduction (*with Maxine Paetro*) • 17th Suspect (*with Maxine Paetro*) • 18th Abduction (*with Maxine Paetro*) • 19th Christmas (*with Maxine Paetro*) • 20th Victim (*with Maxine Paetro*) • 21st Birthday (*with Maxine Paetro*) • 22 Seconds (*with Maxine Paetro*) • 23rd Midnight (*with Maxine Paetro*) • The 24th Hour (*with Maxine Paetro*)

DETECTIVE MICHAEL BENNETT SERIES

Step on a Crack (*with Michael Ledwidge*) • Run for Your Life (*with Michael Ledwidge*) • Worst Case (*with Michael Ledwidge*) • Tick Tock (*with Michael Ledwidge*) • I, Michael Bennett (*with Michael Ledwidge*) • Gone (*with Michael Ledwidge*) • Burn (*with*

Michael Ledwidge) • Alert (*with Michael Ledwidge*) • Bullseye (*with Michael Ledwidge*) • Haunted (*with James O. Born*) • Ambush (*with James O. Born*) • Blindside (*with James O. Born*) • The Russian (*with James O. Born*) • Shattered (*with James O. Born*) • Obsessed (*with James O. Born*) • Crosshairs (*with James O. Born*)

PRIVATE NOVELS

Private (*with Maxine Paetro*) • Private London (*with Mark Pearson*) • Private Games (*with Mark Sullivan*) • Private: No. 1 Suspect (*with Maxine Paetro*) • Private Berlin (*with Mark Sullivan*) • Private Down Under (*with Michael White*) • Private L.A. (*with Mark Sullivan*) • Private India (*with Ashwin Sanghi*) • Private Vegas (*with Maxine Paetro*) • Private Sydney (*with Kathryn Fox*) • Private Paris (*with Mark Sullivan*) • The Games (*with Mark Sullivan*) • Private Delhi (*with Ashwin Sanghi*) • Private Princess (*with Rees Jones*) • Private Moscow (*with Adam Hamdy*) • Private Rogue (*with Adam Hamdy*) • Private Beijing (*with Adam Hamdy*) • Private Rome (*with Adam Hamdy*) • Private Monaco (*with Adam Hamdy*)

NYPD RED SERIES

NYPD Red (*with Marshall Karp*) • NYPD Red 2 (*with Marshall Karp*) • NYPD Red 3 (*with Marshall Karp*) • NYPD Red 4 (*with Marshall Karp*) • NYPD Red 5 (*with Marshall Karp*) • NYPD Red 6 (*with Marshall Karp*)

DETECTIVE HARRIET BLUE SERIES

Never Never (*with Candice Fox*) • Fifty Fifty (*with Candice Fox*) • Liar Liar (*with Candice Fox*) • Hush Hush (*with Candice Fox*)

INSTINCT SERIES

Instinct (*with Howard Roughan, previously published as* Murder Games) • Killer Instinct (*with Howard Roughan*) • Steal (*with Howard Roughan*)

THE BLACK BOOK SERIES

The Black Book (*with David Ellis*) • The Red Book (*with David Ellis*) • Escape (*with David Ellis*)

STAND-ALONE THRILLERS

The Thomas Berryman Number • Hide and Seek • Black Market • The Midnight Club • Sail (*with Howard Roughan*) • Swimsuit (*with Maxine Paetro*) • Don't Blink (*with Howard Roughan*) • Postcard Killers (*with Liza Marklund*) • Toys (*with Neil McMahon*) • Now You See Her (*with Michael Ledwidge*) • Kill Me If You Can (*with Marshall Karp*) • Guilty Wives (*with David Ellis*) • Zoo (*with Michael Ledwidge*) • Second Honeymoon (*with Howard Roughan*) • Mistress (*with David Ellis*) • Invisible (*with David Ellis*) • Truth or Die (*with Howard Roughan*) • Murder House (*with David Ellis*) • The Store (*with Richard DiLallo*) • Texas Ranger (*with Andrew Bourelle*) • The President Is Missing (*with Bill Clinton*) • Revenge (*with Andrew Holmes*) • Juror No. 3 (*with Nancy Allen*) • The First Lady (*with Brendan DuBois*) • The Chef (*with Max DiLallo*) • Out of Sight (*with Brendan DuBois*) • Unsolved (*with David Ellis*) • The Inn (*with Candice Fox*) • Lost (*with James O. Born*) • Texas Outlaw (*with Andrew Bourelle*) • The Summer House (*with Brendan DuBois*) • 1st Case (*with Chris Tebbetts*) • Cajun Justice (*with Tucker Axum*)• The Midwife Murders (*with Richard DiLallo*) • The Coast-to-Coast Murders (*with J.D. Barker*) • Three Women Disappear (*with Shan Serafin*) • The President's Daughter (*with Bill Clinton*) • The Shadow (*with Brian Sitts*) • The Noise (*with J.D. Barker*) • 2 Sisters Detective Agency (*with Candice Fox*) • Jailhouse Lawyer (*with Nancy Allen*) • The Horsewoman (*with Mike Lupica*) • Run Rose Run (*with Dolly Parton*) • Death of the Black Widow (*with J.D. Barker*) • The Ninth Month (*with Richard DiLallo*) • The Girl in the Castle (*with Emily Raymond*) • Blowback (*with Brendan DuBois*) • The Twelve Topsy-Turvy, Very Messy Days of Christmas (*with Tad Safran*) • The Perfect Assassin (*with Brian Sitts*) • House of Wolves (*with Mike Lupica*) • Countdown (*with Brendan DuBois*) • Cross Down (*with Brendan DuBois*) • Circle of Death (*with Brian Sitts*) • Lion & Lamb (with *Duane Swierczynski*) • 12 Months to Live (*with Mike Lupica*) • Holmes, Margaret and Poe (*with Brian Sitts*) • The No. 1 Lawyer (*with Nancy Allen*) • The Murder Inn (*with Candice Fox*) • Confessions of the Dead (*with J.D. Barker*) • 8 Months Left (*with Mike Lupica*) • Lies He Told Me (*with David Ellis*)

NON-FICTION

Torn Apart (*with Hal and Cory Friedman*) • The Murder of King Tut (*with Martin Dugard*) • All-American Murder (*with Alex Abramovich and Mike Harvkey*) • The Kennedy Curse (*with Cynthia Fagen*) • The Last Days of John Lennon (*with Casey Sherman and Dave Wedge*) • Walk in My Combat Boots (*with Matt Eversmann and Chris Mooney*) • ER Nurses (*with Matt Eversmann*) • James Patterson by James Patterson: The Stories of My Life • Diana, William and Harry (*with Chris Mooney*) • American Cops (*with Matt Eversmann*) • What Really Happens in Vegas (*with Mark Seal*) • The Secret Lives of Booksellers and Librarians (*with Matt Eversmann*) • Tiger, Tiger (*with Peter de Jonge*)

MURDER IS FOREVER TRUE CRIME

Murder, Interrupted (*with Alex Abramovich and Christopher Charles*) • Home Sweet Murder (*with Andrew Bourelle and Scott Slaven*) • Murder Beyond the Grave (*with Andrew Bourelle and Christopher Charles*) • Murder Thy Neighbour (*with Andrew Bourelle and Max DiLallo*) • Murder of Innocence (*with Max DiLallo and Andrew Bourelle*) • Till Murder Do Us Part (*with Andrew Bourelle and Max DiLallo*)

COLLECTIONS

Triple Threat (*with Max DiLallo and Andrew Bourelle*) • Kill or Be Killed (*with Maxine Paetro, Rees Jones, Shan Serafin and Emily Raymond*) • The Moores Are Missing (*with Loren D. Estleman, Sam Hawken and Ed Chatterton*) • The Family Lawyer (*with Robert Rotstein, Christopher Charles and Rachel Howzell Hall*) •

Murder in Paradise (*with Doug Allyn, Connor Hyde and Duane Swierczynski*) • The House Next Door (*with Susan DiLallo, Max DiLallo and Brendan DuBois*) • 13-Minute Murder (*with Shan Serafin, Christopher Farnsworth and Scott Slaven*) • The River Murders (*with James O. Born*) • The Palm Beach Murders (*with James O. Born, Duane Swierczynski and Tim Arnold*) • Paris Detective • 3 Days to Live • 23 ½ Lies (*with Maxine Paetro*)

For more information about James Patterson's novels, visit www.penguin.co.uk.